The WIDOW'S FATE

THE POISONER OF KINGFOUNTAIN

JEFF WHEELER

Text copyright © 2023 by Jeff Wheeler

Cover Art by Dar Albert

Published by Oliver Heber Books

0 9 8 7 6 5 4 3 2 1

ALSO BY JEFF WHEELER

YOUR FIRST MILLION WORDS

*Tales from Kingfountain, Muirwood, and Beyond: The Worlds of
Jeff Wheeler*

The Dresden Codex

Doomsday Match

Jaguar Prophecies

Final Strike

The Dawning of Muirwood Trilogy

The Druid

The Hunted

The Betrayed

The First Argentines Series

Knight's Ransom

Warrior's Ransom

Lady's Ransom

Fate's Ransom

The Grave Kingdom Series

The Killing Fog

The Buried World

The Immortal Words

The Harbinger Series

Storm Glass

Mirror Gate

KING FOUNTAIN MAP

To Kristin, Ankarette's biggest fangirl

KINGFOUNTAIN MAP

There is nothing so dangerous as a man who craves a kingdom. . . and is thwarted. I was sixteen when Duke Warrewik decided to rebel against the king. I helped Eredur reclaim his lost crown and prevented his brother from wearing it. Powerful men are not known for their propensity for forgiveness. Yet I persuaded Eredur to forgive his brother Dunsdworth for coveting the throne.

I suspected, even then, that certain sins ought not be forgiven. When one has had a sip from the cup of power, it is impossible to forget the taste.

— ANKARETTE TRYNEOWY, POISONER
OF KINGFOUNTAIN

CHAPTER
ONE
THE KING'S THREAT

"Wh-who are you?" asked King Iago of Atabyrion, his voice quavering with fear.

Ankarette had slipped from behind the curtains, exposing herself to the light from the hearth and the flame of the candle trembling in the king's hand. She held his gaze, knowing the door to his private chamber was still unlocked. His knights were in the corridor beyond. One cry for help would summon them.

"You know who I am, my lord," she answered softly. The dull ache in her abdomen presaged her growing need for a sip from the tincture that was prolonging her life. She was the poisoner of King Eredur of Kingfountain. And she had many enemies.

"You're Eredur's poisoner?" Iago said. Slowly, he set the candle down on the table. His eyes darted involuntarily to the sword and scabbard belt slung over a nearby chair. She'd waited until he'd disarmed himself before revealing her presence.

Although it was a royal dwelling, Rune Castle was hardly a castle at all, for the kingdom of Atabyrion was not wealthy. Rather, it was a single square tower that had been built in the Atabyrion hinterlands, then surrounded by an elegant manor house with chimneys and a single weathercock. The tower was defensible, with a few arrow slits in the walls and a thick balustrade at the top. But the royal residence wasn't there—it was in the corner room with the gabled window overlooking the gardens and twin chimneys. Infiltrating it hadn't been a challenge at all. At least, not for someone with Ankarette's skills.

"I'm grateful for the chance to meet you, my lord," she said.

He lunged for his weapon, and in a moment, the naked blade was hoisted from the scabbard. His arm stretched out, the tip of the blade extended toward her. She didn't flinch. She didn't move a muscle.

She tilted her head slightly. "Do you feel better holding a sword? Do you think that will save you?"

"I know your reputation, Poisoner," he said, lips contorting. "And yes, I feel better holding it, thank you."

The king's accent was strong, as was common with his countrymen. Ankarette had been raised in North Cumbria, which had often exchanged hands between the Argentine kings and Iago's Atabyrion ancestors. The poisoner school had removed all trace of her own accent, although she could feign the brogues of many kingdoms when she desired it. For now, she did not.

"I come with a message from my king," she said. "Will you hear it?"

"I could have you dragged from this castle and drawn and quartered, my dear," he said, his tone full of bravado. "You chose a poor time to reveal yourself."

Sweat had beaded on his brow and began to drip. Though his eyebrows furrowed with concentration, his arm started to shake, as if the weight of the sword were getting heavier by the moment.

"I lured you away from Edonburick easily enough," Ankarette said. "You think I don't know how many knights you brought? Or whether they are too sick at the moment to stand up? Or where your son is sleeping tonight?"

She didn't like her threats to involve children. She'd been raised by a midwife and a spy and had learned the trades of both her parents. She had killed for her king. But she refused to kill children for any reason. Still, Iago of Atabyrion didn't know that.

He blanched. "Don't. . . harm my child."

"I'm here to deliver a message, Iago. It's up to you whether our conversation ends poorly or not. Put the blade down before you drop it."

His arm was shaking badly now. And as his eyebrows lifted in sudden understanding, he set the sword on the table and began massaging his palm.

"Now you're spreading the poison to your *other* hand," she said. "That won't do."

"You. . . you came to deliver a message or to kill me?" he gasped. Fear was a powerful tool. She'd applied the poisoned oil to the hilt of the sword after he'd gone to use the privy in the corner of the room, which had been a rather noisy affair. She'd had plenty of time to figure out a hundred ways to kill him if she'd wanted to.

"I could have killed you and stuffed your body in the privy hole if that had been my aim, my lord. No, I come with a warning. This time."

"The itch is insufferable!" Iago said, grabbing a rag from the table and using that to try to stanch the itching feeling, which must have been flaming up his entire arm. And it would now inflict his other hand too. Anywhere he touched, actually.

"But not fatal, fortunately for you," she responded. "Your incursion into North Cumbria. Withdraw immediately. That is my message. And your only warning."

"Those lands belonged to my grandfather," Iago spat, his mouth twisting with offense.

"Aye, and he's dead now. Your son is too young to rule, and your nobles are too fractious to trust. You've heeded the counsel of the treacherous king of Occitania who cares nothing for you. Or for the son who bears your name, as you bear your own father's. Instead of making an enemy of Kingfountain, you should consider making an alliance. King Lewis is not your friend."

"Are you saying you're here to negotiate a truce, lass?" He looked defiant but hopeful. Atabyrions were stubborn and proud but keen on intrigue. All these things she'd learned from Pisan and had found them to be true from her own experience.

Ankarette shook her head. "I'm no royal herald, my lord. Just a poisoner. Let your itching hands remind you of the cost of your greed. The king needs the duke of the North for higher duties than fending you off. Withdraw. Bide your time. Then consider alternatives to arrows and swords to grow your power and your son's future." She narrowed her gaze at him. "If I come to Atabyrion again, it will be to kill you, and you won't even know I was here. Good night."

He was still scrubbing at his red-streaked palm. Welts were already forming on his hands. This particular poison was made from the oil of a rare weed added to a tincture that accelerated its effects. It would irritate the king for at least a week, annoying and incapacitating him from fighting. There were other concoctions

4

she could have chosen, but she'd determined this one would get his attention the most. The memory of his itching hands would linger.

"Are my knights truly incapacitated? How were you planning to leave?" he asked challengingly. "Or were you hoping to get a safe-conduct from me?"

"I don't leave things to chance, my lord. I had a way out prepared long ago. Hopefully, we will never need to meet again."

She returned to the rustling curtains. The window was still open.

"Save me from this infernal itching!" he yelled.

She didn't think it prudent to respond. Some people could not endure discomfort. It made them irrational. And irrational men could be dangerous.

She grabbed the rope dangling outside the window. Clenching it with her hand, she leaped into the darkness outside. The rope was rigged to a block and tackle attached to a sack of grain brought by one of Eredur's Espion, who had helped her set it up. As her weight pulled down, the grain countered it, which slowed her fall. As soon as she reached the bottom, a cloaked man approached with two horses, saddled and ready to flee to a boat waiting off the coast. She didn't trust Iago not to try to hunt her down, so she'd arranged for a hasty escape.

As soon as her feet touched the ground, she let go of the rope, and the sack of grain came plummeting down, rattling the block and tackle. The sack ruptured when it collided with the ground, spilling wheat seeds everywhere.

"Shall we, my lady?" the Espion asked, handing the reins to her.

Ankarette quickly mounted, and the two rode off

through the gardens and into the trees. She'd walked the grounds herself for a few days, both day and night, so that she'd be able to find her way in the dark. Things always appeared different at night. Her gut clenched again, but she didn't have time to stop for a sip.

The poison Lord Hux had given her two years ago would kill her eventually. It was a delayed death. She'd sought the source, of course, but to no avail. No one knew about it at the school, nor anywhere else. Hux had given her a tincture to delay the inevitable. And, on occasion, he arranged for fresh supplies to appear for her use. It wasn't a kindness. The king Ankarette served had taken the throne from his mad uncle. His aunt, Queen Morvared, sister to the King of Occitania, had then attempted to grab power for herself. She was now a prisoner in his tower, and Lord Hux had made it very clear that if anything happened to the queen, then Ankarette would die as well. The supply of antidote would stop, and the poison inside her would reach its climax in days or weeks.

Lord Hux worked for the King of Occitania. He was the best poisoner in all the kingdoms, but Ankarette was coming into her own. She'd found that she could still achieve the king's ends without murdering all his rivals. And they had a deal. For every life she had to take in his service, she would use her midwifery skills to save someone.

"You think they will chase us, my lady?" the Espion asked gruffly.

"I don't. But discretion is still the better part of valor."

After riding for nearly a league, they arrived at the inlet where the Espion ship was waiting to take them back to Kingfountain. Since they hadn't been pursued, they'd be able to bring the horses too.

A man with a hooded lantern produced a few bursts of light to help guide them. Ankarette and her escort slowed to a trot as they approached the crashing surf. The cliff walls were being pummeled by the waves, but she saw the ship at anchor in the moonlight. A crew of sailors were on shore with a rowboat to carry them back to the main ship and bring the animals too.

Ankarette dismounted swiftly, anxious to be underway. The cloaked man with the lantern had a familiar gait. Her hand reached for one of her daggers and drew it.

"Och, lass, I forgot you had the eyes of a falcon," he said, holding up the lantern with one hand. He tugged his cowl down and then lifted his palm to show he was unarmed.

It was Sir Thomas. Sir Thomas Mortimer.

The man she'd loved and lost.

Ankarette wasn't often surprised. She and Sir Thomas boarded the rowboat without taking the horses. He'd told her King Eredur wanted her to return in all haste. After a brief slog through choppy waters, they were hoisted up and were soon on their way back to Kingfountain. They'd be there before dawn if they timed the tides right. The skiff was sleeker and faster than the galley vessel she'd left on days before.

Sir Thomas and the crew, and the Espion who'd accompanied Ankarette on her mission, were given some food to ease their hunger, and she hunkered down on a bench to eat, enjoying the wind on her face. After she ate a few hasty bites, her stomach panged again with discomfort, so she surreptitiously withdrew the vial of tincture that staved the pain for a few days. She took a quick, measured sip of the bitter drink.

Sir Thomas sidled up next to her on the bench, so close that the sway of the waves made them bump shoulders. He offered her a steaming mug.

"Maybe this will chase away the ichor's nasty flavor," he said.

8

She arched an eyebrow at him and then accepted the cup. She smelled it first, inhaling the fragrance of lemon, herbs, and honey. A poisoner could never be too cautious.

"Tea?" she asked.

He chuckled ruefully. "Don't you trust me, Ankarette?"

Sir Thomas was part of her history. Fate had entwined them together. He'd served Eredur's uncle, Duke Warrewik, as his trusted man, and in that capacity, he'd recruited Ankarette into the duke's service, first as a companion to the man's daughters, Isybelle and Nanette. Then the duke had sent Ankarette to Pisan, at great expense, to study at the poisoner school. Having a poisoner was a near necessity in these turbulent times. After the mad king's reign ended, and his wife, Morvared, tried to seize power, Warrewik had cast his allegiance with her, forcing his daughter Nanette to marry the mad king's son.

Thomas had remained loyal to the crown. Ankarette too. They'd been loyal to each other too, friends and confidants, and their feelings had deepened to love. But when Sir Thomas had been given his dream of marrying Lord Horwath's daughter, his heir, which would someday grant him the title of Duke of North Cumbria. . . well, he'd seized the opportunity. Some nights, when she was feeling especially sorry for herself, Ankarette remembered their last kiss.

She'd let her thoughts wander, his question dangling, unanswered. "I'm surprised is all," she confessed. "I thought you were in the North with Lord Horwath's army?"

"Aye. And I was. I'm here on Espion business, Ankarette. I'm sick of that life, truly. But my father-in-law dispatched me to court with news on the Atabyrion conflict. When I got there, the king asked for a special favor. He sent me to get *you*."

His voice still held the subtle accent of a man from the North. She adored hearing it. But those feelings had to be quelled. He was married to Horwath's proud and vain daughter. There could be nothing between them now.

Ankarette lifted the mug to her lips and took a small sip. The honey did as Sir Thomas had promised, soothing the bad flavor still in her mouth. She experimented with it before swallowing, breathing in through her nose again to judge whether anything toxic might be in the brew. It was just tea. She'd become more distrustful in this life of hers. That couldn't be helped. She swallowed.

"I was already on his errand," she said with confusion. "Why interrupt it? I accomplished the mission, but he didn't know that."

"This is more important than threatening the King of Atabyrion. Which, I'm not surprised to hear, you succeeded at. That means I can go back to Dundrennan."

Ankarette shrugged. "I believe he took the threat to heart. He also didn't chase me."

"He would be foolish to play in one of King Lewis's intrigues. And I've never doubted your skills of persuasion, Ankarette. Only a fool would."

She sipped more tea, calming her heart from the effects of his praise. The last thing she wanted to do was to flush in front of him.

"So what's the matter? Why was this so urgent?" she pressed.

"The king's brothers are at each other's throats."

Ankarette sighed. "What is it this time? Is there another title Dunsdworth wants forfeited?"

"Eredur wouldn't have sent for you if that were the case. I'll admit I've been too preoccupied with this business in the North to follow the latest tantrums amongst the Argentine siblings, but this particular snit is about Warrewik's daughters."

"Why would they be the cause of so much ire?" Ankarette asked.

"Severn wants to marry Nanette."

Both of Eredur's younger brothers had been under the influence of Duke Warrewik. They were all cousins, but it was common for royalty to intermarry. Dunsdworth, Duke of Clare, had already married Warrewik's eldest daughter, Isybelle.

When they were younger, Ankarette had witnessed Severn and Nanette flirting with each other. But that was before Warrewik's rebellion. Before the young girl had become a prince's widow.

Ankarette had the cup halfway to her mouth and paused at his words. "Oh."

"You're not surprised?"

"They were fond of each other as children. But I didn't think Severn would still want her. Not after the war. Not after her. . . marriage."

"You're not the first to think so. Warrewik's daughters are notable heiresses in their own right through their mother's line. There are many nobles of Ceredigion who've asked for her hand. But for naught. The king forbade it at first, just to be sure Nanette wasn't with child. When she remained unmarried, I thought Eredur had submitted her fate to Dunsdworth because he's Warrewik's heir, and thus she's his ward. But I was wrong. The king forbade any marriages out of respect for Severn's feelings."

"The Duke of Glosstyr has feelings?" Ankarette said with a wry smile. "Or is this really about her inheritance?"

The skiff lunged down a wave, causing their shoulders to collide again and Ankarette to nearly slip off the bench, but Sir Thomas put his arm around her to steady her.

"I'm fine, Sir Thomas," she said, disentangling his arm.

He looked abashed. "Pardon. I didn't want you to fall."

How gallant. But where was that trait when it had come to his love for her? In the end, his pride had meant more to him. She'd forgiven him, but she still had regrets. Did he as well?

"I won't, Sir Thomas. Just answer me. Why would Severn be so desperate for Warrewik's daughter?"

"Am I a Wizr to read a man's mind?" he said jokingly. "The duke could have chosen any lass in any kingdom, for certain. His brother would have allowed it. His loyalty and faithfulness are being rewarded. He's the most powerful man in the realm, next to the king. Dunsdworth resents it. And with Nanette under his guardianship, he can spend her part of the inheritance as he sees fit. He has no motivation to let her go. But I don't think pique is what emboldened Severn to ask for Nanette. Truly, I think he cares for her. The connection remained despite the obstacles. He asked the king to marry her, and the king said yes."

"How does any of this involve me?" Ankarette asked, perplexed. She didn't give two figs about whom Severn married, but she did think it somewhat romantic that the childhood yearnings had blossomed.

"Dunsdworth refused."

Ankarette tilted her head. "Can he. . . *do* that?"

"Legally. . . yes. But if he's not the Fountain's biggest fool, I don't know who is. I need not remind you that he rebelled against his brother. That he was mercifully pardoned because of your intercession. If you hadn't persuaded him to turn against Warrewik, then Eredur's present circumstances might have been very different. But as they say in Legault, only the most grievous of eejits would lord that over a king. Instead of being grateful for being pardoned, Dunsdworth has done naught but complain that he wasn't rewarded *enough*."

"By the Lady, his behavior is appalling," Ankarette said.

"And obtuse and reckless and contemptible. Severn is as implacable as the glaciers in the North, though. He refuses to give way this time. He has demanded that the king legally wrest the wardship away from Dunsdworth. That was done. Accomplished yesterday, in fact. I saw the seal on the parchment with my own eyes." He looked at Ankarette expectantly.

"And?"

"What do you think happened, Ankarette?"

"I presume Glosstyr took the writ to Dunsdworth's castle in Clare and demanded that he release Nanette?"

"All the brothers are in Kingfountain at present. So you're nearly right. Glosstyr went to Dunsdworth's manor, the Arbon. The one Warrewik used to reside at in Kingfountain. He took enough men with him to enforce the order."

"That sounds ominous," Ankarette murmured.

"Dunsdworth let him in. He flung open the door

13

and told his brother to enter and find the lass if he could. When the writ was signed and sealed, Dunsdworth said he no longer had custody of the girl. She is gone, and he knows not where she went. They almost came to blows, so I'm told. Glosstyr's men searched the Arbon from one end to the other, looked in every barrel in the cellar, and even climbed inside the attic. The barns, of course, were also searched. As were the gardens. The servants were interrogated, though they were too abashed and frightened to speak."

"Eredur must be furious," Ankarette said. "This is defiance. Contempt."

"Aye. And the reason the king sent me to get you. Glosstyr is ready to rampage through the city to find her. And if she'd dead, Ankarette, another murder will need to be committed to sate Severn's rage."

"Surely the king summoned Dunsdworth to the castle."

Sir Thomas nodded. "He did. And Dunsdworth brought a deconeus of Our Lady with him and swore on the blessed Lady's *hair* that he had harmed her not. . . nor does he know where she is."

He reached out and put his hand on Ankarette's shoulder. "That is why the king sent me to bring you back to Kingfountain. He knows you have certain. . . powders. . . which can make a man speak the truth."

That made sense, but it was also a distasteful errand. Ankarette did not care for either of the king's younger brothers. Dunsdworth was a greedy, ungrateful sot, and although Severn was loyal, he was also ill-tempered and bitingly sarcastic.

"It's not easy to know when a man is lying," Ankarette said. "Even someone as distrustful as Dunsdworth may be telling the truth."

"Aye. We learned that the hard way with Warrewik, didn't we? He smiled and pretended, all while secretly corresponding with the King of Occitania. Even the Espion, with all their training, are hardly capable of discerning the truth when lies are so abundant and persistent. But you. You can get to the bottom of this faster than anyone."

"I see. The king wants me to poison his brother. He wants me to find out what happened to Nanette. Whether she's alive or dead."

"That's the gist of it." He squeezed her shoulder, his eyes stern and serious. "If the lass is dead, the Duke of Clare will pay the price for it. Nothing less will appease Glosstyr. And that's *my* worry, Ankarette. Someone else may be pulling the strings here to create war between the brothers. Find the widow. Before it's too late."

THREE

THE FATE OF A MARCHER LORD

They made good time and arrived at the docks of Kingfountain just as the city was bathed in morning light. The famous castle, perched atop a hill, was the pinnacle seat of the Argentines' power. The river emptied next to it, forming a staggering waterfall, the roar of which could be heard throughout the city. A stone bridge straddled the river, connecting the castle to a rocky landmass, where sat the sanctuary of Our Lady amidst the turbulent waters. The bridge had houses, taverns, and stores built on it, cramped and soot-choked, and ended at Bridge Street along the outer edge of the island. Multiple wooden bridges met up with the street and spanned the other side of the river, connecting to the teeming city, which was composed of various districts or wards run by the mayor and his constables under the command and authority of Lord Axelrod, lord high constable of Ceredigion. Ankarette gazed at the haze of smoke rising from the tenements and their broken streets. A feeling of gloom settled over her heart. Many of those crooked streets were dangerous places, all the more so because of the sanctuary men who preyed on the unwary, the lost. Ankarette thought the king—or at least the lord high constable—could be doing more to safeguard them.

The deconeus of the sanctuary was a powerful man, nearly as powerful as the king. That little island in the middle of the river had the right of sanctuary. It granted those who trod there immunity from the king's justice. Where the tradition had originated from was lost to the mists of history, but deconeuses past and present had affirmed it with ironclad resolve. That meant a man could steal in the city, and if he made it inside the sanctuary gates before being caught, there was nothing the king's men, the constables, or the night watch could do to force him out. Some criminals were so notorious that guards were posted outside the gates to bring them to justice if they ever left the grounds. In effect, they were still imprisoned, only not in chains or stocks.

"Do you think there's a chance Lady Nanette went to the sanctuary?" Ankarette asked Sir Thomas as they left the quay. Their skiff had pulled into the king's docks, which were less crowded and provided a direct route to the palace.

"If she had, wouldn't the deconeus have mentioned it when Dunsdworth was declaring his innocence?"

"Do we have any Espion inside the sanctuary yet?"

Thomas shrugged. "I don't think Master Nichols has managed it yet. I never dared when I ran the Espion. The deconeus would not approve, and they'd be vulnerable to his authority. Do you remember the story of the Marcher lord who was thrown into the falls for attempting to violate sanctuary?"

"I haven't heard that story before," she replied, intrigued. "What is a Marcher lord?"

"Oh, long ago, the borderland between Occitania and Ceredigion was called the Marcher lands. The Occitanians called it La Marche. We called it the Marches. The ruler back then had a mistress. A servant girl. I don't recall all the details, but this lord was conspiring against the king. He beat the girl savagely for some perceived indiscretion, and she fled to the sanctuary of Our Lady. He feared she'd reveal his plotting, so he sent his men to the sanctuary to force her out.

"The deconeus was incensed. When his armed guards stormed the gate, the bells were rung, and the people swarmed out from their homes. The knights were taken and thrown into the river and perished going over the falls. Then the mob stormed the Marcher lord's manor, and he was carried off too. The king granted a safe-conduct to the girl, who related the story of the Marcher lord's treason. But there was nothing left for him to do. The justice of the Fountain had been far swifter than his own could be."

"I'd never heard that before. Thank you."

"The Duke of Warrewik told me about it. I hadn't known, at the time, that he was plotting treason too."

They climbed the stairs leading from the quay and entered a postern gate at the base of the hill. Ankarette didn't need to flash her Espion ring to gain admittance since the man recognized her and offered a polite greeting. The main road to the palace was controlled by the king's guard, but the Espion had other ways of getting inside the tunnels leading to the palace. The castle was filled with secret passageways and nooks that allowed the Espion to spy on guests. Those same passageways would provide the royal family with a means of escape in case of an attack from within. However, the castle itself would be beyond difficult to siege. They had food stores aplenty, and an enormous cistern had been built beneath the castle to gather enough rainwater to maintain the castle year-round.

After passing the sentinels who guarded the entrances, Sir Thomas and Ankarette appeared through a secret door and approached the king and queen's private rooms through the main corridor. The knights posted at the door recognized them both and hurriedly interrupted the royal breakfast.

"Ah, this marks the start of an auspicious day," Eredur said, wiping his mouth on a napkin. A hearty breakfast was laid out before him—fresh trout, buttered rolls, and an assortment of cakes and fruit. He was wearing a royal tunic emblazoned with his insignia— the Sun and Rose—and seemed ready for the demands of the day. Rising, he shook Thomas's hand firmly. Queen Elyse was sitting in front of a looking glass, a maid arranging her hair.

"Ankarette," the queen said with warmth. She then dismissed the maid and the squires, leaving the four of them alone.

Eredur took Ankarette's hands in his in a gesture of warmth and tenderness. She was more than just a pawn, a weapon in his arsenal. She'd saved his life and rescued his throne, and neither the queen nor king would ever forget it. Elyse embraced her, kissing her cheek.

"I'm sorry I had to interrupt your last mission," the king apologized. "But as you know, there was good reason for it."

"Actually, she finished the mission. Shall I return to the North?" Sir Thomas asked. He was spying the leftovers on the table with thinly veiled interest. "I did as you asked."

"In such a hurry to leave, Thomas? Stay a moment longer."

Sir Thomas sighed, then wandered to a chair and sat down.

"I won't keep you long, my dear," Eredur said to Ankarette. "I need you to go to the Arbon straight-away and find out what happened to our missing cousin."

"Why didn't you keep the duke in custody?" Ankarette said. "It would be easier if he were already here."

"He came on safe-conduct with the deconeus. Which was vexing, to say the least. He's afraid, Ankarette. But I tell you, sometimes I think my brother has lost his mind. Is he being truthful? I don't know for sure. But if he lied to the deconeus, he risks not only the king's justice but the Fountain's. Why would a man risk both? It makes no sense."

"When someone loses something of importance," Ankarette said, "they think irrationally. Good judgment is impaired in those situations. If you're going to be exe-cuted for stealing a lamb, you may as well steal a horse."

The king chuckled. "Too true." He glanced at Elyse. "She will see this right. I know it." Turning back to Ankarette, he said, "I know you have a powder that can loosen the tongue. What's it called?"

"Nightshade," Ankarette said hesitantly. "There are risks in using it, though." Too much and she'd kill the Duke of Clare. Too little and he'd be able to fight off the stupor and refuse to speak. Worse—he'd remember what she'd done to him. Men weren't forgiving of such things.

"What risks?" the queen asked.

"I think she means, delicately, the fatal kind," Sir Thomas observed dryly.

The king's brow furrowed with alarm. "Is that so?"

"Indeed. I don't use nightshade recklessly."

"You used it before, if I remember correctly," Eredur said.

"True. And I've not killed anyone with it, to my knowledge. But I must state this as a risk. His physical health is a factor. Whether he is suffering any ailments."

The queen looked startled and then touched Eredur's arm. "He reeked of malmsey when he came in with the deconeus."

Malmsey was an expensive white wine from Genevar. It was noted for its strong sweetness. It was also a good wine to use to hide the flavor of certain poisons.

"My brother is something of a drunkard," Eredur said dispassionately, his lips pursed with disapproval. "I'd assumed that was all it was."

"Too much drink can affect not only his body but also his wits," Ankarette said. "It would require a stronger dose. That means a greater risk."

"Isn't there another way you could get him to talk?" Sir Thomas asked, leaning forward in the chair.

Seduction was an effective tool of the trade, but Ankarette had told the king previously that she would not be using it in his service. He'd never asked it of her, and the thought of manipulating his brother that way made her stomach ache worse than Hux's poison.

"None nearly so effective," she hedged.

Eredur sighed and began to pace. "The Fountain knows my brother is a vexation to me these days. If he did something to harm Warrewik's daughter, I'd see

21

justice on him done without hesitation. But if he died under suspicious circumstances, it would endanger my reputation abroad." He paused and looked back at Ankarette. "That's why I didn't want you to kill Iago. Just... threaten."

"And so I did. We'll see if the effort bears the right fruit."

"We'll see. Ankarette, I'm going to leave it to your judgment. If you think he'll be susceptible to night-shade, use it. If you feel it's too dangerous, don't." He glanced at his wife and then at Sir Thomas. "I *would* like to know if he's lied to me, but the more important consideration is finding Nanette. Are we agreed?"

The queen walked to her husband and squeezed his hand. "Yes. I think Ankarette will know the right course of action."

"Thomas?" the king asked. "What do you think?"

"It's your decision to make, Eredur. I trust Ankarette implicitly, though. I'd trust her with my life. And your brother's."

Eredur nodded. "I told Dunsdworth not to leave Kingfountain. I warned him not to interfere in my efforts to find Nanette. He may have a blistering headache this morning, so you'll probably find him still abed. You have the Espion as a resource if you need anything, but knowing you, I suppose you'd prefer to do things your own way. Besides, more than half of the Espion are new, and Nichols is still unsure about the loyalties of everyone. If you have trouble getting into the Arbon, let me know, and I'll send Axelrod to knock the door open."

Master Bensen Nichols was the new head of the Espion after Sir Thomas had stepped down. The deconeus, Tunmore, had recommended him.

"There are no Espion stationed there?"

Eredur shook his head. "I've tried. He's too suspicious by nature and too harsh on his servants."

Ankarette glanced at Thomas, remembering the story of the Marcher lord.

"I haven't been to the Arbon recently," she said, "but I know its general location. Many of the streets have changed since I was last there."

Eredur shook his head. "I'll save you time. It's in between Dowgate Hill Road and Bush Lane in the Vintrey ward. Do you know where that is?"

"I'm not familiar with all the wards of the city," Ankarette said, "but I do know where Vintrey is. I should leave now. I'm assuming the constable honors the Espion?"

"The constable, yes, because he's my man. The people in that ward, no. They were loyal to Warrewik. It was his little enclave, complete with its own night watch. Be careful, Ankarette. It's always been a dangerous part of town." He grinned at her. "But nothing you can't handle."

She nodded to him and said with a strong Yuorkish accent, dormant but still ready to use, "I shall do my best, milord."

"Are you finished with that breakfast?" Thomas asked, coming to his feet and ambling over to the table.

"I am now, Thomas," Eredur said. Then, to Ankarette, "Send word when you've found her. I know you will."

"I'll walk with you," Elyse offered, hurrying to join Ankarette as she made her way to the door. That was unusual. But she accepted the company, and the two walked down the corridor, turning toward the door leading to the queen's interior garden near the cistern opening.

They emerged into the garden together, Ankarette pausing with curiosity. Was there something the queen knew and hadn't told her husband?

"How was it being with him again?" Elyse asked, looking at Ankarette with sympathy. She took both of Ankarette's hands and clasped them.

Now Ankarette understood. She'd been so focused on her mission that she hadn't realized Elyse would be worried about her and Sir Thomas. Elyse was one of the few who knew Ankarette's feelings for him. It helped having such a confidante. Especially when the grief had first come crashing in on her.

"I'm fine, truly," Ankarette said. "There's no need to worry."

Elyse looked doubtful. "I told Eredur to send anyone else. Not him. Thomas isn't even part of the Espion anymore. He should have chosen someone else to find you."

"Truly, it is fine. I don't think about him much anymore."

The queen sighed and shook her head. "He would have done better if he'd chosen you, Ankarette. Their marriage isn't a happy one."

Ankarette winced and pulled her hands away. "I didn't need to hear that."

"I'm sorry. Maybe I should have said nothing. It's only that I hurt for you. Whenever they come to court, it makes me writhe with frustration the way she treats him. She's never at his side, always flouncing off with other ladies. And yet she'll interrupt him in the middle of a conversation to attend to her needs." She sighed. "But he chose her. We must accept the consequences of what we desire, is that not so?"

"He made his choice," Ankarette said, feeling more

uncomfortable now than she had with Thomas. "And she can give him something I cannot."

Children.

One of the terrible side effects of the poison Lord Hux had unleashed on her was the harm it was doing *inside* her. It had stopped her monthly flux, and it would kill anything that grew inside her.

Elyse's face was raw with grief. She stroked Ankarette's hair. "I'm so sorry, Ankarette. We owe you more than we can ever repay."

"I have made my peace with it," Ankarette said. "I hope Thomas has as well. I'll serve your family as long as I am able."

In Pisan, I learned that half a truth is often the greatest lie. I was taught not only to lie with words, but in the tone in which the words were spoken. The wearing of clothes contributes to a lie. A pretended wound or scar is a lie. People are so used to believing what they see and what they hear that they are vulnerable to the subtlest deceptions. I've often gained access to a home or castle just by walking through the front door as if I were supposed to be there.

— ANKARETTE TRYNEOWY

FOUR

THE ARBON

A smudge of dirt can say a lot. So can a scarf to cover hair, a wicker basket, and a load of freshly scrubbed laundry. Ankarette's disguise had only cost her a few farthings. She'd lived among the nobles of Ceredigion since the Duke of Warrewik had hired her. Even then, as a confidante to the duke's eldest daughter, Ankarette had noticed the scullions, the laundry girls, and the waifs who swept ashes from hearths and labored at endless tasks in the periphery. Ignored. Dismissed. Unnoticed.

She adjusted the basket against her hip as she walked up Dowgate Hill Road toward the Arbon. It was an unfriendly part of town, and she'd had more than a few leers sent her way from the idlers and shifty men who roamed the streets. No one accosted her, though, because a lass carrying clean laundry hadn't been paid for it yet, and it was coin these louts were after more than anything. The smell of bread and sausages was strong in the air, along with smoke from hundreds of fires and the subtle aroma of wine. Vintrey was the center of the wine trade in the city. It didn't require a poisoner's gifts of observation to have figured that out.

"Whatcha got there, lass?" asked a menacing young man with a scarred face, leaning against a wall.

Ankarette gave him a dismissive expression and a curt, "Are ye daft?"

Criminals were always looking for easy marks. Signs of fear attracted them. A whimper of fright and increasing speed would only bring a gang of them after her. Instead, she radiated that she *belonged* in Vintrey. Her accent said she was one of them. A local. Not to be bothered. It worked. She could feel him watching her as she passed, but she didn't look back. That would have kept his attention.

She reached the walled estate of the Arbon after sidestepping piles of fresh sewage cluttering the murky street. Dowgate Hill Road was steep, and she was perspiring by the time she reached the crest of it. She'd already passed the Arbon's main entrance gate and found it guarded by men wearing the livery of the Duke of Clare. That was the gate that Severn and his men would have entered. But not servants.

All manor houses had back or side entrances for the servants to come and go through. She found an arch set into a stone wall thick with ivy and broad-leafed plants. If it had been after nightfall, it would have been easy to climb the wall from the outside. As she approached the wrought-iron gate with her basket on her hip, she glanced at the foliage for signs of someone having done just that.

"What's this?" asked a grumpy voice from the gate's shadow. A man was sitting on a stool there. The porter guard. "Who are ye?"

"I'm the new gull," Ankarette said with a haughty sniff and a toss of her head. "You gonna make me stand here all day?" She'd adopted a Northern accent deliberately. The porter sentry was definitely from North Cumbria.

"Where'd you grow up, lass? Yuork?"

"Aye. What about you? A dung stable?" Servants insulted each other depending on their station in the hierarchy of power.

"Don't be saucy, wench. Don't be saucy." He grunted as he eased off the stool and rattled a key in the gate's lock. He opened it without hesitation.

"Fetch me a biscuit from the kitchen if you might," he asked her, scratching his whiskers.

"I might do that if cook's not lookin'," she said. It didn't help to be mean all the time. And it was harder getting information that way too.

The gate squealed noisily as it was opened just wide enough for her to enter. As she did, she brought the basket in front of her and used it to wedge more space between him and herself. Sometimes the servants could be a little too familiar with one another, and she didn't fancy having him touch her as she passed.

"Were you at your post when the Duke of Glosstyr's men came?" she asked with a twinkle in her eye. Excitement like that would be talked about for days.

"Indeed, I was! The Fountain spite that man and his ilk. Duke of Glosstyr—he's no duke at all!"

"Did his knights come to your gate, then?"

"The duke himself did! I've served this place for years. Too saucy, I say. Too saucy. But he gots nothin' out of me. Nothin'. I'm loyal, you see. You'd best be loyal too, lass, if you know what's good."

"I know what's good and where my coin comes from," Ankarette said. She backed away from him until she'd passed under the thick arch. The gravel crunched against her shoes, but there were paving stones and a garden beyond that and an easy path to a sturdy wooden door.

She'd have another little *chat* with the porter on the way out. If someone had left through his gate, he'd know about it, although she had no doubt that he would have lied through his teeth to the Duke of Glosstyr, probably groveling while he was at it.

Ankarette walked purposefully and quickly past the overgrown hedges and cluttered yard. There were buckets left haphazardly about and some rusty gardening tools. A fruit tree of some kind off to her right looked like it hadn't been tended in years. The lawns were choked with weeds. The Duke of Warrewik had been a fastidious man. He would not have been pleased to see how the Arbon had been neglected under his son-in-law's stewardship.

Ivy crept up the stone wall face at the rear of the manor. There were three triangular roofs, two walls of stone, one of stucco. A wolfhound was roaming the yard and piddling on the brush. It heard her and then loped away as if afraid she'd scold it.

Ankarette reached the door and opened it, hearing the gate squeal and shut behind her. It was early enough in the morning that servants were scuttling around everywhere, but they were being unusually quiet. There was an atmosphere of fear in the air that she noticed immediately. Everyone was doing their own thing, carrying candles or woodbins. There was a mess throughout the manor. Ankarette sidestepped debris on the main hall floor as she passed by several servants who didn't regard her at all.

She'd noticed smoke coming from most of the chimneys, except for one—the chimney connected to the duke and duchess's private chambers. She knew the manor house well enough to remember its layout. Ankarette found the main hall easily. It was a vaulted room, two stories tall. On the wall above the massive hearth was a huge decorative shield with two halberds crossing above it. Beautiful but dusty wainscoting adorned the far wall, and massive windows on the adjacent one would have been facing the front facade of the manor. Chairs and couches were placed on bear rugs that decorated the floor. There were wine casks to the side. A huge tapestry hung from the stucco-and-beam wall above the wainscoting.

What surprised her was the lack of men-at-arms. The Arbon was vulnerable. Too vulnerable. She didn't want to peer out the front door in case there were any knights guarding it, but the lack of protection was troubling. Even so, it would make her assignment easier.

She glanced at the spiraling staircase and immediately started going up it.

"What are you doing, lass?" hissed a woman's voice in distress.

Ankarette looked back. The woman beneath her was obviously an authority figure. She was older, sharper, and dressed more nicely than the other servants.

"I've got Lady Isybelle's laundry," Ankarette said back in a half whisper.

"She's not been out of bed yet," said the other woman, beckoning for Ankarette to come back down the steps. "You don't want to go up there."

"I was told to be quiet," Ankarette said, giving off a confused expression. "Her ladyship wanted a stain cleaned first thing."

"Oh, better hurry, then," replied the woman, shooing Ankarette up. There was enough chaos in the house that Ankarette's little lie had been completely believable. "But be gentle and still. Don't wake the duke. He's a terror in the mornings."

"Don't I know it," Ankarette huffed and then turned and hurried up the stairs, treading softly.

The upper floor was easy to navigate, and Ankarette walked to the massive double doors marking the master suite, turning her back on the single doors down the other way. The smell of sour wine grew stronger as she approached them.

Ankarette adjusted the basket on her hip again and paused at the threshold, listening. It was quiet. Deathly quiet. She waited longer, straining for sound. With no one in the great hall below and the servants busy behind closed doors, there was nothing to hear. Ankarette tried the handle and pushed it open. It was common for nobles to leave their bedrooms unlocked so servants could come in to restoke fires, bring food, and carry warm water for bathing. The interior smelled of human waste—an indicator the chamber pots were still full—which made her wrinkle her nose. It was dark, the curtains all drawn.

Ankarette entered quietly after testing the hinges and discovering they were better oiled than the gate at the porter door. There was a crossbar latch on the inside. She slid it into place to block it against intruders. The fire was out. No one had come with wood to tend it. The distinct sound of snoring was coming from a curtained bed, a mammoth structure made of fluted timbers and covered in veils.

Ankarette waited by the door, hoping her eyes would adjust to the darkness swiftly. Shapes began to form in the gloom. A couch. A stuffed chair. A changing screen with clothes strewn haphazardly around it. A sword and belt on the floor.

"Ankarette?"

The voice came from the couch. It was Isybelle's.

The poisoner set the basket down by the door and walked to the couch. Isybelle wore a nightdress and had a blanket covering her lap. In the dimness, Ankarette couldn't see the other woman's eyes.

After Eredur had reclaimed his throne, Ankarette had been sent by the king to serve Isybelle again. But that arrangement had been short-lived. Dunsdworth knew who Ankarette was and had rejected the idea about a fortnight later, but he had given his wife permission to summon Ankarette if she became pregnant in order to help with the childbirth. The duke and duchess had lost their firstborn during premature labor on a ship outside Callait. It grieved Ankarette that she hadn't been there to help.

"What are you doing here?" Isybelle asked in a fearful whisper.

The snoring halted, and Ankarette glanced at the bed for a moment before it started up again. She gazed at her friend. It had been almost a year since they'd seen each other. There was a little bulge on her friend's abdomen. It was early still.

"You're with child?" Ankarette whispered.

Isybelle nodded worriedly. "Did Eredur send you?"

Ankarette nodded. "Where's your sister?"

Isybelle covered her mouth, glancing worriedly at the bed. "We can't talk here. Not like this. If he wakes up. . . he'll be furious."

"Do you know where she is?" Ankarette pressed.

Isybelle shook her head. "Let's go to another room. Where he won't—"

"Who's there?" barked a slurred, angry voice. Ankarette's stomach tightened with dread.

FIVE

SINS OF THE BROTHERS

The Duke of Clare could be charming when he chose to be. But since he'd lost his gambit to seize the throne of Ceredigion, he'd grown more selfish, defensive, and passionate about perceived slights to his status. Ankarette wasn't sure how he would react to finding a poisoner in his bedchamber.

"I'm here, Dunne," Isybelle said coaxingly, using her husband's pet name. "Go back to sleep."

"You're talking to someone. Who? I said I didn't want to be disturbed!"

The sound of the bedsheets moving brought Ankarette to her feet. Isybelle's eyes flashed with dread.

After jerking aside the bed curtains, Dunsdworth emerged with an obvious hangover. His eyes were bloodshot, his forehead crumpled with pain from a likely headache. He looked at Ankarette in anger, showing no sign of recognition.

He came off the bed, stumbled slightly, still wearing his breeches and an untucked shirt open at the collar. He reeked of wine.

"When I say I don't wish to be disturbed," he said

with a glower, advancing swiftly to Ankarette, "I expect my commands to be obeyed."

"Please, Dunne!" Isybelle pleaded. "You don't recognize her."

"If she works in this manor, she must do as I say!" he blustered. He reached for Ankarette's arm, his muscles tense, his cheek twitching.

Ankarette caught his littlest finger before he could get a grip on her arm. She torqued it back and watched his face light up with surprise and a new source of pain.

She continued the pressure, deliberately, firmly, until she had him on his knees in front of her. "You don't recognize me, my lord," she said stiffly.

"It's Ankarette," Isybelle said, coming to her husband's side, kneeling next to him. "Please, try to be calm!"

"Ankarette?" he gasped, his arm shaking with excruciating pain.

She didn't release the hold, not yet. She wanted him to see that he was entirely in her power. By the smell of his breath, the sallow skin, and a little burst of Fountain magic from inside her, she knew that nightshade would be deadly to him in this state. He had too many toxins in his body already. His paleness told her that he was keeping late hours, not venturing outdoors as often.

Her ability to tap into the power of the Fountain was her most precious skill and had nothing to do with her gifts as a poisoner. She'd discovered the gift earlier in life and had learned to trust the impulses it gave her, the insight into the character and motivations of others. She used it sparingly, for anyone else who was Fountain-blessed could sense it when she used the magic. Just as she could sense their use of the power.

She felt the magic the most not when she was at a

fountain with coin in hand but when she assisted in childbirth. There was something about the birthing process, the struggle between life and death, that aroused Ankarette's deepest feelings. Helping a child and mother survive that ordeal was deeply gratifying. She wanted to continue doing it for as many years as she had left.

But she didn't want to underestimate him. He was a noble's son—had trained with swords and shields and halberds since he was young. He'd been brought up in Duke Warrewik's household and had his first lessons of knighthood from the man. Then, two years before, he'd fought alongside Eredur and Severn against Queen Morvared's army. She'd heard it said since then that Dunsdworth was savage on the battlefield.

Some men quailed from shedding blood. Others enjoyed it.

"Release me," Dunsdworth snarled amidst the pain, "or I'll call for my knights!"

"Dunne, don't!"

"They aren't here, my lord," Ankarette said. "And your sword is over against that table, well out of reach. Consider the situation carefully. Why am I here?"

"To *kill* me?" he spat.

"Dunne, she's not," Isybelle said. "Ankarette isn't here for that." But her voice didn't sound certain.

Ankarette released her hold on his finger, and he began to massage his hand. His eyes flicked to the sword and scabbard, but she positioned herself to block his path to it in case he tried something foolish. He was just unhinged enough that he might.

"You're here about Nanette?" Dunsdworth said, slowly rising to his feet. Isybelle stood up with him, clutching his arm protectively. "Search the manor, by all means! If my idiot brother couldn't find her here, you think you can?"

"I don't think she's here," Ankarette said.

"I don't *know* where she is," Dunsdworth affirmed. "I swore it on the name of the Lady of the Fountain in front of the deconeus of the sanctuary!"

"I know you did. Still. . . I'm here."

"Our knights have been scouring the streets of King-fountain looking for her," Isybelle said nervously. "That's why. . . that's why they're not here. Dunne was leading the search, and he didn't arrive home until a few hours ago, when the morning bells tolled. He hadn't slept all night."

"Eredur threatened me," Dunsdworth said. "But he gave me time to find her. Or has he taken back his vow?"

"I'm here," Ankarette said, "for the *truth*. And I have ways of making men talk. Pour him a cup of wine. Just a little," she said to Isybelle.

"What. . . what are you going to do?" Isybelle quailed.

"There's a poison called nightshade," Ankarette said. "It frees the tongue. Too much can be. . . harmful. I need to assure the king that you are telling the truth. Surely with your history, it's an understandable concern."

Dunsdworth's nostrils flared. "This is outrageous!"

"I can *make* you drink it," Ankarette said. "But that will make your heart race, make you see things that aren't really there. Rave like a madman. It's gentler if you drink it willingly. But it's your choice, my lord duke. Either way, you're drinking it."

Dunsdworth hesitated and then glanced toward the sword once more.

JEFF WHEELER

"I see we have to do this the unpleasant way," Ankarette declared and stepped toward him.

"No! No! I'll drink it," he said, panicking.

"Fetch the wine, my lady," Ankarette said, eyes fixed on the duke in a threatening stare.

Isybelle hastily splashed some white wine in a goblet and brought it to Ankarette. She withdrew a vial from her bodice and unstopped it. Holding the wine cup, she gazed at the volume of liquid in the cup, then at the vial. Dunsdworth stroked his chin in anticipation, watching her with feverish eyes.

Ankarette gently added a few drops from one of her vials into the wine. She smelled a lemony scent from it. To be cautious, she added one more. Then she handed the cup to Dunsdworth.

"Drink it all."

"What will it do to me?" he asked, alarmed.

"If you don't fight it, nightshade will relax you. It won't harm you unless you become too agitated."

"I'm *already* agitated."

"I've taken that into account, my lord. Drink it."

"Are you going to make Severn drink it too? Maybe he kidnapped Nanette and is blaming me for it!"

"Drink it," Ankarette insisted.

Dunsdworth held the cup to his nose, sniffed, and then gulped it down quickly.

"You'd best sit down while the poison does its work," Ankarette said, gesturing to the couch. Dunsdworth and Isybelle both sat down nervously, side by side, holding hands.

Ankarette watched the look on Dunsdworth's face as the poison began to work. It was fast-acting, even diluted in wine.

40

"I feel strange," he mumbled. His eyelids began to droop.

"Don't resist it," Ankarette said. "Take deep and shallow breaths."

"Deep. . . and shallow? That doesn't make. . . sense. . ."

"Close your eyes," Ankarette whispered. "Breathe in and out."

Dunsdworth slumped against Isybelle, his jaw suddenly slack.

"Dunne? Dunne!" she cried in a panic.

"It was a sleeping draft," Ankarette said. "Not nightshade. That's a powder. You blow it in someone's face. He needs some rest, and now we can talk. Lay his head down."

Isybelle clutched her chest with relief and then helped get Dunsdworth settled on the couch, his arms and neck against the rest.

While Isybelle did that, Ankarette slipped the vial back into her bodice. She pulled a chair up to the couch and then sat across from Isybelle. Dunsdworth started to snore.

"You tricked us," Isybelle commented.

"In his state, nightshade would have been toxic," Ankarette replied. "I'm not here to harm him. Or you. I have no doubt he would have lied to the king or the deconeus to save himself. Tell me what happened. I know you love your sister."

"I do love Nanette," Isybelle said, reaching for Ankarette's hand. "I just. . . don't understand her sometimes."

"Why do you say that?"

"She and Dunne were often at odds. She'd speak too boldly to him."

"Are we talking about your sister?" Ankarette asked, confused. She'd always been a rather docile creature. Inhibited.

"Yes! She. . . what happened in Occitania. . . caused her immense grief. She didn't love her husband. She *hated* him. She was forced into the marriage by Father and Queen Morvared. I believe. . . I believe they poisoned her to get her to say yes at the ceremony. And the prince was cruel to her because she didn't want him."

Ankarette sighed. It had been a short-lived marriage. Morvared's son was slain on the battlefield of Hawk Moor. His father had been poisoned by Ankarette herself while in prison. The mad king's widow, Morvared, was now in the dungeon where he'd been held.

"You don't know how Nanette disappeared?"

Isybelle shook her head. "It happened after an. . . an argument with Dunne."

The hesitation in her voice implied much. "Oh?"

Isybelle looked down. "Nanette knew that Severn loved her. That he'd win her freedom from Dunne's control. She. . . she provoked him. One night. He was drunk and said some mean things."

"What kind of things?"

Isybelle flinched. "About our father's death. They were hurtful, Ankarette. Hurtful to me as well. But. . . but he's like that when he drinks. He says things he doesn't remember. That he doesn't mean. He said he'd hide her in the cistern where Severn would never find her. She's afraid of the dark. And afraid of drowning. Remember that boulder by Dundrennan? The one we'd use to jump into the river?"

Ankarette did remember it.

"Nanette was always terrified of it. But Dunne was

angry with her. He wouldn't have done it, of course. I wouldn't have let him."

"Does this manor have a cistern? Or did he mean the one at the palace?"

Isybelle shook her head. "We don't have one. The next morning, she was gone. The gates were still locked."

"Even the porter gate?"

"Yes, even that one. No one had seen her. That was the day Severn came for her. But she was already gone, you see. And Severn and Dunne got into a row. It was... was awful. I thought... I feared they would try and kill each other." Isybelle wrung her hands. "I'm frightened, Ankarette. We've been searching for her ever since. So have Severn's men. I know my husband doesn't want her to marry his brother. It would divide the inheritance, you see. But I don't begrudge it. It's hers by right, and Severn wants her... even knowing..."

"What?" Ankarette put a gentle hand on Isybelle's shoulder.

"She's still... frightened of men. It was never tender for her. Severn is... patient. I never knew he could be."

That was news to Ankarette too. "I'll find her, Isybelle. I don't think it's a coincidence that she disappeared the same day that Eredur took custody of her wardship. I need to find out how she left. And I have a feeling the guard at the porter door may know something. I think I'll use the nightshade on *him*."

Isybelle's brow wrinkled. "Moser? He's loyal to my family. *My* family."

"I'll talk to him as I leave. Your husband will be asleep for several hours. He needs the rest. The draft I used will also help purge the effects of the wine in his

43

blood. Thank you, Belle. I wish we could see more of each other." She stroked Isybelle's hair.

"We shall, I hope," replied her friend. "I reminded Dunne that he promised you could be there to help with another baby. I think. . . I pray to the Lady. . . it will be another little boy." Her eyes glistened with tears.

The two women hugged each other. Ankarette departed without the basket but not before collecting the dagger hidden within it. She slid it into a thigh sheath under her skirt and then retraced her way back through the manor. Part of her wished she'd been called in to investigate earlier. With the Duke of Glosstyr's men ransacking the Arbon, any helpful clues had probably been ruined. She stopped by the kitchen, took a biscuit, and wrapped it in a napkin for Moser. She heard the second morning bell ringing as she left the back door and started toward the alcove and gate. He was sitting on his stool, leaning against the inner wall and facing the gate, his back to her.

When she reached the arch, she held out the napkin. "I brought you a bisc—"

Something heavy struck Ankarette in the head. A sharp blow. It stunned her.

Then blackness.

CHAPTER

SIX

THE NIGHT WATCHMAN

A nkarette was roused by the fervent jostling of a quick pace and the guttural, curt words of the man handling her. A throbbing pain in the back of her skull reminded her of the injury. Her wrists were bound tight. Her ankles too. A smelly rag had been crammed inside her mouth, pushing against her tongue.

"Have a care, have a care!" hissed her captor, his hands holding her legs against his shoulder. She was being carried like a sack of grain. Dull pain throbbed. The instinct of panic was strong, but she'd been trained for circumstances like this. For being incapacitated. It was always best to feign unconsciousness. Learn as much as she could.

"It's clear yonder," said another rough voice. "We should take Rat Street."

"Too risky," said another man. "Brogan's gang is always there."

"Hush, fools," said the man holding her. "We need a blanket or some sheets to hide her. Steal something, Beggar. Be quick about it!"

"Aye, Snatch. I will." It was a fourth voice, and the

45

sound of running steps could be heard. Ankarette's upper body flopped against the man's back. She'd heard four distinct voices. She trained her ears, trying to discern if anyone else was present. Now that the one man, Beggar, had run, she counted three sets of footsteps. Criminals, judging by their nicknames. Were these sanctuary men? Thieves and murderers who hid from justice at the sanctuary of Our Lady? She wasn't wearing her Espion ring. She felt it crushed against the skin of her chest, along with her poisoner rings and vial. They hadn't searched her yet. She could still feel the dagger against her leg. But with her hands bound and secured, it was useless to her.

Under normal circumstances, she could handle four men. But not when she was tied up. That put her at a distinct disadvantage.

"What was she doing at the duke's manor, you think?" asked a worried man.

"We'll find out soon enough," barked the man holding her.

The sound of running steps returned shortly after. "Gots a blanket!" announced the runner, panting.

"Well done, lad. Let's ditch to the alley and roll her up in it. Come on!"

Ankarette opened her eyes. The swaying motion was disorienting. She was somewhere deep in the slums of Kingfountain. The road they were on was a back street, narrow and littered with debris. The smell of offal was strong. The four men turned the corner, and then she was hoisted down onto the cobblestones. She closed her eyes again but parted her eyelids just slightly to get a measure of the men. They were furtive, skulking types. The largest one, the one holding her, had a thick beard and soot stains on his face and hands.

She summoned her Fountain magic to try to understand the situation clearly. She felt the magic build up inside her. It revealed quickly that her life was in real danger. If they took her to their lair, she might not come out alive.

"Hold it out, I'll lift her in," the big one commanded. Two of the others grabbed a ragged quilt and held it out.

"Someone's coming," said the runner.

"Hurry on!" growled the big man. "Who is it?"

The runner hastened back to the mouth of the alley. "A night watchman!" he hissed back.

"Club him and leave his body in the alley. He's no threat to us."

Ankarette heard the distinct sound of another man approaching from the street. He wasn't making noise or trying to hide his approach. It was morning still. The sun hadn't risen high enough to dispel all the shadows, at least not in the western part of town. Ankarette tested the bonds at her wrists, still feigning sleep. The rope was sturdy. It would take time to twist her way free. But she could remove the gag and warn the watchman of the ambush. One man against four. Not good odds. Hopefully he was armed.

"I'll help him," whispered another of her assailants.

Ankarette moved quickly. She brought up her wrists and tugged the gag from her mouth.

"Help!" she yelled, driving the volume from deep in her abdomen. Not a waif's cry of terror, but a full-throated roar of alarm. It was the type of cry that would put anyone on the defensive.

The man who'd carried her cursed under his breath and tried to slam his fist down against her head. She was expecting that and shielded her head with her arms. The strike hurt her forearm, but it didn't knock her out again.

The sound of a sword clearing a scabbard came from the road. Maybe it wasn't a man from the night watch. Maybe it was an Espion who had followed her. She prayed to the Lady it was.

The big man lifted his fist to strike her again, only this time he hit her in the stomach. She tried to block it, but the blow landed hard and forcefully, knocking the wind from her. She rolled onto her stomach, tucking in her legs to try to strike out. He punched at her a third time, but she changed positions quickly to make it harder for him to target her.

A groan sounded from the alley mouth, and a body slumped to the ground. Cries of rage sounded, and the other men joined in the attack. Ankarette was trying to protect herself from the blows of the big man, but she caught a glimpse of the swordsman in the alley mouth. He'd killed the runner already, stabbed him through. He dispatched the other two assailants with brutal efficiency. She caught the glimpse of a scar on his face by his eye and noticed the dangerous look on his countenance. Reaching out with her magic again, she tried to gauge whether her situation was going from bad to worse. He was a soldier. Possibly a knight. He was a seasoned warrior.

The third man slid off the watchman's sword point, knees buckling as he spilled into the street.

The big man rose to his feet, leaving Ankarette on the ground.

"Your turn," said the watchman.

The big man drew a cudgel from his belt. No. . . it was a knobbed mace. He was the bigger of the two. "I'm not afraid, watchman."

Ankarette was about to kick the big man in the knee, but he rushed the watchman right at that moment. She began twisting her wrists in circular patterns, trying to stretch any slack in the ropes so she could free herself. With her hands loose, she could use one of her poisoned rings. As she wrestled with her bonds, she observed the fight. The two men were evenly matched, despite the larger one's size. She sensed with her magic that both had fought on the battlefields. It was not the lopsided contest it had been with the other three thieves. The big man was the leader, the most cunning of the four.

The mace crashed against the watchman's shoulder, causing him to growl in pain. But the watchman kneed his opponent in the stomach, and then the two crashed against the alley wall, where the sword clattered onto the cobblestones. Ankarette grimaced as she tried to work the bonds loose, but they were still tight. She rubbed her wrists together, tried to open more room. The two men crashed into the other side of the alley against the wall. The mace fell next as the two grappled each other with their bare hands.

She saw a dagger flash.

The big man coughed in surprise, backing away, a blade buried to the hilt in his belly. Then the watchman kicked him hard, and he crumpled.

Breathing fast, the watchman retrieved his sword, then pulled his dagger from the dying man's stomach. He nodded to the big man, like a mark of respect to a worthy opponent, and then shuffled over to Ankarette.

"Stop squirming, lass, let me help you," he said, panting as he lowered to a squat. He set the sword down by her, and she offered her wrists. He wiped the blood from the dagger on the discarded quilt first and then cut the bonds on her wrists and her ankles. He had a close-cropped beard, black, and shorn hair. A soldier's cut. His chainmail hood, lowered about his neck and shoulders, also denoted his profession. She had a better look at his scar—a crescent-shaped mark extending from his eyebrow back to his ear, part of which was missing. He looked stern, serious, and she already knew he was dangerous.

"Thank you," Ankarette said, panting. "I was stolen."

"I can tell, lass. What's your name?"

Now that he was talking again, she recognized the Northern accent. He was probably from Yuork.

"Krysia," she answered.

His brow wrinkled. "That's a Northern name. Are you from Yuork?"

"Aye," she said, giving a smile. "What's yours?"

"John Thursby, at your service," he said. He sheathed the dagger in his boot, grabbed his sword with one hand, and then rose and extended the other to help her stand.

His hand was very calloused. She saw scars on his knuckles.

"Thank you, John Thursby," Ankarette said. She meant it. Most night watchmen were doddering old men in need of coins to maintain a meager lifestyle. They were paid neighborhood by neighborhood to patrol the streets and warn of fires or robberies, not to battle sanctuary men.

"What ward of the city do you live in?" he asked her, sheathing his blade. "I can escort you home."

"I'm a midwife," Ankarette said. "I was visiting the Duchess of Clare."

"Vintrey, then. You're quite a ways off from there, lass."

"I don't know where I am," she said, glancing at the dead men nearby. The big man's eyes were still open, vacant, head tilted to one side.

"You're at the edge of my ward now," he said with a chuckle. "It's normally quiet, so they call it the Hermitage. We don't get many cutthroats here. Most are smarter than this lot. Vintrey is south of here. I'll take you."

"I can manage to find it," she said.

He cocked his head. "Your head's bleeding. That won't do. Come on, lass. Let's get you patched up first. Old Rose is my neighbor. She's an apothecary. Come on. No fuss. Then I'll report these men to the constable's men and have the bodies removed." He sighed and gripped her by the arm. Not forcefully, but firmly enough to provide a stable hand for her to walk. "Then I can finally get some rest."

She was grateful to leave the alley behind and the dead-eyed men that John Thursby had killed. She was intrigued by him and what he was doing in such a quiet quarter. It gave her an idea. If he was a night watchman, he could tell her who patrolled the streets by the Arbon.

Nanette had vanished during the night. Ankarette was convinced of it.

And she still needed to go back there and have a talk with Moser and learn why he'd had those men ambush her.

I've found that it is better to listen than to speak. And when speaking, say only what is necessary and in few words. I learn more by listening. People reveal themselves in what they say and how they say it.

— ANKARETTE TRYNEOWY

CHAPTER
SEVEN
DEAD END

"Isn't that the way to Dowgate Hill?" Ankarette asked, pointing to the rise in the land. They were still in an unfamiliar part of the city, but she was beginning to have glimpses of familiar features.

"Dowgate is that way," the night watchman answered. "But if we cut through Crooke Street, we'll get there faster."

"You know the city very well, John," she complimented. She hoped he was right and thought she'd let him prove it. He'd already taken her to the apothecary, who had tended to Ankarette's wound with skill and courtesy and given her a little salve to aid in the healing. The watchman's quarters were part of Old Rose's business, a single attached room, and he'd fetched himself something to drink. Once she'd been tended to, they'd begun the walk back to the Arbon. He took another street to the left, one with a narrow alley where the windows of the upper floors were nearly touching.

"Call me John Thursby, if you please," he said.

"Oh?"

"Thursby is the town I'm from, on the outskirts of

Yuork. I like to remember the North. The land of my birth. Have you heard of it? Thursby?"

"Nay," Ankarette said. "I grew up on Chequers Lane."

"I know it well. The midwife lived between a barber and an apothecary."

"She was my mother," Ankarette said.

He nodded in recognition. "Her husband died in the war. Your father?"

"Aye. What brought you to Kingfountain, John Thursby?"

"The war," he sighed. "I joined the true king's army as a lad of fifteen."

"The true king?" She felt a murmur in her heart, a warning.

"Henricus Argentine," he said firmly.

The mad king. The one Ankarette had poisoned. She kept her expression interested, even though her heart felt pangs of disappointment. Ankarette served Eredur, the king who had toppled his cousin Henricus and seized his throne. If John Thursby had known who she really was, he wouldn't have saved her life in the alley.

"Why didn't you go back to the North when the war was over?" Ankarette said.

"I tried but couldn't get any work. Lord Horwath is the duke of the North now. He wouldn't take me because of my previous loyalties. Neither would any of the others. I tried joining the city watch of Kingfountain, but there were too many of us. So I volunteered for the night watch."

"Volunteered? Why?"

"Had to prove myself somehow. I'm a man of my word. They put me in the roughest part of the city at first. But I did my duty."

"And now you've settled in the quietest part?"

He glanced at her and looked away. "It is now. That's why they call it the Hermitage, it's so quiet now."

She understood. He'd worked hard and tamed the ward. That was impressive, but he wasn't boasting about it. His modesty was also impressive.

"I wish the night watch in Vintrey were as diligent as you."

"The sanctuary men know the tolling of the bells," he said. "They plan their crimes around when the sanctuary gates open and shut. I don't walk my ward at the same times or in the same places."

"Clever of you. I take it the other night watchmen do?"

He shrugged. "One thing I like about this alley is the planter boxes overhead. The smells coming down from them. Do you recognize them?"

Ankarette had been so engrossed in the conversation that she'd barely noticed the fragrant scent of fresh herbs. "Rosemary?"

"Aye. And lavender. And mint, thyme, marjoram."

She smelled again and caught the various fragrances. "You know your herbs, John Thursby."

"I love plants and their smells. Flowers especially, though none grow in an alley. I could walk the city blindfolded, I think."

That was a little boastful, but Ankarette let him have it. When they reached the end of the alley after several curves, she recognized the neighborhood.

"I know my way from here," she said. "Thank you for escorting me."

"I'll see you to the gate." He had a little flushed look on his cheeks and gave her a surreptitious glance.

She touched his arm. "I can manage, thank you. I

appreciate your help. I'll tell my lady what you did. I think she'll reward you."

He pursed his lips. "I did my duty, lass. I don't need a reward." He nodded to her. She noticed, in the change of lighting, how blue his eyes were, but he abruptly turned on his heel and walked briskly away. Had she offended him by mentioning a reward?

"John Thursby," she called.

He paused but didn't turn back.

"Thank you."

He didn't look at her, but she saw his profile. "Fare ye well." Then he strode away briskly again.

Ankarette wondered at his sudden shift in mood. It had been a pleasant walk, even though her head was still throbbing. But that was common for such an injury.

She walked to the porter gate, staying out of sight, but then noticed two knights outfitted with Dunsdworth's bull badge guarding it from the outside. They hadn't been there before.

Ankarette's brow furrowed, but she smoothed it and then walked up to the knights. There was no stool on the other side. No sign of the gate keeper.

"Where's Moser?" she asked one of the knights. She'd walked up to them as though she belonged.

"Broken skull," replied the man gruffly.

"Had to carry him to a healer," said the other knight, pointing. "Might not make it, poor sod."

WHEN ANKARETTE AWOKE FROM A NAP, the pain in her skull had subsided considerably. The long night coming from Atabyrion, along with the morning's adventures, had convinced her to take a room at the inn on Bridge Street. An Espion safe house. She gazed at the midafternoon light coming from the glazed window, then scooted off the bed, and removed the peasant's dress, replacing it with one of her own. She was gentle brushing her hair, especially near the wound, and then applied more of the salve she'd gotten from John Thursby's neighbor.

The memory of him tickled her mind, especially his abrupt change in behavior. And the flush on his cheeks.

One of the things she'd learned in the poisoner school was that men, in general, were prone to mistake a listening and sympathetic ear as a sign of romantic interest. She'd asked about his background in order to learn more about him. Maybe he'd interpreted her motives one way and her offer to reward him had then offended his pride. Ankarette knew she was attractive. Alluring even. Several cocksure young men in the Espion had made a few brazen attempts to get her interest, but she'd disabused them of the notion quickly enough.

Her heart had belonged to Sir Thomas. After he'd chosen Lord Horwath's daughter and Ankarette had been debilitated by Lord Hux's poison, she'd locked up her heart.

Ankarette gazed at herself in the mirror, turning her chin to one side to get a look at the wound. The apothecary had cleaned the blood from her hair, applied sutures, and put on a layer of the salve to help clean the wound and block more bleeding. It would take several weeks of healing before she could have them removed.

Old Rose was a decent healer, but she didn't know how to do sutures.

In her mind, she remembered John Thursby's blue eyes and then shook her head. It was not like her to allow a man to distract her.

After securing her cloak, she unlocked the door of the room and then wandered toward the Espion chief's office and knocked the code.

"Enter."

She twisted the handle and stepped into Hugh Bardulf's chamber. Hugh was an older man, with a distinguished white mustache and goatee, and trimmed hair combed forward in the Occitanian style. He was seventy years old and one of the oldest spies in the Espion, stationed at the inn near the gates of the sanctuary of Our Lady.

"How are you feeling?" he asked, poring over scrolls and pushing aside a missive he'd been in the middle of writing.

"Better now that I've slept," she answered. He was a father figure to all the Espion stationed there, training the new generation.

"Good, I'm glad to hear it. I haven't told the king you took a wallop. Thought I'd spare your dignity for a while longer."

"It's appreciated." She sat down in the chair opposite him. "What news?"

"The lord high constable was here but an hour ago. Glosstyr's and Dunsdworth's men nearly got into a fight in Highbury. They're both scouring the city and making fools of themselves. That's why the constable was so late in answering my summons." He tapped his finger on the desk. "He knows John Thursby. A soldier who fought on the wrong side of the last war. What he said was true. The man's from Yuork. Was grievously wounded in the Battle of Borehamwood and laid up at an apothecary for months with an infection. Wandered Ceredigion looking for work and finally volunteered at the night watch to prove himself. The story checked out based on what you told me."

Ankarette had known it would. Her assessment of the man was that he was trustworthy. "Who is the night watchman for the Vintrey ward?"

"There are two. Bolger and Derrow. They were both sought out by Severn and interviewed. They didn't have any information. And that gatekeeper, Moser, is unconscious and may be for some time if he doesn't perish from the blow. You're blessed by the Lady not to be in the same predicament."

Ankarette sighed. Moser had been her most promising lead.

"What apothecary is he staying at?"

"I can have one of the boys take you there."

"Just tell me."

"The one on Wrexham. It's near the Arbon. What do you make of the attack?"

"It may not be related to Nanette," Ankarette replied. "When I went to the Arbon this morning, there were no knights guarding it. Obviously, they're all out searching for the duke's daughter. It's possible the sanctuary men were looking for an opportunity to rob the place."

"It's also possible they were bribing Moser for information," Hugh said. "His body was found abandoned in the street, so we're assuming they made it through the gate."

"Well, they're all dead now," she mused. Thanks to

John Thursby. "Any thoughts about where she might be?"

"Kingfountain is a big city. There are many possibilities."

"Aye, and for all we know, she could be on her way to Pree by now," Ankarette said worriedly. "But I think she's still in the city. If it was done by King Lewis's spies, they would know we'd be watching the gates and the docks."

"And we *are*."

"I need someone who knows this city. Who knows the alleys and all the cracks in the walls."

"The sanctuary men. But we don't operate there."

Ankarette shook her head and rose from the chair. "Not them. Someone they're afraid of."

She needed someone like John Thursby. But she'd already lied to him about who she was and whom she worked for. To get his cooperation, she had a feeling she'd need to tell him more of the truth about herself.

Her insides tightened. She wasn't sure if it was a result of the lingering poison or another feeling entirely.

EIGHT

THE LOST GIRLS

Danner Tye ran a fine apothecary shop in the wealthy Queenshithe ward. Ankarette went there to restock her poisons. He knew who she was, and everything she needed was paid for by the king's treasury. Fastidious in both his housekeeping and his personal grooming, Danner had a neatly trimmed beard the color of chestnuts and the high doublet of a well-to-do tradesman.

When she entered through the front, he was at a workbench with a mortar and pestle, grinding something into powder.

"Ah, Ankarette. Good to see you. It's been a fortnight, at least."

"Hello, Danner."

He brushed off his hands and rose from the workbench and then washed his hands vigorously in a dish before drying them on a towel. He was always conscious of not contaminating his work.

"What are you in need of?" he asked.

"I took a blow to the head this morning," she said.

"Ah, some red nettle and vinegar for the pain, then? What else?"

"I need a soporific as well. The one with hemlock and mandrake."

"I always keep that in stock for you," he said with a rueful smile. "And for wives with snoring husbands! Anything else? I ground up some nightshade recently."

"I have enough but may need more soon. Any news about the sample I gave you?"

His brow furrowed, and a disappointed look came on his face. "I still can't identify the poison you're suffering from. It has an. . . acute scent to it. Very distinctive and unusual. It could be from a native plant in Occitania for all we know. Or farther afield. I'm sorry I haven't been able to unmask it."

"It doesn't hurt to hope," Ankarette said.

"Indeed. Let me get your things."

Shortly after, she bid Danner Tye farewell and went out into the city again. This time she was dressed more in her normal fashion, no longer a laundress but a well-groomed woman with braided hair and a cloak. She'd discussed the location of the Hermitage with one of Hugh's streetwise young men and proceeded to walk there, bypassing Vintrey and heading to John Thursby's humble quarters. She didn't know what time he began the night watch, but she wanted to speak to him before he began his rounds.

As she passed through the city this time, she wasn't given the leers or whistles that she'd been greeted with that morning when in disguise. She walked with the confident stride of a businesswoman. Her clothes showed she was a woman of means, but not a lady—who wouldn't dare walk the streets of Kingfountain without an armed escort or by carriage. The appearance of wealth brought some measure of protection from obscene remarks. Her daggers gave her more.

When she reached the Hermitage ward, she recognized the cramped streets and nearly touching roofs. She noticed a boy crouching on a roofline, hunkering low, watching her pass. He was a barefoot lad, probably using the roofs to sneak from house to house with a light foot and deft hand.

She found John Thursby's place where she'd remembered it, part of Old Rose's apothecary. It was time to reveal the truth to him. After rapping gently on the door, she waited a moment, then heard the clunk of boots approaching. She noticed the curtain by the window parting, saw a glimpse of John Thursby's face, and then he opened the door.

He seemed disappointed to see her. He also looked like he hadn't slept a wink.

"It's you," he said sullenly.

That was not the greeting she'd expected.

"I was hoping we could—" she started, but he interrupted.

"I went to the Arbon earlier. Came to check on you. I was worried about you. Imagine my surprise." His tone was cold, yet she sensed the pang of injured pride.

"Did you speak to Lady Isybelle?" Ankarette asked. She hadn't anticipated this. Had he even gone to bed?

"I did. Some of what you told me was true. But you're not who I thought you were." Again she sensed his disappointment.

"What did she tell you about me?" Ankarette asked.

He crossed his arms and leaned against the doorjamb. "What does it matter? You need my help?"

"I did come to ask for it, yes."

"I went to the constable afterward. He knew about you too. Said if you came asking, it was the king's business, and I should do what you say."

Ankarette was used to being in more control of a situation. She'd offended John Thursby. She wasn't sure why his opinion mattered to her, but it did. It wasn't often she felt the stirrings of defensiveness, but they were more than stirring now. They were seething.

"It's not my practice to reveal myself and my identity to just anyone," she said, then regretted it instantly. Her feelings were getting in the way of her task.

"I imagine not. You're here. And I have information that'll be helpful to you."

"What information?"

"You're looking for someone. A lass. Knights have been scouring the streets like a scullion does her kitchen pots for the last two days. Everyone in the night watch has been talking of it. Someone important, though her name hasn't been shared. I think I know where she might be."

Ankarette's eyes widened with surprise. She wanted to ask about it straightaway, but first she felt she needed to repair things with John Thursby.

"There's something I would say to you first, John Thursby," she said, reaching out and touching his arm.

He visibly flinched but didn't withdraw. "Whatever you need to say, all I ask is it be—"

"The truth," she cut in. She stepped closer to him, looking him directly in the eyes, her hand still on his arm. "My name is Ankarette Tryneowy. Not Krysia. That's a name of a girl I knew in Yuork. A childhood friend who died of the pox. I'm the king's poisoner."

His lips pursed, and she felt his body stiffen.

"I trained at the poisoner school in Pisan. Duke Warrewik sent me. I have an Espion ring, although I don't report to their master. We are allies. I'm here on the king's business, and it's urgent. When I heard you were loyal to Henricus Argentine, I thought it prudent to keep my identity secret." She released her grip on his arm. "I've told you the truth. And I ask that you guard it."

He'd kept his blue eyes fixed on hers. Now he looked down at the floor, a little abashed. "I believe you."

"And I do need your help, John Thursby. But if we are to work together, we need to trust each other. At least as much as we can. Are you loyal to Eredur?"

He chuckled darkly. "I don't think highly of him. I didn't think highly of Warrewik either. But I keep the king's peace in the city because it is my duty. The men who attacked you were criminals. Sanctuary men. They've been kidnapping lasses in recent weeks and taking them to a dangerous man. A miscreant of the foulest sort. Bidigen Grimmer."

That name meant nothing to Ankarette. She shook her head. "And he escapes justice by staying at the sanctuary of Our Lady?"

"No. Not even the deconeus could countenance what this man does. I spoke to the night watchmen of Vintrey. Their names are Bolger and Derrow."

"Have you slept at all since we parted this morning?"

He chuffed. "A little. I don't require much. Derrow saw a girl in a cloak get abducted the other night in his ward. He didn't tell Bolger, nor Glosstyr's men. He was too afraid."

"Why did he tell you?" Ankarette asked, cocking her head.

"Because I beat him half to death and threatened to spill his gizzards on the street if he didn't. He told me Grimmer's been purchasing a few stolen young ladies throughout the city. They believe he's going to send them to Genevar to be sold for sport." His face twisted with revulsion. "One of those chaps I felled in the alley was still alive when I went back. I asked him about Grimmer. They worked for him. Those men. . . this morning. . . were going to do that to *you*. By the time you woke up, you might have been on a ship and gone with the tide."

Ankarette's heart clenched with dread. "Do you know where to find him?"

"No, lass. But I know someone who might."

"Oh?"

"I can't threaten *him*, though. The deconeus wouldn't allow it, and I'm not fancying a swim over the falls."

"Who?" she pressed. Someone already at the sanctuary.

"There's a blighter in there. A pickpocket. A thief. They call him Dragan. If anyone knows where Bidigen Grimmer is skulking, it's him. I suggest we hurry to the sanctuary before they bar the gates for the night."

Ankarette knew that name. The deconeus, Tunmore, had spoken to her about him years before when she'd encountered his special ability.

Dragan was Fountain-blessed and could become invisible at will. He'd be able to sense her coming just as she could sense him.

CHAPTER

NINE

TOSSING A COIN

Ankarette saw no good reason not to tell John Thursby about her mission while they hurried toward the bridge and the sanctuary. The urgency of the situation made her suspend her typical penchant for secrecy. Having a night watchman to assist her would allow them to continue the search after dark. She told him, briefly, about the Duke of Clare's sister-in-law Nanette and the conflict with the Duke of Glosstyr. She also admitted that she thought Moser knew more than he'd said. If he didn't survive the blow to the head, there would be no further information from him, though, which meant pursuing Dragan was now their highest priority.

"Do you agree?" she asked him, dodging past a cart and their fellow travelers on High Street.

"You're right sharp," he answered with a nod of agreement. "Grimmer might not know who the lass really is. If he's not a fool, he'll try to get a reward for her if he finds out. Do you think one of the duke's men had her abducted? Without his knowledge? One of his enterprising servants could have spawned the idea, I suppose."

"I don't know. But I do believe she was stolen away at night so none of the servants would know of it. Her sister, the duke's wife, clearly isn't aware. Nor has she any motive to injure her sister."

"What I've heard of the Duke of Clare isn't to his honor. He rules the Vintrey ward with a bit of a heavy hand, they say. It being the king's city and all."

"I'm not surprised," Ankarette replied. "He is a powerful man. And ambitious."

"I could say more, but I won't," John Thursby muttered. "Lest I offend."

"I'm not easily offended."

"That may be, but you still serve the king."

She touched his arm to get him to meet her eyes and then removed her hand. "If you know something, please tell me."

He sighed. "I served Lord Devereaux, lord high constable of Ceredigion. What I know of Lord Dunsdworth, I learned from him."

Ankarette knew little of Devereaux, except for what Sir Thomas had told her. Lord Devereaux had been chosen by Eredur as lord high constable to try to win his allegiance. He'd served for two years before joining Queen Morvared's rebellion. After Eredur had reclaimed his throne, Devereaux had fled the realm. No one knew where or what he was up to.

"Do you know where Lord Devereaux is?" Ankarette asked. It was information the Espion would want to know.

"No, lass. I haven't seen him since the day I fell in battle. The battle *your* king won. Nor have I heard of him. But whilst we were in Occitania, Devereaux said that the Duke of Clare could not be trusted. Said he's a weathercock, always yanked about by the wind. He has no scruples."

"Not many men with ambition do," Ankarette said. She wanted to tell John Thursby that she was the one who had infiltrated Occitania and convinced Dunsdworth to realign himself with his brother over his uncle. Secrets were like that, always wanting to wriggle free. But there was no point in telling him other than trying to impress him. And, to be honest, he probably wouldn't have been since that action had led to the battle his side had lost. Lives were like ripples in a pond, touching each other in distant ways.

Her eyes found the hooked scar by John Thursby's eye. She'd helped cause it. Then again, he'd made his own choices.

"What I'm saying, Ankarette, is the duke won't give up power without being compelled to. He *wanted* to be king. He'll see Glosstyr's interest in the girl as a threat. Muddle his mind with wine, and he'd consider things he wouldn't have in sober moments."

"You think he *sold* her to Grimmer? If the king found out. . ."

"Aye. He'd be a dead man. I've no evidence, but after working as a night watchman, I've seen the worst sorts in this world." She saw his cheek muscles tighten, his eyes grow cold with a winter's fury. "I've heard screams in the night when all are abed, and then heard the neighbor's shutters bolted. I've seen the bruised cheekbones the next day. The cowering children." She could see his mind was reliving memories he'd rather forget. And she understood why he didn't sleep much. It made her heart pang for him. This was brutal truth, spilling from a wounded man.

70

He stopped speaking, eyes fixed on the road. They reached the bridge, which was crowded with merchant stalls and carts, the hive of trade mingling with the roar of the waterfall.

"We're nearly there," he muttered darkly, his mood gloomy.

Ankarette noticed a young man passing by, giving her an Espion hand signal, asking if she needed help. She made a subtle gesture that all was well. No one in the crowd would have noticed the exchange.

The Espion ruled the bridge. But not what lay beyond the gates of the sanctuary.

They reached those gates amidst a throng of people and carts and had to walk very close to each other in order to slip in through the gaps. When they entered, the flow of people ebbed, and she could hear the pattering of the fountains. It was normally more crowded at night, after the sanctuary men returned with their plunder. She honed her senses, trying to detect the ripple of Fountain magic that would reveal Dragan's presence. She felt nothing, so she decided to draw him out with a manifestation of her own power.

She reached into her purse and withdrew a coin, which she handed to John Thursby. "Let's petition the Lady to help in our search. Throw it in that fountain." She gestured to one of the pools in the yard.

John Thursby shrugged and followed her lead. To petition the Fountain for blessings was the primary reason people came inside the sanctuary grounds. There were some standing around it, some alone, some holding hands. A mother with three children.

As the night watchman bowed his head, Ankarette reached inside herself, triggering the Fountain magic within her. For each Fountain-blessed, the gift manifested itself in different ways, but when the power was used, it rang like a bell for other Fountain-blessed to hear. Ankarette's greatest gift was discernment. It helped her understand a person's weaknesses and also to tend a pregnant woman in the middle of delivering a baby.

Standing by the fountain, she used her power on John Thursby as he tossed the coin into the burbling waters, and she immediately regretted it.

Her magic could strip away pretention. He had none. It could weave through layers of self-justification. Again, he had none. John Thursby was an honest man and a soldier. He enjoyed smells—a well-cooked sausage oozing with grease, the scent of the rain in the street, the tender fragrance of flowers. And he was being driven mad with longing by the scent of Ankarette's perfume after walking next to her for so long.

She could see right through him, exposed, vulnerable. When he'd rescued her the previous day, he'd taken a fancy to her, had hoped against hope that his service to her would help her overlook his scars, his grim countenance, his past. But now he knew who she was, and he was cursing himself for being a fool. He still wanted to help her. To be near her. And it tortured him every time she touched him.

Ankarette shut off the flow of her magic, momentarily stunned by the power of his feelings. He'd gone that afternoon to look in on her, to see if there was anything he could do to help her. Then he'd found out the truth, and the blow had been severe.

He had no way of knowing that she'd infiltrated his

thoughts. Part of her was charmed by the simplicity of them. By *him*. But she was dying, slowly and implacably, and she'd barred her heart from feeling anything.

The coin sank to the bottom of the water. He turned and cocked his head at her. "I hope we find the lass," he said forcefully. "She doesn't deserve any of this."

Abashed by her newfound knowledge, she simply nodded, looking down at the rippling waters. Then she waited, senses attuned for a reply.

It came. A power she could sense but not see began to intrude on her thoughts and slip past her defenses. She felt conscious of it and keenly uncomfortable. Turning around, she searched the courtyard, looking for him.

There he was, standing by the gates, arms folded, head tilted slightly. He had a scraggy beard and dark hair. The clothes of a beggar. But she felt his gift. He had special powers of observation in addition to his ability to become invisible, and he was studying her cautiously, trying to determine how serious a threat she was since she was *inside* the sanctuary grounds.

Dragan leaned away from the gate and began to saunter toward them.

"He's coming," Ankarette said, turning to face him. John Thursby pivoted and glanced across the crowd. "The beggar?"

"He's the one." She was impressed at how quickly the watchman had sized Dragan up.

Dragan prolonged his contact with the Fountain magic. They both knew he was doing it, and it felt. . . rude. Deliberately so. She invaded his privacy as well, learning things about him that she'd only suspected. He was a coward at heart. A liar. And probably the best thief in Kingfountain. He had two lives in the city, including two wives—one inside the sanctuary and one without—who did not know of each other. He grinned, showing discolored teeth, when he reached them.

"Pleasure meeting you in person," Dragan said in an oily voice. He walked around her, his fingers brushing against her cloak hood, then John Thursby's sword pommel. He kept moving, not holding still, affable and gregarious. "And what brings this fine pair to the sanctuary of Our Lady of Kingfountain? Not just to toss a coin, I think? You want information. But information will cost you." His hand surreptitiously went for John Thursby's purse, but the watchman batted it away.

"We'll decide the price we pay, thank you," John Thursby said, grunting with displeasure.

Ankarette still felt the magic swirling around her, but it began to lessen. "We're looking for Bidigen Grimmer."

The thief continued to make a circuit around them both. He ran his eyes over Ankarette's body, admiring the rings, the necklace. She felt like pressing the necklace against her bosom for fear he might snatch it out from under her nose and run away.

"You think you're a match for him, do you?" Dragan sneered.

"Why do you say that?" she countered.

"I know of Bidigen Grimmer. He's not like us, lass. Not like you and I. He's. . . different. He'll suck it right out of you."

"You're making no sense," John Thursby said. "Do you know where he can be found or not?"

"I know. But as I said, it'll cost you." He deftly patted John Thursby on the cheek before whisking his hand away as the watchman tried to grab it.

"It's important we find him," Ankarette said. "But you know more than just where he is."

"Aye. And as I say, he's more than a match for you, lass."

"You think so?" Ankarette said, feeling piqued by his attitude and wandering hands. She wanted to smack him, but she kept turning to face him, not wanting him to get behind her.

He suddenly stepped very close, his chest brushing hers. He was doing this to rile her up. "I want a pardon from the king. That's my price."

"For what crime?"

"Any crime. If I'm caught, which I doubt I will be, I want to hand it over to one of those sniveling Espion. They'll open the bars, unlock the irons, and I'll walk free. One pardon. Any crime. Get it for me. And I'll tell you where you can find Grimmer."

The man's breath was awful, as if he were rotten inside. John Thursby put his hand on Dragan's shoulder, his nose twitching with raw anger.

"You can't hurt me here," Dragan said coldly. "You raise a finger, you'll be swimming off the bridge. I know the value of information. The Espion don't even know about Bidigen Grimmer. But *I* do. And I know his lair. Get me a pardon, and I'll tell you what I know about his. . . *trade*."

John Thursby lowered his hand and clenched it into a fist. "The gate will be locked soon."

Dragan shrugged. "That's not a problem. I'll meet you at the gate and talk to you from this side. What I have to tell you is only words. You show me the king's seal, and then we'll talk."

The Fountain magic dropped, ending the annoying probing feeling. Ankarette was sick inside and angry.

She wanted to throw this man off the falls herself. But she kept her expression innocuous.

"I'll be watching for you tonight," Dragan said, backing away from the pair. "You'd best hurry. Some secrets are worth even less at dawn."

The heart is a fickle thing.

— ANKARETTE TRYNEOWY

CHAPTER
TEN

WHEN IN DARKNESS

"**C**an I bring you something to drink? A mug of ale?" The serving girl was friendly, inquisitive, and definitely part of the Espion.

John Thursby waved the question aside with a half-lifted hand and a curt shake of his head. He leaned his elbows on the table, gazing at Ankarette, who sat across from him at a small table in the corner of the inn's common room.

"A soldier who doesn't drink?" Ankarette asked curiously. She still regretted using her Fountain magic on him. The unexpected glimpse into his soul had broken past some of her defenses. She'd found a warm ember glowing inside what she'd assumed to be a dark vault. She wasn't entirely sure whether to smother the warm feelings or coax them.

"There was a time I welcomed the rush to oblivion," he said with a wrinkled lip. "It dulled the terror of battle. Made boredom bearable. It was the morning *after* that became insufferable."

"You have a gift for words, John Thursby."

Her compliment had pleased him. She saw a little flush rise to his cheeks, and he suddenly couldn't meet

78

her eyes. He fidgeted for a moment and then sighed. "You do me too much credit, lass. Some men steal wealth. I'm a thief of words."

"Oh? And who do you steal them from?"

"Master Caxton of Brugia."

Ankarette had heard of him. A merchant from East Stowe who had gone to Brugia to learn the occult craft of printing books. He was known for printing legends of King Andrew.

"A soldier who reads?"

"Don't mock me, lass."

"You mistake me. I'm impressed."

He squirmed some more, looking uncomfortable and pleased. "My mother taught me to read and write. It helped me rise in Devereaux's service, while earning scorn among others. I have a little collection of books. Six, I think? I'd rather spend my wages on things that last longer than a night of merriment and a morning of malady."

"Master Caxton has stories of the legends of Our Lady. Of the knights of the Ring Table. Do you fancy those?"

"I prefer his book of poems."

That pleased Ankarette in a way that surprised her.

"Do you have a favorite line? One you know by heart?"

His eyes widened with surprise at her questions. He drilled his fingertips on the wooden table. "Too many. Since sleep is often suffering, I read some over and over so I can repeat them while roaming the streets at night. Let me think." His eyebrows knitted together, and then he flattened his palms on the table.

"Pride, o flower of warriors, beware of that trap. Do not give way. For a brief while, your strength is in bloom. But it fades quickly. Soon follows illness or the sword to lay thee low. Or a sudden surge of fire, a plume of water, or jabbing blade or javelin from the air. Or repellent age. Soon thy piercing eye will dim. And darken. Death will arrive for thee, dear warrior, to sweep you away over the falls."

His eyes met hers after saying it, and she felt an involuntary shiver prickle down her arms. He'd said it reverently, like a prayer at a fountain.

"That was lovely," she murmured. The ember inside her grew a little brighter. She spent many evenings doing embroidery. The precision of the needlework helped her restore her Fountain magic, which was depleted by use. A task of nimble fingers and deep thought, it kept her mind sharp. But she thought she might get the same benefit from listening to this man speak poetry to her. Either way, she would enjoy it very much.

"They are but stolen words," he said. "Written by men much wiser than I."

Ankarette noticed Hugh Bardulf entering the common room. He spotted them at the table and then strode forward, holding a sealed scroll in his hand.

"This was an errand better suited for daylight hours," Hugh complained, plopping the scroll on the table in front of her. "And a younger man."

Ankarette smiled at him. "Thank you," she said. She unrolled the scroll and quickly read the royal pardon. It was addressed to one Dragan of the sanctuary of Our Lady. That way, it could not be bartered or sold to someone else. The king's seal was affixed to the bottom of the page.

"I will have men on alert in case you need them," Hugh said.

"That will be helpful." Ankarette pushed away from the table and rose, and John Thursby followed suit. She rolled up the scroll, and the two of them left the inn. Even though it was after dark, the bridge was still busy with people going about their work. The evening bell hadn't tolled yet, but it would soon. Their shadows intermingled on the cobblestone street as they walked briskly to the gates of the sanctuary of Our Lady.

The gates were shut and locked, but they found Dragan skulking there. He was eager to get his pardon. Ankarette saw it in his eyes.

"I knew you'd get it, lass," he said with a wicked smile.

She approached the gate but held it firmly in hand. The last thing she wanted was for him to snatch it away and run off into the darkness inside the sanctuary grounds.

"Your information had better be worth such a prize," she said.

He pressed against the bars. "You'll know soon enough. Bidigen Grimmer is a brute of a man. Bigger than yon soldier next to you. Thick as a boar. Angry as one too."

"Tell me where to find him."

"Give me the scroll first."

Ankarette stepped up to the bars but kept her hand on it. She could smell his rancid breath again.

"The advantage is all on your side," she said. "I cannot trust you'll not run off."

"Show me the king's seal first."

Ankarette unrolled the scroll and revealed the glob of wax with the seal. "I've delivered what I promised. Now tell me what I want to know."

"I'll whisper it you lass."

John Thursby grunted with displeasure, shaking his head in frustration. He looked ready to reach through the bars and throttle Dragan.

Ankarette turned her head and leaned closer. But she didn't release her grip on the scroll. She prepared for him to yank it away and grabbed his belt with her left hand.

"You want to get friendly, lass?" he sneered at her. He wrapped his hand around the scroll.

"If I burn the scroll, you get nothing," she said.

"Very well, very well! Listen carefully." He was being more dramatic on purpose. He whispered his words. "Grimmer is one of the dockmen. Works on the Anchor wharf. But you'll not oft find him there. Has a lodging at the Flyte Tavern in Queenshithe. Not common housing for a dockman, eh? That's where you'll find him at night. A man will take any lass for a wench in that place. It's rowdy. You'll know the bull when you see him. Cinnamon beard. Squints a lot. That's your man."

It was an apt enough description of half the population of Kingfountain. But Ankarette knew Queenshithe. It serviced a higher-end clientele.

The Flyte was unfamiliar to her. Danner Tye, her apothecary, might know of it, though.

She let go of the scroll and then of Dragan's belt. He tapped it against his forehead in a little salute and backed away from the gate.

"Don't say I didn't warn you," he crowed and then walked into the shadows.

John Thursby had his arms folded and a distasteful look on his face. "I didn't catch what he said. Where is Grimmer?"

"The Flyte Tavern in Queenshithe."

"I know it," he murmured. "It's popular among the officers. I'll take you there."

"I was hoping you'd heard of it. Thank you."

If Bidigen Grimmer were such a mountain of a man, it would require a stronger dose of poison to render him unconscious. From the description he'd given, Dragan had made it sound like a brothel as well as a tavern. If that was where Nanette had been taken, then her situation was dire. Or, since she was noble born, perhaps Grimmer would smuggle her away from Ceredigion, where a higher stakes player would be able to afford her. Either way, Ankarette felt they were running out of time.

After crossing the bridge, they entered the wards of Kingfountain, and John Thursby took a shortcut. The buildings were all wedged thickly together, providing few alleys and byways. The primary architecture style consisted of beams and stucco, each building typically three stories with gabled rooms at the roofline. A few brick chimneys dotted the roofs. The slumping rooflines and debris in the street showed the ramshackle nature of the place. The growth of trade in Ceredigion had brought new wealth to the kingdom. That wealth had, in turn, attracted a slew of workers from the countryside; however, few accommodations had been made for them, and they were paid just enough to survive another day. These squalid streets were a consequence of a desire for profit over the lives of the workers.

"I appreciate you going with me," Ankarette said. "I'm not as familiar with the streets at night."

"I'm equally comfortable day or night," he said. "I know the night watchmen for Queenshithe ward as well. They'll give us no trouble."

"I've seen you handle a sword. I wasn't worried about that."

He laughed. "The average night watchman is sixty or seventy years old. Blind in one eye, crippled in one or both legs, and deaf as a post."

"Oh, so how did you get the job?" she said with a grin.

"I'm blind in one eye."

"Are you?"

"It's a little dim, but I'm mostly jesting. As I said, it was hard for a soldier on the wrong side to get a job."

"I might be able to help on that front. You're doing the king a service."

"No, Ankarette. I'm doing the service for *you*."

If she hadn't already discovered his true feelings, that admission would have been enough of a hint. A silence hung between them as they walked, but it was not a terrible one. The night grew darker, and only the lights from inside the closed shops and houses spilled into the street.

"This way," he said, gesturing at a crossroads.

"How can you tell?" she asked. "You've walked it a hundred times?"

"No. We just passed the butcher. Can't you smell the offal?"

She'd noticed it but hadn't made the connection to the butcher. Her magic had been correct about his sense of smell.

As soon as they turned the street and started down it, they were plunged into darkness. There were no lights on in this part of town. The air became heavier, more stained with mildew. The road curved down, and homes bunched tightly together. A cat hissed at them.

Then the clop of hooves came from behind, loud

enough that it had to be several riders. Ankarette and John Thursby turned and saw a group of four knights coming after them, all on horseback. One held a lantern to chase away the shadows.

"Hoy," shouted one of them. "Stop in the duke's name!"

CHAPTER ELEVEN

BROTHERS OF THE BLOOD

When Ankarette heard the order, she felt a prickle of apprehension go down her spine. It was dark, and the buildings on either side of the gently sloping street offered no alleys to duck into. The doors were probably all locked. Fleeing from armed, mounted knights wasn't a good strategy anyway.

"Which duke?" John Thursby wondered aloud, his tone betraying his misgivings about their situation.

"Let me handle them," Ankarette said. She turned to face the oncoming knights, adjusting her cowl slightly to hear their approach better. They were probably looking for Nanette as well, and if someone had thought the poisoner and night watchman suspicious enough, their report may have triggered a search of the area. Or it could just be happenstance their paths had crossed.

Soon the knights arrived, and the lead man holding the lantern hoisted it higher to expose them. He wore the badge of the bear and the staff. Warrewik's badge. He wasn't the officer, though. She recognized that knight immediately, for he'd served in the Duke of Warrewik's personal guard and wore his badge. His name was Sir Rigby. A proud man, one still embittered by the fall of his master. Still, she knew him to be loyal to the duke's daughters.

"Shine the light on her face," Sir Rigby ordered. "Is it you, Nan?"

Ankarette lowered her cowl, spilling out her nest of braided hair. Nanette was dark-haired, like her sister.

"Ankarette?" Sir Rigby said with startled surprise. "What are *you* doing here?" The edge in his voice spoke of disdain. All of Warrewik's household knew about her betrayal of the duke. But Ankarette and Sir Thomas had thought treason a higher crime.

"We're searching for the same person," she answered. "You go your way. I'll go mine."

"And who's that with you?" Rigby demanded. "Shine the light on him."

The knight with the lantern obeyed, and the glare fell on the soldier. Rigby snorted. "Is that you, Thursby?"

The night watchman said nothing, only scowled. His hand rested on his sword hilt.

"We're on the king's errand," Ankarette said firmly. "Begone."

Rigby's expression filled with anger. "I'm on the duke's business, and the king knows it. Where are you headed?"

"Is that any of your concern?"

"If I make it mine, yes. I could drag you both back to the Arbon for questioning."

"You could try," John Thursby said darkly.

Ankarette knew the situation needed some delicacy. Men could be so thick-headed sometimes. She took a step closer to Sir Rigby's horse, keeping her eye on the knight, and moved within reach of the bridle. If she could yank the reins from his hands, he'd be unable to control his mount. Two against four weren't bad odds, but Ankarette would prefer to avoid a confrontation.

"Sir Rigby, I applaud your diligence," Ankarette said, trying to smooth things over. "Have you had any leads? Is Moser still unconscious?"

"Aye, he took a nasty blow to the head. And from what I heard, a night watchman from the *Hermitage* killed the only witnesses."

"He was protecting me," Ankarette said.

"I didn't think a poisoner required protection?" challenged Rigby. "The duke said you threatened him this morning. You'd best tread carefully, lass. Very carefully."

John Thursby took a bold step forward, and Ankarette put her hand out to flag him to stop.

"So you have no information on where Nanette is?"

"I wouldn't tell you if I did. We'll find her, though. Be assured of that."

She didn't like his tone, but he seemed on the verge of backing off.

Ankarette measured her voice soothingly. "Best if we both continue our search, then. She is in real danger. We should not be at odds."

"You should have considered that when you snuck into the Arbon today and drugged my master." He sighed and then twitched the reins. "Let's go, men." He turned and gave John Thursby a contemptible glare. "Lucky for you, lass, there's no fog in the streets tonight. Else he might attack you by mistake."

He'd poked a raw wound, and Ankarette heard the night watchman suck in his breath. She could also hear the snick of a blade coming out of his scabbard.

"Don't," she said, keeping her eyes on Sir Rigby.

Sir Rigby didn't look fearful. He was trying to provoke Ankarette's partner. To get him to behave rashly and offer an excuse for further violence.

At that moment of alarm, the sound of more horses came from farther down the street. Ankarette turned, saw the weapon gleaming in the night watchman's hand and another group of knights approaching. Rigby squinted with wariness as five knights appeared, wearing the badge of the boar. Severn Argentine's standard.

"What's this commotion about?" asked the officer in charge of the newcomers. Ankarette didn't know his name or recognize him.

"None of your concern, Sir Brent," said Rigby.

"Did you find her? Is that Lady Nanette?"

"Don't be daft," said one of Rigby's men.

"Who are you calling daft?" came a fierce challenge.

"Gentlemen," Ankarette said, dreading what would happen should their hostility continue to mount. "This is the king's city. Your authority resides elsewhere."

"Who's the tart?" asked one of Glosstyr's men.

"The king's poisoner," Rigby said. "Now tuck your piggy tails and leave before things get ugly."

Ankarette's eyes flashed with anger. She heard the sound of blades being drawn all around her. It was not a good strategy to be standing betwixt the antagonists.

"Shut your rotting mouth!" barked Glosstyr's captain.

"Go back to your pigsty," shouted one of Clare's men.

Ankarette lunged forward and snatched the reins from Sir Rigby. She tugged the horse in a half circle as the knight shouted in surprise, then swatted the animal on the rump to send it running back up the street. There was no more time to negotiate a peace between the rival factions. They were determined to brawl. Best to get the leader out of the way.

As Rigby's horse charged away, a melee broke out. Ankarette withdrew from the circle of knights as they charged each other, sword clanging against sword. Hooves struck sparks on the cobblestones. As one of Clare's knights rode past her, she grabbed his tunic and yanked him off the horse. He crashed hard, and then she stuck him with a poisoned needle to paralyze him.

John Thursby was in the middle of the conflict, deflecting blows from the men higher than him. A horse reared and screamed, the hooves flailing. It was chaos.

Someone grabbed her by the arm and tried to lift her up onto a saddle. Ankarette punched him in the throat. Gasping for air, he let go, and she fell to the street. She rolled to one side to avoid getting trampled by one of Glosstyr's horses, then sprang at the man passing by and slammed her hand against his leg, hoping there was enough poison still on the needle in her ring to affect him.

She heard someone coming up behind her and fished a dagger from her belt. Whirling, she raised it and saw John Thursby there, sword in hand.

"You fight well," he complimented. "Back-to-back," he suggested.

She agreed, and the two of them faced off against their opponents, back-to-back. The two sides were mostly angry with each other, but she and Thursby were trapped in the middle, a dangerous place to be. A knight rode up to her with his sword, and she took a pinch of powder from her stash and flung it at the animal's face. The horse screamed and began to buck and thrash, throwing the rider from the saddle. She clubbed the man in the temple with her dagger hilt.

Sir Rigby came charging at her on foot. He must have thrown himself off his horse as it bolted and had run back to join the fray. He came straight at her. Ankarette ducked low and swept her boot around, catching him mid-ankle and knocking him down. He dropped his sword, and she kicked it away, then grabbed him by the tunic and held the dagger to his neck.

"Call off your men," she ordered.

He stared at her in fear, unsure whether she'd slit his throat or not.

"Y-you wouldn't!" he gasped.

She nicked his neck to draw blood and prove she was capable of greater violence. "Last chance before you can't speak!" She gave him a threatening glare.

"Stand down!" Rigby shouted. "Stand down!"

Ankarette rose, holding her knife out still, watching as a few drops of blood from it pattered down onto Rigby's face. A glance revealed that the Duke of Clare's men were already beaten. Severn's knights were winning.

"I knew Dunsdworth's ilk were cowards," said one of Glosstyr's knights.

"Stand down," John Thursby warned, approaching the man.

"And who are you?" sneered the knight.

"I'm the night watch. These are my streets. This is my city. Stand down."

"Or what?" came a cry of challenge from another one of Severn's knights.

John Thursby kicked him in the groin. It was three on one, and before Ankarette could intervene, he'd engaged all three, sword in one hand, dagger in the other.

Glosstyr's men were well trained. They were all warriors, but none of them could stand up to John Thursby. Ankarette watched, once again, as he quickly disabled his foes. He didn't kill them, but he drew blood, stabbing arms and shoulders, slashing at legs.

Ankarette felt a premonition of warning from her Fountain magic and turned just as Sir Rigby was grabbing for her hair. She caught his outstretched hand and spun around, hoisting him onto her back before slamming his body onto the cobblestones. In the poisoner school, she'd fought off men much larger than herself. She knew how to use their weight against them. The bone-jarring impact knocked the air from Rigby's lungs. It knocked him unconscious too.

When she straightened, she saw the other knights flattened out. Some were groaning. Some were bleeding. Ankarette felt sweat trickle down her ribs, between her breasts. She was breathing hard but not winded. So was John Thursby. He gave her an approving nod and beckoned that they should leave the scene.

"We'll cover more distance with horses," she said. All the knights had been brought down, and there were several beasts from both camps milling about. She grabbed one while John Thursby took another, and they both mounted. Once again, her partner had proven an able fellow. Her admiration for him increased.

They rode down the shadow-strewn street, Ankarette following his lead. No sound of pursuit followed them. She wondered if the fight would even be related back to their masters. One tended not to brag about losing. Or interfering with the king's business. With the additional speed brought on by the steeds, they crossed the different wards until they reached Queenshithe, or what she assumed was the place, for she didn't recognize it in the dark, coming from a part of town she was unfamiliar with.

But John Thursby knew the way and guided them to the Flyte. As they moved, Ankarette started feeling the pangs inside her again. She'd only taken a little sip of the antidote when she'd come from Atabyrion. Extra effort, like the street brawl, tended to make its effects wear off sooner rather than later, which was why she didn't like to exert herself more than was needed. She'd have to take a stronger dose before the debilitating effects of Lord Hux's poison got the better of her and made it too painful to even walk.

"This is the place," he told her, reining in his horse in front of a large three-story building, which looked no different than the others on the street. There were glowing windows in the upper floors. The lowest floor was made of stonework, no windows at all. Ankarette gazed at the stonework and realized it would be easy to climb. Maybe she should do some exploring before going straight through the front door.

John Thursby dismounted and held the reins while reaching out for her horse. She winced as she slung off it, feeling her insides flame with pain. The poison's toll was a constant presence; one she'd grown accustomed to.

"I'll tether the horses yonder," he offered, and took them to a bar where other horses had been tied up by the patrons of the inn who were likely having a drink instead of staying the night.

Ankarette pressed her hand against her abdomen, wishing she knew a way to cure herself. She would have liked to get to know her companion better. To listen to him read poetry or share his love of herbs and sweet-smelling things. She rubbed her stomach and then

JEFF WHEELER

reached into the hidden pouch in her skirts for the vial with the tincture.

It was gone.

Her brow wrinkled with concern. Had it fallen out during the clash with the knights? The way the pocket was designed would have prevented that, for she had to slip her finger around a flap in order to retrieve it. No, it couldn't have just slipped out. It could only have...

Her thoughts stopped with jarring force, along with her breath.

It had been stolen.

Dragan.

CHAPTER
TWELVE
PERILOUS TIMES

The look on her face must have betrayed her emotions. She felt John Thursby's hand on her shoulder.

"You look troubled."

Her heart surged with anger, resentment, confusion, and even disgust, while her mind whirled to come up with a plan. When something was lost, it could render the mind incapable of rational thought. She knew this. But knowing it didn't help in the anguish of the moment. She shook her head, needing a moment to calm herself. That vial was the only thing keeping her alive. If Dragan. . .

Stop it, she thought, rebuking herself. There were too many "ifs" to consider. That way led to paralyzing indecision.

"I just realized something," she said, trying to explain her sudden change of behavior. He'd tethered the horses already, and they nickered softly by the other animals. She began to pace. Even if she rode straight back to the bridge, the gate of the sanctuary would be locked. Would the deconeus help her reclaim the tincture? Would Dragan even be there? It would waste precious time—and risk Nanette's life even further.

And yet, if she did not secure the tincture, her condition would continue to worsen until the cramps became unbearable and she couldn't walk. There'd be no securing it then. Fear shot through her, and she realized she was starting to panic. That wasn't helpful. She walked to the edge of the building and pressed her back against the stone wall. Then she began to measure her breathing. She had to put out the fire in her mind, or she wouldn't be able to think clearly.

One breath. Two breaths. She purged all thought away.

"Ankarette?" John Thursby asked worriedly.

She needed to tell him something, but not yet. Not when she was on the verge of losing control. Holding up her hand to forestall further questions, she motioned for him to back away. Closing her eyes, she thought about the boulder near the river that she'd jumped from when she was younger. That place, that time, had always been a helpful tool in emptying her thoughts. The river had been so cold. She imagined standing on the boulder, staring at the river, and casting her thoughts into it one by one. Letting go of them was the secret to regaining her calm.

With her eyes closed, she could imagine the beautiful green of the North. The scent of pine. The frigid shock of the water. She filled her chest with air, then let it out slowly. Her heartbeat began to settle. The worry began to ebb. It didn't take long before her body responded to the mental exercise.

She opened her eyes again, seeing John Thursby's concerned face. He was standing away from her, as she'd asked, but as soon as her eyes opened, he came closer and put a steadying hand on her shoulder.

"Talk to me," he pleaded.

"Dragan stole something from me. Some. . . medicine that I need. I didn't realize it until just now, and now we're far from the bridge."

"I'll kill that—"

She cut him off. "Not now, John Thursby. Our mission is more important. Without the medicine, I will get weaker. But I'm still capable right now. We need to go in there and find Bidigen Grimmer. There's no time for subtlety. Give me your dagger."

"Why the dagger?" he asked, his brow wrinkling. He slid it out of his belt sheath and handed it to her.

She opened her poisoner's bag and removed some silk gloves, which she quickly put on. Then she produced a tub of ointment and opened it. With her fingertip, she slathered some of the salve on his dagger.

"This cream will cause paralysis if you cut someone. You don't have to stab them through the heart, just a nick anywhere that pierces the skin. I don't have enough to treat your entire sword, and it's better to use a smaller weapon." He nodded in understanding. "It'll also hurt *you*, so be careful how you handle the blade. My dagger sheaths contain it, so my blades are treated already. I also have poisoned pins and rings." She remembered using one of them earlier and paused to re-treat the needle with the toxin before twisting the cover back in place.

She handed him a bag. "This bag contains dust that will temporarily blind opponents. Pour some in your fist before we go in. But be careful to throw it at their faces. Even breathing it in will be harmful."

"We're going to cause a ruckus, then?"

"Yes, that's my plan. I want to empty the place as quickly as possible to avoid being outnumbered. We're going to pretend it's an Espion raid. Give orders, like you're the captain. Trust me, the rats will flee. I'll focus on identifying Grimmer or someone who can lead us to him. By the time they realize it's a ruse, we should have Nanette and be back for the horses. If we're separated, we meet back at Old Rose's."

John Thursby grinned. "I like it. But I'm not leaving you behind."

"I will be fine. And I owe Dragan for his dirty trick."

"We both do. Let's go bash some skulls."

She smiled back, nodded, and then pushed off from the wall and walked to the front door. "Kick it in."

"With pleasure."

He stepped up and planted his boot against the door, cracking it down the middle. It took a second blow to split it open. He hefted the dagger and bellowed out his words in a powerful voice.

"Don't let anyone escape! Take them all!"

He charged in first, and Ankarette came in after, searching the dimly lit room. Ladies in various stages of undress began to scream. A knight with a cup in his hand was trying to stand up from the couch when John Thursby kicked him hard in the chest. Ankarette's plan had the desired effect. There was mass panic.

"Stop in the king's name!" John Thursby roared.

Ankarette caught a glimpse of someone trying to slip past her through the door and made a quick swipe at him with her dagger, cutting him on the arm. He made it two steps before collapsing.

"Back door!" Ankarette shouted. "They're going out the back!" She said it just as a ruse, to add confusion to the mix. She wanted them spilling out windows and jumping into the streets in their haste to escape. Some men ran with only one boot on. Others had abandoned scabbards and swords and tunics on the floor.

She was looking for a big hulk of a man. Her eyes fixed on a rat-faced fellow who disappeared behind the bar counter. Her Fountain magic thrummed to life, and she knew he was important. She charged after him, shoving a harlot out of her way, and then vaulted over the bar counter.

A trap door was open.

The sound of shattering glass came from behind her. Turning, she saw John Thursby had taken a hit from a bottle, but it had broken on his shoulder armor. He flung dust in the attacker's face, and the man began to scream in pain. Then the night watchman stomped on his adversary's foot and clubbed him with the dagger hilt. He looked across the room at her and came charging.

Ankarette saw the ladder into the cellar quivering but ignored it and jumped down inside. She landed on the little man, knocking him to the floor. Grabbing him by the collar, she hoisted him to his feet.

"Where's Grimmer?" she demanded.

"H-how did you f-find. . . ?"

She pushed him against the ladder, her forearm going into his throat. She used her magic again, drawing from her reserves to scour his mind, his soul. He was a cowardly man but ruthless. Profit drove him to do despicable things. He was bought and sold by powerful people. He'd do anything for a price.

Ankarette pressed her face closer to his. "Where is Grimmer?" she repeated coldly.

He raised his arm, trembling, and pointed.

Ankarette sensed him. It wasn't Fountain magic. It

was worse. A feeling of blackness lay in the shadows. A keening sound came to her ears, an otherworldly noise, like the mewling of a cat. Fear bloomed inside her as this man—this *thing*—began to suck her magic away.

She saw a massive shape in the gloom. Heard the thump of a footfall.

She threw her dagger at him.

He caught it and threw it back at her. Ankarette's eyes bulged as she twisted just in time for her own weapon to sail past her cheek, almost nicking her with its poisoned blade.

Bidigen Grimmer was on her in a moment. How could someone so huge be so fast? He collided with her and sent her flying with a boot. The blow was so heavy, so powerful that she couldn't breathe. He'd grabbed her by the head to crush her skull between his meaty hands when John Thursby arrived, landing on the cellar floor.

Ankarette twisted the needle ring and jabbed it into Grimmer's hand. She felt it puncture his skin, grateful she'd managed it despite the pain.

Only, he didn't drop. He let her go, turning to fight the night watchman. Ankarette watched, ears ringing, waiting for him to go down. She'd replenished the dose before coming into the Flyte. Even a man of his size should have. . .

John Thursby crashed into the wall, and then Grimmer was on top of him, boot against his neck. He swore at John Thursby, using the most profane language Ankarette had ever heard. Curses vile and disgusting spilled out of him.

Ankarette drew another dagger and attacked Bidigen Grimmer from behind. She stabbed him in the back twice, but the blade didn't sink very far through the thick sinews of his muscles. He turned to face her, and she saw an ordinary fellow with a cinnamon beard and big cheeks. It was his eyes that terrified her. They were cold and dead. And glowing silver.

He punched her in the throat, knocking her back, and cursed at her. His savage words stung her ears, and again she felt her Fountain magic draining. This man was *cursed* by the Fountain. He was deplorable. Evil. Twisted. Incredibly strong. It was unnatural strength.

But she sensed, through the dregs of her Fountain magic, that he was afraid of justice. Afraid of being caught by the Espion and going over the falls. He shouted more hateful words at her and then slunk into the shadows. Ankarette was still laboring to breathe, to clear the dizziness in her throbbing skull.

He had to have a weakness. If she could only discern it.

The last gasp of her magic revealed it. He wore an amulet around his neck that gave him his dark power. If she broke the chain, it would break his connection to it.

Ankarette rose shakily to her feet, preparing for the struggle of her life.

Her eyes met his silver-cast ones. He knew that she knew, and he hated her for it.

Suddenly, the rat-faced man clamped his ears and started screaming. He charged at Ankarette, slathering and biting, blocking her path. He was all madness and frenzy, stronger than her. She punched and kicked him, trying to deflect, but he wouldn't be deterred. She felt his teeth gnawing into her arm.

John Thursby knocked the rat-faced man out cold with a blow from the hilt of his sword. His own teeth were bared in fury. He tossed the little man aside and then helped Ankarette stand back up. She'd hardly registered that she'd fallen but felt the bite marks on her arm.

"Are you well?" John Thursby gasped. He had discolorations on his neck from the boot.

"I-I think so," Ankarette breathed, panting. She was grateful he was there to steady her.

"Let's get after him," John Thursby said. "He fled up the root cellar chute. He was carrying someone. I saw her hair. Dark—like the duke's daughter."

What worries you masters you. That is one of the greatest lessons I have learned so far in life. What they taught us in the poisoner school is true. You have power over your mind, nothing else. Not outside events. Not other people. Realize this, and you will always find strength. It was true then. It is true now. Fear is just an emotion some choose to hide behind.

— ANKARETTE TRYNEOWY

THIRTEEN

WHEN QUIET SPEAKS

Ankarette pressed her hand against her stomach, gritting her teeth, enduring the pain that was already wreaking havoc inside her. They walked firmly, using a lantern they'd found in the cellar to illuminate the cobblestones and the trail of blood. Whatever uncanny powers Bidigen Grimmer had, he was mortal. He bled.

John Thursby held the lantern aloft as they reached another intersection of alleys. The crooked buildings blotted out the trail of stairs overhead. The moon hadn't risen yet, so they carried the only source of light.

Ankarette slowed and then stopped next to him, studying the street. He backed up a few steps and then discovered the trail plunging into the narrowest street on their right.

"That way," he said. Then he caught sight of her expression. "You're in pain."

"I'm all right," she answered, trying to sound calm. It felt like daggers were plunging in and out of her stomach.

"Ankarette," he sighed, shaking his head.

"We're close. I feel it." She started down the narrow

alley, and he joined her. A feral cat hissed at them from a heap of trash, making Ankarette clench her drawn dagger more tightly.

She was afraid of Bidigen Grimmer. He'd not succumbed to her poison, and his size and girth made him more than a match for John Thursby. Still, she would find him, and she would defeat him. She knew his weakness now.

Gathering reinforcements would have been helpful, but there was no time for that. It was her and John Thursby. That had to be enough.

"What kind of medicine is it?"

His voice cut into her thoughts.

"For an illness related to my profession. Now's not the time to discuss it."

"I'm sorry."

"There's no need to be. When we faced Grimmer, I could tell he's wearing a necklace of some sort. One that gives him power. It might have made him impervious to the poison. I'm not sure. What I do know is if we take it from him, he'll be vulnerable."

"How exactly do you know this, Ankarette?"

She wouldn't lie to him. Not anymore. "Because I'm Fountain-blessed."

He was silent for a few steps. "I don't believe in the Fountain anymore."

"Oh? Would you tell me why?"

"I've seen the sextons rake coins from the fountains throughout the city. At night. They leave a few, offering the illusion that prayers were sent. But I lost my faith during the war. Everything that's happened since has just confirmed my doubts."

"War destroys everything. I don't judge you for it. It was a difficult time for all of us."

He chuffed. "So what is this blessing you have? I've read about such things in the legends but didn't believe there'd been anyone like that since the Maid."

"You believe she was Fountain-blessed?"

"I did. At first. But if she was, why did the power leave her to die on that mountain?"

"They say it's the only way to kill a Fountain-blessed. But that's just a rumor. We can die like anyone else." There was no magical power sustaining Ankarette's life. She knew the poison would eventually kill her. She just chose not to think or worry about it.

John Thursby sniffed. "I saw him go around that corner. I think I know where he's going."

The stench was growing fouler the deeper into the alley they went.

"A cesspit?" she asked, wrinkling her nose.

"No. We're too close to the river. On the west side of town, they cart the dung off. On this side, they purge it into the river. We're near an entrance to the sewers."

Ankarette's skin crawled.

Just ahead, a walled dead end blocked the way forward. There was a man-sized grate on the ground. The street sloped down toward it. Ankarette could see the grime and sludge getting thicker the closer they got. People would toss the contents of their chamber pots out the windows into the alley. Rain and muckers would then bring it down to the grate and the plumbing below the street.

When they reached the grate, she could hear the echo of something banging on metal down below.

John Thursby squatted on his haunches and shone the light on the grate. It had been moved very recently, dragged over a patch of filth. Something had been set down nearby. A burden he'd been carrying had been set on a pile of rubbish, leaving an indentation.

He'd gone underground.

Ankarette looked down at the grate and frowned. Then nodded. John Thursby handed her the lantern, and he heaved up on the grate. It was rusted and caked with muck. He set it down gently and then backed away. It hadn't rained in weeks, so the rotting smell was awful. There was only a little trickle in the sludge-gray waters below. She could hear the sound of the river and the ping of a hammer on metal.

John Thursby drew his sword and then jumped down into the shaft. Ankarette felt a shudder of dread and a stab of pain inside. She lowered the lantern down to him and then made the jump herself. The tunnel was narrow but tall enough that the night watchman could barely stand full height. It had to be tall enough for men to shovel and push the filth toward the river. A trench was cut in the middle, which was deeper and murkier. Two stone rails on either side offered footing for them.

Leading the way, John Thursby marched ahead, straddling the trench. Ankarette kept to one side of it, pressing her back against the wall. Another shock of pain made her gasp involuntarily. He turned and gazed back at her worriedly, but she motioned for him to keep going.

The pinging of the hammer stopped. Ankarette knew they had to hurry. Her magic was drained, but her senses told her Bidigen Grimmer was just ahead.

Fear crawled inside Ankarette. Their shadows cast on the moldering walls made creatures of imagination in her mind.

She lifted the lantern and saw him at the end of the straight tunnel. The hulking man was bent over, barely fitting inside. A woman had been deposited on the footing on one side. Behind Grimmer was a metal gate and beyond that, the river that led to the falls. The smell was intense and strong, but the feeling of blackness exuding from him was even stronger.

"End of the road, friend," John Thursby said menacingly.

Bidigen Grimmer's back was to them. When he turned, Ankarette saw his eyes glowing silver. Fear filled her again, an irrational, wild fear. But she'd learned to control her emotions.

"Keep her," grunted the brute. He pushed the gate open and leaped into the river. The current whisked him away. Only the bravest or the most foolish entered the river this close to the falls. It was said only someone who was innocent of any wrongdoing or a Fountain-blessed would survive a plummet off the waterfall at Kingfountain. Ankarette didn't want to risk it.

John Thursby hurried toward the woman. He crouched near her and then turned to look at Ankarette. His face had hardened.

"She's dead."

Ankarette's chest heaved with disappointment and regret. If only they'd come faster. She approached the woman and saw no motion of the chest rising up or down. Dark hair covered part of her face.

She handed John Thursby the lantern and crouched beside the body. She felt the woman's neck. No throb of a heartbeat. There was the stain of a bruise on her brow from where the hammer had struck. Bidigen Grimmer had killed her deliberately.

Ankarette tilted the woman's face and brushed away her dark hair.

It wasn't the Duke of Warrewik's daughter. It was someone else.

"AND TAKE the body to the coroner," John Thursby said to the other night watchman. "There's a blow to the skull. Maybe more was done. Have her examined."

"Awright," muttered the other man. He was bald with a thick beard. "D'you hear about the trouble at the Flyte tonight? Espion raid?"

"Oh?" John Thursby said. "That's none of our affair, is it?"

"By the Lady's legs, no. One murder tonight awready. The lord high constable will be cheeked."

"Aye. That he will."

The sound of a cart clacking on stone came down the dead-end alley. John Thursby had lifted Ankarette out first and then handed the body up to her. He then went to get help and found a night watchman from that ward to come assist. The body would be taken away and studied for more clues.

"Well, I'll leave you to it, then," John Thursby said, nodding to his fellow watchman and motioning for Ankarette to walk back up the alley with him.

The pain inside was growing steadily worse. By the time they passed the cart and mule and reached the mouth of the alley, Ankarette had to rest, pressing her back against a building's wall. She looked up at the sky, seeing the trail of stars more clearly now. They'd left the lantern with the other watchman.

"I'm going to fetch those horses from the Flyte," he announced. "You're no in condition to walk back."

"I'll be fine," she said, breathing hard.

"I'll be back in a trice. Then I'm taking you to Old Rose's. You need help."

"She won't be able to help me," Ankarette said. "Just take me to the palace."

"If that's where you want to go," he said with a shrug. "You realize the duke's going to want answers about our ambush at the Flyte—"

"I know," Ankarette said, cutting him off. "Just. . . hurry."

He began to jog down the street, and Ankarette slid down the wall. She wrapped her smelly cloak around herself tightly. It would be hours before dawn, before the gates of the sanctuary opened. Would the deconeus assist her in getting her vial back? If the king commanded it? Tunmore wouldn't force Dragan to leave sanctuary, but he might demand what had been stolen. And what if Dragan had emptied the vial? Her mind wandered in and out. How long would John Thursby be gone?

She listened to the noise coming from the alley and the workers retrieving the body. She began to shiver. Her mouth tasted strange. Spots were dancing before her eyes. Was she going to faint? How embarrassing. She tried to stand, then gasped and sank back down as the sharpness of the pain increased.

Clopping hooves announced the arrival of the two horses. She was grateful John Thursby had run there so quickly. Grunting, she tried to stand again and only made it partway before he was there, hoisting her off her feet and lifting her up onto the horse.

"Can you hold on?" he asked her. "Or should you ride with me?"

"I can manage," she whispered, breathing fast. He took the guide rope from her horse and dragged hers over to his before mounting. He'd provide the pace and direction for both animals. She gripped the saddle horn tightly, and the two beasts hurried into the night. Dizziness washed over her. In a moment of panic, she thought she'd fall off and crash onto the street. She hunched forward, gripping the saddle with all her strength, focusing on watching the cobblestones flying beneath her.

It wasn't until they reached the stone and timber house that smelled of herbs that she realized John Thursby hadn't taken her to the palace at all. They were back in the Hermitage, at Old Rose's. He quickly dismounted and came to her horse.

"You need to take me to the palace," she said.

He lifted her from the saddle and carried her to the entrance. Old Rose opened the door, undoubtedly having heard the commotion. A candle splashed light on them.

"Her *again*?" Old Rose said with a grunt of bemusement.

Ankarette could see John Thursby's teeth as he hefted her onto the treatment table in the middle of the shop. She tried to sit up, but he pushed her back down.

"There's nothing she can do that can help me," Ankarette said.

"I don't doubt it," he responded. "But she'll look after you, and that's all I need." He looked at Old Rose. "Get her something else to wear. She can sleep in my bed while I'm gone."

Ankarette reached out and seized his wrist. "And *where* are you going?"

He twisted free of her grip easily enough and backed away. The look of determination on his face was frightening in its intensity. "I'm getting your medicine back."

CHAPTER
FOURTEEN
THE FOUNTAIN'S JUSTICE

The pain was not subsiding, so Ankarette did what she could to endure it, to distract herself from it. Old Rose offered some tea, but it could not remove the agony. The old apothecary had taken Ankarette's cloak, dress, and boots and washed them in a basin. She'd given the poisoner a nightdress with little embroidered flowers along the collar and hem. Those details had inspired Ankarette to ask for needle and thread. When she was working with her hands, it helped her think. It replenished her Fountain magic. But it didn't make the pain cease.

Even though it was the middle of the night, Old Rose stayed with her. She had a healer's heart, a tenderness toward all creatures, including a black cat with snow-colored paws and underbelly who had transfixing yellow eyes. The cat's name was Ani, and it was a curious and trusting creature that purred whenever Ankarette paused in her needlework to stroke her soft fur.

"She likes you," Old Rose said from the chair with a twinkle in her smile. "Methinks John Thursby does too."

Ankarette already knew the truth on that front, so she didn't brush it off. "Does he always bring home strays in the middle of the night?"

"Sometimes," Old Rose said. "One night, he heard a ruckus in a home. A husband was beating his wife, and the children were frightened. He thrashed the husband, beat him good. Served him right. Then the fellow up and disappeared. Left everyone behind. Soon the wife and little ones couldn't pay, so they left too. He fretted for weeks afterward about whether he'd done the right thing to get involved. I think he did. It was the Fountain's justice. And we can't always see what's going to happen next."

Ankarette listened and smiled at the story. No matter how wise someone was, the future was mercurial. There were always unintended consequences. Another kind of pain stabbed inside her chest.

"I'm worried about him now," Ankarette confessed.

"He's no fool," Old Rose said.

"But he's doing something very foolish. If he violates sanctuary, the people will kill him." In the darkness of the night, her ears dreaded the sound of the bells tolling. If that happened, it would summon a mob. So far, all was quiet.

"He's not the kind of man who walks away from trouble."

"I know. How long has he lived here?"

"Two years? It feels like months. This ward used to be very dangerous until he became the night watchman. Some of them take bribes to turn a blind eye. Some are *actually* blind." She chuckled softly. "He needed another place to live, and a friend recommended him. I have this spare room." She gestured around them. It was such humble quarters. A single small bed. A chair and table for meals. There were books piled on the floor beneath it. His private collection.

"You should try to get some sleep," Old Rose suggested. "He could be gone a while."

Ankarette nodded, but she knew she wouldn't be able to fall asleep. "I need to get a message to the king," she said. "Could you have someone send it when it's morning?"

"Aye. I could do that. John Thursby keeps some paper and ink for writing reports to the constable. On the table."

She saw it and winced as she scooted off the edge of the bed. Hunched forward, she went to the table and scrawled a note for Hugh about her actions at the Flyte. She asked that the Espion arrest the rat-faced man who had attacked her in the cellar and hold him for questioning. She also advised him that Grimmer and Dragan had stolen something from her. She asked for someone to be sent to Old Rose's to check in on her. After signing it, she folded the note and handed it to Old Rose, giving her instructions to deliver it to the correct inn on Bridge Street.

Once Old Rose was gone, Ankarette lay back down on the bed. The pillow and blankets smelled like a man. It wasn't unpleasant. She tried to doze, but the cramps kept pulling her back awake. She lay there, watching the candle flame dance.

Then the bells of the sanctuary started to toll. She closed her eyes, her heart suffering even more. The little embers inside of her snuffed out. She wanted to cry. But she wouldn't let herself. Not yet.

THERE WAS no noise of a horse. Just the running steps of boots. Ankarette lifted herself up onto her elbow. The candlewick was near the basin of melted wax, offering just a glimmer of light. The sound of the steps approached Old Rose's home, and Ankarette reached for her dagger.

The door burst open, and she saw John Thursby framed in the entrance, his face dripping with sweat.

For a moment, they stared at each other in stunned silence.

"You're alive," she breathed in wonder.

"So are you," he said, grinning with apparent relief. He rushed to the bed and held out the precious vial. She'd not even described it to him, but he'd found it. Against all odds, he'd found it!

She couldn't believe her change in fortune. After sitting upright, she accepted the vial as he sank to his knees, breathing hard and fast as if he'd run all the way from the bridge. She untwisted the stopper and smelled the liquid to be sure it was right. It was. She took a deep swallow, more than her usual preventative dose. The flavor made her nose wrinkle, but as she felt it glide down her throat, she anticipated the relief it was soon to bring. He was panting, but his face showed a look of triumph.

She sealed the vial again and reached down, putting her hand on his. "How can I thank you? I'm. . . I'm just so relieved you're all right. When I heard the bells. . ."

He shook his head. "Think not of it, Ankarette. You look weary."

"So do you."

"I'm very tired," he said. "We can talk in the morning. It's still a few hours until sunrise."

"But how did you get it?"

"I'll tell you. I was praying to the Fountain the whole time. I haven't done that in *years*. I must have been quite desperate."

Ankarette bit her lip, understanding the meaning behind the words. Words he couldn't bring himself to confess.

"This is your bed. You should—"

"No. You need it. It's so small. It's not like the accommodations in the king's palace, I'm sure. I'll be fine on the floor. I'd prefer it."

A warm, glowing feeling was spreading inside her. Was it from the antidote or something even more powerful?

Ankarette was exhausted, but now that he'd made it back safely, she finally felt like she could rest. They'd both need their wits if they were going to hunt down Bidigen Grimmer and, hopefully, Nanette. She stretched out on the small bed, and he did so on the floor, still huffing. She listened to his breathing calm, and then a little snore escaped him. He'd fallen asleep so fast. Gratitude welled up inside her heart and spilled over. Closing her eyes, she drifted off, savoring the bliss while the bitterness of the antidote lay sour in her throat.

She awoke at dawn with light streaming in from the windows. Blinking, she rubbed her eyes, amazed that the pain in her stomach was absent, save for the memory of the ache. To her surprise, she saw John Thursby sitting against the wall by the table, a book in his hands.

"How long did you sleep?" she asked, stifling a

yawn. She brought her legs around and touched her bare feet to the cold stone floor.

"I don't require much," he answered. He was about to close the book and stand, but she stopped him.

"What were you reading?"

"A poem," he said. "One of my favorites."

"Share it with me?"

"You may think me morbid for liking it."

"That only makes me want to hear it all the more." She gave him an encouraging expression.

He sighed and cocked the book in his lap. The light streaming in from the window illuminated the page in his hand. His brow furrowed slightly in concentration. When he spoke, his voice grew a little more husky. She loved the sound of it.

"'Death is not easily escaped, try it who will. But every living soul among the children of men dwelling upon the Fountain's earth must go, of necessity, unto his destined place. Where the body, fast in its narrow bed, sleepeth. . . as if after a feast.'"

The book slumped down on his lap, and his cheeks burned a little. "When I woke and saw you lying in my bed, I thought you were dead. It reminded me of the poem. I didn't want to wake you. I did notice you breathing."

"You're very kind, John Thursby."

"I'm glad you are well again. I don't see the pain in your eyes."

"It's gone. Now tell me what happened. How did you persuade Dragan to give it to you?"

He cocked his head slightly. "I'm a soldier. And he's a thief. All it required was thinking like he does."

"And?"

"I had time to think while I rode there. Stopped by a

brothel near Bridge Street." He held up his hand. "I needed an accomplice. Someone he wouldn't fear. I paid her to braid her hair like you do. To wear a dress and cloak, as you do."

"You tricked him?"

"He wasn't happy about it. I hid along the wall by the gate. She came up and asked to speak to him. Promised money for more information. He came along quick enough when his stooges told him. She held out the pouch of coins. My purse, actually. I was hidden at the edge of the gate by the wall. When he reached for it, I seized his arm."

Ankarette's eyes widened.

"I drew my sword and told him I'd cut off that part of him which was outside the sanctuary if he didn't hand over what he'd stolen from you."

She pressed her hand against her mouth, surprised at the threat and how quickly it had achieved results. "And he gave it to you?"

"He had it in his pocket," he said, bemused. "He didn't want to risk losing his arm." He scratched the back of his neck. "We exchanged few words. I got the medicine. Then he raised the alarm. I had to get the woman to safety when the bells started ringing, then the horse went lame, and I had to run the rest of the way back, which is what took so long. I was terrified you'd die ere I got back because of a badly shod horse."

He'd been worried about her. Worried sick. It didn't require Fountain magic to see that.

"I hope your clothes are dry," he said. "Now that it's light, we should investigate that sewer again and see if we can discover where he went."

"Before we walk in that muck again," she said, "I

119

asked the Espion to arrest that little man who led us to him. I'd like to see if they found him."

"I should change my tunic," he said, rising. He set his book on the table, his fingers grazing the binding. "I can't stand the smell of myself right now."

She rose from the bed and walked up to him. She took his hand, feeling the calluses. "You did me a service, John Thursby. Again. Thank you."

"I did it for you, not your king," he muttered.

"I know. And I thank you." She leaned up and kissed his bearded cheek. It tickled her lips, and she felt a flush of warmth go through her.

He stared at her in surprise, and then the most foolish grin spread across his mouth.

She left him standing like that to go find her clothes.

CHAPTER

FIFTEEN

KINGFOUNTAIN BURNING

After Ankarette finished lacing up her boots and checking the embedded sheaths, she noticed John Thursby outside the window of the apothecary shop. He knocked at the window, as if requesting permission to enter, and she nodded to him. A new tunic covered his hauberk. The sword and dagger belted at his waist were slung low.

Ankarette's gown was still damp from the washing Old Rose had provided for her. The embroidered nightdress sat neatly folded on the counter.

"Where's Rose?" the night watchman asked. He didn't look as stark as when they'd first met. His eyes were softer too.

"Getting us some food to eat on the way," Ankarette answered. "I told her it wasn't necessary, but she insisted."

"She's that way," he said with a shrug.

There was noise in the street outside. Carts clacking, the murmur of street conversations. Ankarette pressed her hand against her stomach, grateful that the sharp pangs were over. She didn't know how Dragan had stolen the vial from her, but he was clearly Fountain-blessed at stealing. Maybe his magic had revealed to him the thing she needed most. She was still brimming with gratitude that John Thursby had coerced him into giving it back.

Old Rose came in with bread, a cold sausage, and some apples. "It isn't much, but I don't like anyone suffering with hunger. Take it with you."

"Thank you," John Thursby said, accepting the offering wrapped in a frayed cheesecloth.

The door of the apothecary burst open, and a young boy entered, probably eight years old. He had big tears in his eyes. "Mama! Mama's hurt!"

"Where is she?" Old Rose said patiently, going to the boy.

He pointed to the door, and they all looked out and saw a woman with a bloodied rag clamped to her hand. Two little ones, both girls, toddled after her in the street.

The black cat Ani came up and sidled by the boy, making little chirping sounds.

John Thursby held the door open for the woman who came walking up, her face white and strained with worry.

"What happened, Agnes?" Old Rose asked, clucking her tongue sympathetically.

"Cut my hand," the woman said, wincing with pain. "Didn't mean to, the knife slipped."

"I thought you had a new scullion to help out? Let's have a look at it," Old Rose said.

"I was showin' her how to cut faster. She was so slow and fearful. Then I go and make a fool of myself."

John Thursby picked up the two little girls and set them on the countertop. The boy wiped his eyes and then dropped down to stroke the cat.

Ankarette was close enough that when Old Rose removed the rag, she saw the cut ran deep. It looked like a common kitchen injury, but one that could get infected and risk the woman's health later on.

"You'll need a barber for it," Old Rose said. "I can make a poultice of yarrow and mint, but that'll need to be held closed in order to heal. You should go to Sessions the Barber. He can fix it."

"I tried him, but he didn't answer the door," the woman said. "Is there anyone else?"

"I can help," Ankarette said. She'd brought the needle and embroidery thread back with her from the other room, and they still sat on the counter.

Old Rose looked at Ankarette in surprise.

"I was trained as a midwife. I know how to sew a wound."

"The Lady bless you, lass," Old Rose said.

Ankarette fetched the needle and some thread and went to work. The woman, Agnes, was brave and endured the pain from the needle piercing her skin with poise. With efficient and steady hands, Ankarette closed the wound and stanched the bleeding.

"Make that poultice," Ankarette said. "It'll help with the healing."

"I'm thankful to ye," Agnes said, smiling through tears. The boy was sitting cross-legged on the ground, the cat coiled in his lap. The little girls were looking at the herbs and jars assembled on the counter. John Thursby helped them both down.

"I'll take care of the bandage," Old Rose said. "You should get going. But thank you for staying."

Ankarette smiled, feeling the thrill that her often deadly talents could also be put to use for saving lives.

John Thursby gave her an affirming nod before they left and went for the horse.

"We'll have to share," he said apologetically.

She could think of worse things. "I'll ride behind."

John Thursby swung up into the saddle. The horse nickered and stepped a bit, getting a verbal reprimand from the rider. Then he reached down for her, and she grabbed his hand and let him pull her up behind him. It was a tight squeeze, but she wrapped her arms around him and smelled the scent she'd encountered on his pillow. It was a pleasant one.

John Thursby started the horse at a walk and picked up the pace to a trot. He turned his head slightly so she could hear him better over the noisy street. "Agnes has been a widow nigh on a year now."

"What happened to her husband?"

"Fell ill last autumn. Fever burned him through. Left her with three little ones."

"Do you know all the families in your ward?"

"Naw, not by half. I hear Old Rose talking about them. Making hints. She thinks I should find a wife." He chuckled.

"She was a handsome woman," Ankarette said teasingly.

"Agnes? I wouldn't take a lass out of pity. I admire her. But admiration doesn't rise to love."

It was a commendable sentiment, but Ankarette knew that most marriages in Ceredigion were made out of necessity. If love happened, it was considered a rare blessing. That was why she admired Eredur and Elyse so much. They'd fallen in love first, and even though many in the realm thought the queen had risen above her station, Eredur had never faltered in his devotion to her. That same kind of devotion seemed to be what drew Severn and Nanette to each other. Their childhood friendship had survived a civil war and contest of succession.

When they reached the Espion tavern on Bridge Street, John Thursby helped her down and then dismounted and tied up the animal. Ankarette gazed at the sanctuary gates, looking for a sign of Dragan. Or a feeling that he was close. She'd concealed the vial in a different place, tucking it into her tight bodice. It was uncomfortable, to be sure, but she was constantly aware of it now.

Upon entering, they were hailed by an exasperated Hugh Bardulf.

"Beware what the tide brings in! Here you are!" he said, frowning at her.

"Did you get my message?" she asked him, wrinkling her brow in confusion.

"Aye. And several others as well, including the king's first thing this morning. He heard a rumor Nanette was slain. That you found her body in the street, her skull smashed in. The Duke of Glosstyr is about to wage war on his brother!"

"That's not true," Ankarette said. "It wasn't her. I saw the body myself."

"Well, those at court believe it. The Duke of Clare proclaims he was poisoned by you and that you and twenty Espion took vengeance on some of his knights."

"Twenty?" John Thursby said with a chuckle.

"All of Kingfountain is in an uproar! The king wishes you to come and put the matter at rest."

"I can't," Ankarette said, shaking her head. "I'm on a trail that grows colder by the hour. I believe I found the criminal who abducted Lady Nanette. But he eluded us last night."

"Shall we fetch the hounds to hunt him down?" Hugh asked. She wasn't sure whether he was being serious. "Let's add some barking dogs to all this mayhem."

"He went through the sewers," John Thursby said. "He won't have left a trail a dog can follow. And what's this business at the Flyte last night?"

"Did you arrest that man I asked for?" Ankarette asked.

Hugh tossed up his hands.

"Aye. He's in a cell in the cellar. But he's no use. A fearful man—won't say anything about what happened last night."

"I think he'll talk to *me*," Ankarette said. She still had some nightshade with her.

"You should go to the palace first, Ankarette. The king needs you. His two brothers are nearly coming to blows."

"I'm close to finding her, Hugh. If I delay, we could lose her. That man, Grimmer, killed an unarmed girl with a blow to the head just to prevent us from taking her from him."

"He has no feelings," John Thursby said. "And he's strong. Wicked strong."

"Some men are just like that," Hugh said. "They're beyond any remorse."

It wasn't just his strength and size and cruelty that posed a problem. It was that medallion he wore around his neck. The one that could wrench her Fountain magic away. During the night, she'd just started to restore her power. Interestingly, listening to John Thursby recite the poem had increased the trickling return of the magic, just as she'd thought it might.

She was afraid of meeting Grimmer again. But next time, she'd have more to help in the hunt.

"Let me speak to the man from the Flyte," Ankarette said. "If he knows where to find him, that's the most important thing. The conflict between the dukes can wait."

"If the king summoned *me*, I would go straight-away," Hugh said warningly.

Ankarette met his gaze. "He trusts me. He knows I wouldn't disobey without a good reason."

"You know him better than I, Ankarette. But if you're wrong, the next time you come here, I may have to put you in irons and bring you to him. I don't know any man, king or not, who likes to be disobeyed. Or who endures it."

John Thursby had a nervous look in his eye. Was he worrying about himself or her?

She knew the answer already. He wasn't loyal to the king. He was loyal to the king's poisoner.

TRUTH IS CONFIRMED *by inspection and delay. Falsehood by haste and uncertainty. We make our greatest mistakes when we are rushed.*

—Ankarette Tryneowy

CHAPTER

SIXTEEN

THE CORFE

The cellar of the inn contained rooms for confinement and interrogation as well as stores of wine, ale, and other spirits. Down there, the vibration of the waterfall could be felt even more strongly. In the past, Ankarette had been shown the trapdoor where someone could be sent into the falls surreptitiously. Sometimes the king's justice needed to be performed discreetly.

The Espion on guard, a man named Clement, opened the cell door for her, and she and John Thursby entered. The rat-faced little man hunkered on the floor, eyes darting with apprehension at the noises around him. He saw them, recognition flooding his eyes, then he turned his head away.

"I'm not talking to you," he said with a jittery voice.

John Thursby leaned in the doorframe, arms folded, his expression sour.

"What is your name?" Ankarette asked, coming closer to the man.

"W-what does it matter? You're going to k-kill me anyway."

"But you have a name. What is it? I like to know who I'm speaking with." Ankarette lowered herself to his level. He didn't look at her, his eyes wild with fear. He pressed himself into the corner of the cell. Then he started to weep.

"It's not my fault," he moaned.

"Just tell me your name."

"P-Paul Rarick."

He was a wiry fellow. In height, he could pass as a lad, but the flecks of gray in his hair showed he was much older, perhaps forty? He was very thin, of a sallow complexion. She estimated the proper dose of the drug in her mind, judging by his weight and build.

"I w-won't talk," he said. "You may as well just th-throw me in the river. I'm doomed anyway."

"I think you're more afraid of Bidigen Grimmer than of us," Ankarette said.

Paul Rarick shuddered, wiping his eyes. "It's not my fault! What was I supposed to do?"

"He's very powerful."

"He'll kill me. Even if you don't. And I'd rather die quickly. I don't want to die." He began to moan softly.

Ankarette glanced up at John Thursby and saw the disgust in his eyes and in the twist of his mouth. He had no compassion for the man. He was the scum of the city.

But he likely had useful information. Ankarette opened the pouch of nightshade and emptied a little into her palm. It wouldn't take much to get him talking. Judging by the smell of his breath, he had no health conditions, and his build did not cause her concern. He looked at the powder.

"Look at me," she said coaxingly.

He didn't want to and turned his face so that his cheek pressed against the wall of the cell. "D-don't hurt me."

"I'm not going to hurt you, Paul Rarick. I just have some questions for you. Do you want to leave? I have friends in the North who can help you."

He turned instantly, eyes blazing with hope. "R-really?"

She blew the powder into his face. He shrieked with surprise, batting at the dust wildly. Standing slowly, she gazed down at him, watching as the powdered nightshade took over his mind. The worried and afraid look turned into an expression of bliss.

"W-what was that?" he asked, giggling softly and then covering his mouth in shock at having done so. His eyes were soon delirious.

"We're looking for Nanette. The Duke of Clare's ward. Do you know where she is?"

"Wh-who?" he asked, giggling again.

"A noblewoman. Dark hair. She's young."

"The duke's sister. I don't know where she is. No one does."

"Not even Bidigen Grimmer?"

"He does not. She's gone. Now it's all ruined."

Ankarette assumed he was referring to a plan and that Nanette's abduction had been part of a larger plot. Ankarette's instincts screamed it was so. They'd hoped to exchange her for someone valuable enough that Eredur would pay a heavy price. A price he'd been unwilling to pay up until that point.

"Yes, Lady Nanette," she said slowly. "She was the young prince's wife. Morvared's son."

"M-Morvared," he said haltingly. "She is. . . she is in prison at the palace."

"How is Grimmer connected to her?"

"He was a soldier for her. A henchman. He wants to free her."

Ankarette glanced back at John Thursby again. She was right. This was not just a ransom situation. Morvared wanted to escape her tower. Maybe she also wanted a little revenge because of her son's death.

John Thursby wasn't leaning in the doorframe anymore. He was interested.

"How was Bidigen Grimmer trying to free her?"

"He. . . he has a plan. I don't know it. But he says she's the true queen. That she will rule again."

"Grimmer wears an amulet around his neck. Do you know of it?"

"I've seen it."

"What is it, Paul? Where did he get it?"

"From her."

"From who?"

"From the true queen."

So there was a larger plot afoot. Ankarette knew this was important information. Paul Rarick began to swipe his hand in front of his eyes, as if seeing something that wasn't there. It was a side effect of the poison for some.

"Where is Bidigen Grimmer? Where can I find him?"

"He's at the wharf," Paul said, growing confused.

"Which one?" John Thursby asked.

"The Southwark."

She didn't recognize it, so she looked up again at John Thursby. He nodded.

"Are there a lot of warehouses there? Where can we find him?"

"He will find *you*," Paul said, chuckling.

The words caused a chill down her arms. The tone

of his voice frightened her. His eyes were becoming more lucid. He stared at her fixedly. His head tilted.

She saw a flash of silver go through his irises, and she scrambled back as he suddenly lunged at her. John Thursby kicked him in the chest, hard, knocking him back against the wall. He grabbed the man by the neck, holding him there.

"Don't. . . touch. . . her," he growled menacingly.

Paul began to weep again. The poison had worn off too quickly.

Ankarette felt a buzz of excitement mingled with fear. There was still a connection between Paul Rarick and Bidigen Grimmer. The same dark magic linked them somehow.

"I don't know anything!" he wailed. "Let me go! Just let me go!"

"Quiet!" snarled the night watchman.

Paul Rarick fell silent at the rebuke, weeping softly, trembling from head to foot.

"Let him go," Ankarette said. She was more than able to defend herself.

John Thursby released his grip and stepped to one side, but he stood in a protective stance, ready for another lunge. It was in some men's nature to protect. She appreciated it, even if she didn't need it.

"How large is the Southwark pier?" she asked him.

"It's one of the larger ones," John Thursby said. "It's at the base of the falls. Where they unload ships from Genevar, Brugia, and Occitania. There are no less than a dozen warehouses there. A lot of ground to search. Maybe you should use more of that powder on him."

"N-no," Paul said, trembling violently. "I didn't do anything. It's not my fault!"

There was a risk of using too much nightshade. It

was poisonous in larger doses. But the situation warranted it. This cowardly fellow knew enough that he'd be killed by Grimmer if they just let him go. The safest place for him would be in the Espion dungeon. Until they caught Grimmer.

She opened the pouch again and withdrew another pinch of powder.

"N-no!" wailed the victim.

Ankarette blew it into his face again, and he went calm instantly.

"Tell us where to find him," Ankarette said purposefully. "Where is his hideout?"

"I already told you. He will find *you*."

"Tell us," the night watchman said, growing impatient.

"He knows you, John Thursby. You fought on the same side once. You betray your queen."

Ankarette was growing more uneasy. He was reacting differently from the other people she'd used this poison on.

"Did the Duke of Clare hire Bidigen Grimmer?" she asked.

Paul began to laugh. "He will do anything to become king. But you already knew that, you wicked clump of horse—"

John Thursby shoved his forearm into the man's throat, stopping the words, stopping him from breathing. "Where in Southwark? Where?"

The fear was gone from Paul Rarick's eyes. They didn't glow silver, but there was something dark and insidious in them. "The Corfe. He's at the Corfe. Right now. He's waiting for the tide. Then he'll be gone with her."

THE ANGER and outrage was palpable on the wharf. Ships had been banned from leaving, per the king's orders. That meant fish were rotting in barrels, and the produce from farms in Ceredigion would be spoiled before it reached its destination. The merchants were furious. The dockworkers bored and drunk. Whenever Ankarette came to Kingfountain by ship, she usually docked near the palace; she'd not been to the Southwark before. She stepped on a dead fish because she could no longer see through the press of soldiers. The constable's men were clearing the way to the warehouse. A crowd had gathered on the wharf, men demanding why the ships had been halted.

"Can you tell us when, Constable? At least do that! Can we leave tonight?"

Ankarette walked a few paces behind him, next to John Thursby, and they were flanked by thirty guardsmen wearing armor and carrying pikes.

"I'll be ruined!" complained another man. "Will the king compensate me for spoiled fruit, eh?"

"Stand aside!" Lord Axelrod, the lord high constable, yelled, shoving his way through. Members of the Espion had gone ahead of them to spy on the warehouse. Hugh had led the charge in person after sending word to the king that they were hot on the trail. He'd requested that the constable bring soldiers and come personally to the dock at Southwark.

Ankarette didn't like the feelings coiling inside her chest. Being rushed like this was against her nature. It reminded her of darker days, when Eredur and his uncle were scheming against each other. When the fate of Kingfountain hung in the balance between the iron wills of the two men.

The dock was about five hundred paces long, and the Corfe was at the end of the row. There were eight ships tied up, and the timbers of the wharf were creaking noisily. Gulls squawked and swooped, diving down to steal snatches of food. Some bobbed in the smelly water.

Ankarette gazed at the waterfall in the distance, at the palace cresting the hill on the other side. With the cliff right behind the warehouses, she couldn't even see the sanctuary of Our Lady, which was clearly visible from the wharves on the king's side of the bridge.

This was the grotesque underbelly of Kingfountain. She couldn't feel a connection with her Fountain magic at all. The enmity in the air was thick.

"There he is," grumbled the constable. Ankarette saw Hugh Bardulf approaching through the crowd.

"I've got my men in position around the warehouse," Hugh said. "The windows are thick with grime. Can't see inside. This man kills his victims. Go in quick and fast."

"We know our job," Lord Axelrod said petulantly. Nobles didn't take well to people of inferior rank giving orders. "Ready, men!"

Ankarette grabbed the hilt of her dagger. The soldiers began to jog, and one of them, the biggest man, ran ahead and kicked open the warehouse door. The soldiers poured in with their pikes.

Ankarette was anxious to be inside, to join the fight and save as many as she could. She knew Grimmer's power was dangerous and could affect emotions.

Slipping inside, she found the soldiers standing

agog, staring up. The interior of the building was dark. But it was still light enough to see the bodies swaying, hanging from ropes from the rafters.

CHAPTER
SEVENTEEN
INTO THE DUNGEON

The lord high constable of Ceredigion was not a patient man. Lord Axelrod was a cousin of Eredur, a noble of the realm, and of a peevish temperament. Ankarette saw the smoldering fury in his eyes, the disappointment at his subverted expectations.

"Cut the bodies down," he said, his nose wrinkling with distaste. "Take them to the coroner." He cut a dark look at the poisoner. "The king will hear of this. You may be certain of that."

Ankarette also felt the throb of disappointment mingled with the revulsion at the death scene. This was not the act of a poisoner. It was a rampage. A warning of more violence to come. Trade had already been interrupted. A young widow was missing. Two royal brothers were at each other's throats. And now, a murderer was loose in the city.

Ankarette had hoped the Corfe would be the end of the journey. Instead, it was another dead end—literally. Bidigen Grimmer was always a step or two ahead. And he was proving himself to be dangerous.

Choosing to ignore the lord high constable's pique, Ankarette roamed the warehouse. The building was dilapidated. The floorboards squeaked as she stepped on them, and she could hear the sloshing of the sea down below.

Hugh Bardulf approached her swiftly. "The hanging corpses. What do you make of it?"

"Are any female?"

"No. Dockworkers. Blows to the head. They were killed before being hung."

This was not a random event. She'd learned in the poisoner school that some folk had no conscience. None at all. They were the most dangerous kind. They delighted in killing. Most people had motivation or incentive to do what they did, but this man killed for sport.

"He's sending us a message," Ankarette said, turning to look at Hugh. She saw John Thursby kneeling by one of the bodies that the constable's men had already cut down.

"What kind of message? I've seen my share of carnage on the battlefield. But this feels different to me. I'm uneasy, Ankarette."

"I think he intends it that way," she answered. "To put us off our guard. He's sweeping his trail. Anyone who could report on him or his actions."

"What about that fellow we're keeping in the cell?"

"He'll be a target too," she agreed.

"I'd better go back there with some Espion."

"Good idea." She tapped her heel on the floor. "Is there anything underneath this?"

"Other than the sea? No."

"Are we sure? Have some men check it out. I don't want to overlook anything."

"Very well."

A voice caught her attention. "You served Devereaux. You're that night watchman from the Hermitage."

Ankarette glanced back and saw that four of Axelrod's men had come up to John Thursby while he was examining the body. He'd risen, looking defensive since they'd boxed him in. Hugh noticed the situation and frowned.

"What of it?" John Thursby answered darkly.

One of the soldiers gave him a little shove. "I was at the Battle of Borehamwood. And at Hawk Moor."

She saw John Thursby clench his hand into a fist. "And what's your point?"

Ankarette excused herself from Hugh and started toward the men. She could see their contempt.

"Why are you even here?" challenged another soldier. "Wasn't this fellow, Bidigen Grimmer, *also* one of Devereaux's soldiers? I've heard of him."

Ankarette reached them. John Thursby was glowering at them all. When he caught sight of her, he shook his head just a bit, warning her to keep out of it.

"I brought him. He's been a great help," Ankarette said.

"D'you earn that scar in the battle?" asked the first soldier mockingly. "Was the blow from one of your fellow traitors?"

"They all attacked each other in the mist," chuckled a third man.

"What's going on?" barked the lord high constable. Ankarette was grateful he'd noticed the growing commotion.

"This man served Morvared," one of the soldiers said accusingly. "How do we know he didn't warn Grimmer we were coming?"

John Thursby went pale with anger. He looked like he was about to lash out. But he said nothing.

"Lord Axelrod," Ankarette said, shaking her head.

"He's a *traitor*," sniped another man.

"Enough!" Ankarette said, bristling with anger. "We are hunting the man who killed all these people. Who abducted the king's cousin. This is not the time to bandy words about the past."

"Hold on, Ankarette," said Axelrod with a tone of offense. "He's also the one who killed those sanctuary men. The ones who abducted you."

"Maybe he did this," suggested another.

It was ridiculous. Preposterous. There was no evidence at all. His past alone had aroused their suspicion, even though he'd been with Ankarette all day.

"While you're standing here like brainless fools," John Thursby snarled with outrage, "there's a killer running amok in Kingfountain. I've not seen Lord Devereaux in over two years. I know not where he is. I'm here because she asked me to help. In the king's name."

"Traitor," muttered the soldier again.

John Thursby cocked his fist and punched that man in the mouth so hard he crashed down onto the dead body.

"Not treason, loyalty!" shouted John Thursby, his eyes dancing with fury. "I'll best any man here who declares otherwise!"

Lord Axelrod's eyes glittered with wrath. "Captain Sommersby, arrest him. Take him to the palace dungeon."

"Lord Axelrod, I need—" Ankarette started, but he cut her off with a flippant wave of his hand.

"No, you listen to *me*. He assaulted one of my men. I'm in command here, not you. And if you lift a finger against me or my men, I'll have you incarcerated as well."

There were twenty soldiers, plus a few of Hugh's Espion. She didn't think Hugh would side with her, not against the lord high constable.

"I am on the king's mission," Ankarette said, her voice deadly serious.

"When was the last time you checked with him, eh?" He tossed his head. "Take this blackguard away."

John Thursby's shoulders slumped. He didn't resist when one of the soldiers brought wrist irons and clamped them on his arms. He didn't look at Ankarette. His eyes were fixed on Axelrod, a look that promised revenge.

Ankarette was about to speak again, but she felt Hugh grip her arm. When she looked at him, he made a hand sign. *Not now. Later.*

ANKARETTE WAS STILL CROSS that John Thursby had been arrested. After finishing her search of the Corfe warehouse, she left with Hugh and started back to Bridge Street. She'd have to go to the palace and speak to the king. And it would put her farther behind.

Hugh sighed. "I know you're not happy with Lord Axelrod, but you must understand. He's a noble. He doesn't understand your authority because it doesn't come from blood and right like his does."

"He interfered with my mission," she said hotly.

"Agreed. And he likely doesn't understand all you did to secure the king's throne. Not even everyone in the Espion knows. That's intentional. The less people know about you, Ankarette, the better. You have enough enemies."

He was right, but she was still furious. If Sir Thomas had been with them, he would have quelled Axelrod's posturing. She had to stop thinking about him as *Sir* Thomas. He was a lord of the realm now. An earl. He'd craved a rank his whole life, being born a second son, and now he had it. She realized her concern for John Thursby wasn't entirely due to the injustice of his arrest. She cared for him. He'd tried to save her twice, putting his own life at risk. He deserved commendation, not imprisonment.

"Did your men find anything beneath the dock? Were there any trapdoors?"

"None. I had one man cut a hole through the floor, but there were just brackish waters down there."

Ankarette shook her head in frustration. What had Bidigen Grimmer been doing at the Corfe? There were no crates of cargo. The warehouse had been empty. Maybe something else was going on that she wasn't seeing. A diversion to keep her attention away from the true plot?

"I need your help, Hugh," she said. "I'm missing something."

"We've all had little sleep the last few days. Go ahead. Talk it through."

"Nanette disappeared at night. The man who guarded the back gate, Moser, was struck on the head. So was I, actually. So were the murdered men at the docks and the girl we found. That seems to be Grimmer's primary method of attack. What did he need to stage that scene for? Was he going to smuggle them both away by sea?"

"Smuggle both? I thought we were looking for the duke's daughter?"

"Grimmer was one of Morvared's soldiers. He wants her free. The king won't agree to a ransom price. He dithers, on purpose, because he has no intention of letting her go. But what if he's forced to?"

"Are you certain it's about Morvared? Any number of unscrupulous men would want to abduct Lady Nanette for no other reason than that she's a wealthy heiress."

"In this case, revenge is an additional motive, Hugh. Nanette was forced to marry Morvared's son, the young prince. She and her sister were hostages to Queen Morvared during the battle. Their lives were both always going to be forfeit if Eredur won. It's only been two years since that time."

"Morvared is in Holistern Tower. There is no way King Lewis or anyone can get to her. She's the king's prisoner."

John Thursby was also a prisoner in that dungeon now. He wasn't in the tower, but the path to the tower was through that dungeon.

Her stomach clenched with dread. She was certain John Thursby was honorable—her Fountain magic had revealed that to her—but it was also a striking coincidence nonetheless.

"I know this. King Lewis's poisoner is shrewd. He doesn't do anything he hasn't thought through. If the goal is to rescue Morvared, then the king needs to increase the guard. There could be someone on the inside, someone who has been prepared to act. What's happening at the dock is meant to draw our gaze away from their true mission. Even if they don't have Nanette, they want us to believe they do. Did you search the corpses? Were any Espion rings stolen?"

It didn't take long to discover that several of the fallen men were missing their rings. "We should send a runner to warn the king immediately!" Hugh said in surprise.

"I'll go myself."

They'd reached Bridge Street and began to cross it. Since they'd pass the Espion tavern along the way, Ankarette decided to stop there first and get a horse. She could make it to the palace more swiftly that way.

Hugh stopped abruptly. He stared at the tavern, his eyes narrowing with concern. There were people gathered outside it, staring in through the windows. A few soldiers wearing the king's badge were gathered outside with horses.

"I think they're here for you," Hugh said worriedly.

Ankarette pressed her lips together. Were they going to take her off in irons too? She could easily slip into the crowd and disappear. The guards didn't seem to be paying close attention.

"Better to get it over with," she sighed.

As they approached, one of the knights caught her eye. It was Sir Blaxen. One of Eredur's bodyguards. Did that mean the king himself was present?

She walked up to him while he was still seated on his horse. "Sir Blaxen."

"Ankarette," he said with a look of relief. "You're here!"

His reaction confused her. "I need to see the king."

"Of course. He's worried sick about you."

"Why?" Hugh Bardulf asked.

"There were some murders here," Sir Blaxen said, pointing to the safe house. "One of the Espion sent word to the palace. A large man with a mace went on a rampage. Killed everyone inside and got away."

Hugh looked stunned. "W-what? When?"

"After you left. It was a massacre."

"He's trying to draw our gaze again," Ankarette said to Hugh. "Mark my words, he's going for Morvared."

CHAPTER
EIGHTEEN
DISCERNMENT

As Ankarette walked down the corridor of the palace, she reached out with her limited stores of Fountain magic to sense for danger. She was especially trying to discern the presence of Lord Hux, the Occitanian poisoner. There was no telltale manifestation. He wasn't coming for the queen himself. This time, he was trusting a lackey.

The king and queen were meeting in council in the great hall, so she went to their royal quarters, where she was used to having private meetings with them. She wasn't sure how long she'd have to wait, so she paced inside the room after the steward said he'd let Eredur know she had come.

Her training in Pisan had taught her the precautions needed to protect the royal family from a poisoner infiltrating the castle. The cook, Liona, and her husband were both entirely trusted and personally delivered the royal couple their meals. Doors were regularly locked, and visitors caught wandering the halls were questioned. In a palace so large, it wasn't possible to ascertain that every servant was loyal, but the ones closest to the family all were.

She heard the noise of footfalls coming down the corridor and turned before the door opened. The steward stood aside, and Eredur and Elyse entered, both of them with worried looks.

"Ankarette, are you all right?" Elyse asked, coming to her, taking her hands, and squeezing them.

"She looks hale," Eredur said. "You took a blow to the head?"

"Yes," Ankarette replied. "But I am well."

"Lord Axelrod has said some disturbing things about you," the king went on.

"Please," Elyse interrupted. "Can we not make sure she is well before you start interrogating her?"

"Oh, of course," the king said, chagrined. "Truly, are you well? Should I fetch a healer?"

"I've been to one already," Ankarette said. "Thank you both for your concern, but there are more important matters at hand."

"Lord Axelrod says you've been cavorting with one of Lord Devereaux's men," the king said. "Is that true?"

"That's a misrepresentation," Ankarette said. "A deliberate one. He arrested a member of the night watch who has been assisting me in my mission."

"But he *is* Devereaux's man?" Eredur asked. His tone rang with uneasiness and wariness. Eredur had pardoned Devereaux, made him lord high constable, only to be betrayed by him. So his feelings were entirely natural.

"No," Ankarette said. "Not since the battles of Borehamwood and Hawk Moor."

"Are you sure, Ankarette?" the queen asked. "We don't doubt your loyalty. But even the wisest can be misled. And with your head injury..."

Ankarette squeezed the queen's hands. "You are right to question me. I'm not offended."

"Thank goodness," Eredur said with a sigh. "I was worried you would be. With all the conflict raging in Kingfountain today, the last thing any of us wants is estrangement with you. But tell me. How can you be so sure about this night watchman. What was his name again?"

"John Thursby," Ankarette said patiently.

The queen gave her a sidelong look, just a glance, and then shifted her attention to the king. "Do you know the name?"

Eredur nodded. "What I've heard, until now, is that he's respectable. That he tamed one of the most violent wards in the city."

"And now he's languishing in your dungeon for it," Ankarette said, giving the king a pointed look. "This is how we're rewarding acts of duty?"

"Didn't he strike Lord Axelrod's soldier? If so, Axelrod was well within his rights to arrest and punish him."

"I was there, Eredur," Ankarette said, trying to quell her exasperation. "Axelrod's men provoked him. Called him a traitor."

The king's brow furrowed. "I hadn't heard that part. But. . . how shall I put this. . . Isn't it true? He *did* fight against me."

"Then every soldier who fought for Queen Morvared is also guilty of treason? I remember those days very well. Your victory was never assured. Yes, men chose sides. But we hold the leaders accountable. You pardoned Devereaux once. That is why he fled after the battle, because he knew he would be condemned the second time. A knight is more accountable because of

148

his oath of fealty. A soldier. . . they are not held to the same standard."

"She's right, Eredur," the queen said.

The king's expression was conflicted. No one appreciated being told they were wrong. It summoned rebellious feelings, a desire to justify.

Ankarette released the queen's hands and stepped up to the king. She didn't want him to feel he was being overwhelmed with opposition. "It is your purview, as the monarch, to forgive whom you will. But let me try to satisfy your just concerns. You expected a faster resolution to the crisis between your brothers. The situation is more complicated than we all thought. I believe that this man I'm hunting—the one who stole Nanette—is also trying to free Morvared from the tower. He is incredibly dangerous, as the Espion on Bridge Street just learned. He has magic that I don't understand. It gives him incredible power and, I'm afraid, some immunity to poison."

"By the Lady," Eredur whispered.

"But I have magic of my own," Ankarette said. "I know his weakness. He wears a medallion around his neck, and if that link is severed, his power will be greatly diminished. He's still a man. He bleeds. He's injured. But by the power *I* possess, I can sense things about people." She put her hand over her heart, pausing to weigh her words carefully. "It is my blessing from the Fountain—and it has also told me the truth about John Thursby. He is an honorable man. He fought on the wrong side in the war, so he's perpetually distrusted. But he's earned the trust of the people in the neighborhood he watches over. He does his duty and lives a humble life. *I* trust him. And you should trust *me*. Please, Eredur. Give me orders to release him from the dungeon. And reprimand Lord Axelrod for purposefully interfering in my mission."

The king was staring at her. His expression showed he was still conflicted. But her words had moved him. "What do you think, Elyse?" he asked. He always sought her counsel.

The queen came and stood next to Eredur, looking up into his face. "Without Ankarette, Warrewik would have killed you. If we can't trust her, then we can trust no one."

Eredur rubbed his forehead. "There are so many problems it's all a perplexity. Is one night watchman's involvement so critical when the merchants are near rioting? Many of the shipments are going to spoil. My cousin went missing, and still no one knows where she is. There are causes enough for grave concern."

"When a storm batters against our shores," Ankarette said, "can we stop it or tell it to hit elsewhere? No, we face trouble as it comes. You are the King of Ceredigion. You wear the hollow crown. It is *your* decision to make whether to grant my request to free this man. But yes, the life of one night watchman can make a difference."

She wanted him to feel empowered, that the decision was truly his and his alone. He would bear the brunt of the consequences, for good or ill. Every king wanted to be popular, to make decisions that would benefit the people, not injure them. Sometimes the right thing to do had a grievous cost.

Eredur sighed. "You've never done anything to deliberately harm me, Ankarette. Quite the opposite. You've always kept my interests foremost. Even above your own. If you think this Thursby fellow worthy of reprieve, then I grant it. I just hope every merchant from here to Genevar doesn't petition me for redress. We must get the port open quickly."

The queen smiled at him and kissed his cheek. Ankarette's sense of relief was palpable.

Eredur sighed. "Any thoughts on how this fellow intends to liberate Morvared? I've increased the guard on the tower. What else should I do to prevent it? If she escapes, there's no end to the mischief she can do."

"I have a feeling I've forced Grimmer to alter his plan," Ankarette said. "Like in the game Wizr when an opponent unwittingly crosses your move. He killed the people at the dock because they knew something about him that would help us find him. He attacked the Espion tavern when it was weak because he needed to kill Paul Rarick, or he needs that man for his own purposes. Also, by killing Espion, he claimed some of their rings and can thus bypass palace guards."

The king's eyes widened. "I hadn't thought of that!"

"It's going to happen soon. While I don't know all of the particulars of Grimmer's plan, if I'm right about the general details, we may know enough to thwart him."

"If we capture him, then he can take us to Nanette?"

"Precisely."

The secret door to the king's chamber clicked, and a section of the wall opened. An Espion entered, looking worried.

"Sorry to disturb, my lord, but it's important."

"More bad news," the king muttered. "What is it? Speak, man!"

"A message just arrived from Occitania, but it's written in a cipher that none of us can read. It came with a vial, and it was addressed to *her*." Here he nodded at Ankarette.

It was from Lord Hux.

The queen's brow furrowed with concern. "A message from poisoner to poisoner?"

"The last time Lord Hux came to Kingfountain with a message, it was already almost too late," Ankarette said.

"Is Nichols in the Star Chamber?" the king demanded.

"Aye, my lord. Shall I escort her there?"

Eredur nodded, but he took Ankarette by the arm. "How do I keep the tower protected? Should I require a document with my seal for entry?"

"A seal can be forged easily," Ankarette said. "Only someone very astute would recognize it as a forgery. A password, I think. And it must change often."

"Done. When you see Nichols, give him the password. You decide what it is. I trust you."

"Thank you, Your Majesty," she said, defaulting to his title since the Espion was still looking at them.

"I'll have the release papers waiting at the dungeon for you. And I'll box Axelrod's ears as well. You have my permission to poison him the next time he tries something like that."

Ankarette smiled. She nodded to the royal pair and then followed the Espion into the passageway. There was a lantern hanging from a hook to provide light, which they took with them. The young Espion carried it. Even during the daylight hours, the secret passages were dark enough that it was risky to maneuver them without a light source.

"What's your name?" Ankarette asked the young Espion as they started, he in the lead.

"Krupp," he answered. "Are you the king's poisoner, then? We've never met."

"No, we haven't. Where are you from?"

"Westmarch, mum. A border town." He walked at a quick clip, leading the way through the tunnels, but paused at each intersection as if he were unsure of himself.

She reached out with her Fountain magic, probing to learn his abilities. When she'd come to the palace and Sir Thomas had shown her the tunnels, she'd been intrigued and eager to memorize all the passages. This young man wasn't as certain.

As soon as her magic touched him, she realized he was leading her into a trap.

We captured Queen Morvared following the Battle of Hawk Moor. Her son was slain in the battle. I threw a dagger at her arm to prevent her from murdering Isybelle and Nanette out of revenge. Since that time, King Lewis has tried to negotiate a ransom for her release.

I think he's grown tired of negotiations.

— ANKARETTE TRYNEOWY

155

NINETEEN

THE CISTERN

Sir Thomas had tried to root out traitors from among the Espion. Following the war, most of Warrewik's chosen had been easily pruned away. But it was impossible to notice all the weeds growing in a cloistered garden. Krupp had managed to get through somehow.

Now that she knew the truth, Ankarette's mind conjured a way to turn the situation to her advantage. She had no doubt that Lord Hux was involved in the plot, but he wouldn't risk himself. The last time he'd entered Kingfountain, he had escaped through one of the palace fountains. She did not know how he'd managed it, but it was something to do with Fountain magic and the interconnectedness of the shrines of worship. He knew that she could sense his presence, just as he could sense hers. So it made sense that he wasn't coming for Morvared himself. He'd arranged for someone else to free her from Holistern Tower.

If she had to guess, and that's all she could really do at this point, he would use someone who looked like Ankarette. Someone who could convince the guards to let her past. That someone could then *trade* places with

Morvared—and Morvared could walk away disguised in a cloak and gown and wig.

Therefore, Ankarette needed to be removed from the situation.

"Did you work for Lord Kiskaddon?" Ankarette asked the young man innocuously.

"Pardon, mum?"

"Lord Kiskaddon. Did you work for him?"

"No. I was recruited by the Espion at Beestone."

"Oh? For what skills?"

She sensed her questioning was making him nervous. He hadn't anticipated she'd be so chatty.

"I was. . . you know. . . I was good at listening in on conversations. Noticing things."

"Those are helpful skills for any Espion. So just to be clear, we're going to the Star Chamber?"

"Aye, mum. That's where Master Nichols is."

"And where is Bidigen Grimmer waiting?" she asked offhandedly.

He started in surprise, his eyes widening with recognition and shock. Ankarette seized him by the tunic and slammed him into the corridor wall. In a trice, her dagger was in hand and a hair's breadth from his neck.

"I see you know that name," she said in a low, dangerous voice.

"Gorm," he gasped, pupils dancing.

"You were taking me to Nichols, then what?" she demanded. "Where were you going next?"

"D-don't kill me," he burbled. "I d-didn't have a choice!"

"It's the choice you make right now that will save or condemn you. What were you to do next? If I have to force the information from you, it'll become *unpleasant.*"

He pressed himself against the wall, trembling with fear. He was scared out of his wits. She didn't feel endangered by him or his meager skills. He was young in the Espion. She'd known more at fifteen than he did now.

"He's. . . he's skulking in the cistern. There's. . . um. . . ah. . . there's a chamber down there. With a boat."

Ankarette had used that very chamber to escape with Queen Elyse and her daughter. Lord Hux had chased her down there, trying to prevent her from escaping. One of his men had been dragged into the river and perished in the falls. Of course, Hux knew of the location and the secret way to escape into the river.

"What's your role in this?"

"J-just to tell the others when you were going to Master Nichols. One of Lewis's spies is dressed like you. She's going to the tower."

"And Grimmer?"

"He's to get Morvared home."

"How?"

"I don't know. I swear it on the Lady!"

Ankarette imagined they'd use the cistern boat and empty into the river. Just as she'd thought, all of the chaos happening on Bridge Street and the wharf was part of the ploy to help Morvared escape. It was just the wily kind of plot that Lord Hux preferred.

"And what were you going to get out of this? How much did they offer to pay you to betray your king?"

"It was a s-sizable sum."

She imagined it was far less than the ransom

amount Lewis had offered to secure the fallen queen's freedom.

"We're going to the cistern now," she said.

"W-what?"

She gripped him by the shirt collar and held the knife to his back. "If you cry out or warn them, it'll go badly for you."

"I'll do whatever you say," Krupp assured her. She felt through her magic that he was being truthful. He'd been caught. The only way to avoid a harrowing fate would be to switch sides once again.

They reached the junction leading to the Star Chamber and then took the other branch, leading down into the bowels of the castle. The cistern beneath the palace was a cavernous structure, fed by ducts and openings in the upper floors, which diverted water there. At the end nearest the river was a chute and ramp, blocked by a mechanical wall that provided another escape from the palace in case of an emergency. She knew how to get there and guided her willing accomplice to the opening. The cistern door could be locked on both sides, and her goal was to trap Grimmer inside and summon help from the Espion. She wanted crossbowmen to be ready on the palace dock to shoot at anyone escaping by boat. Any delay in Krupp's arrival would alert Grimmer that his plan was in peril.

Krupp's lantern chased away the shadows as they descended some steps. Now there were no arrow slits to provide daylight. All was dark, wreathed in shadow. At the bottom of the steps, the path led to the iron door blocking the way to the cistern.

"Who's there?" asked a sniveling voice from the shadows. Ankarette recognized it instantly. It was Paul Rarick.

"'Tis I," Krupp announced, his voice trembling with fear. "Who are you?"

Rarick hefted his own lantern, and the light shone on them. He sucked in his breath.

"It's her!" he shouted in alarm. "The poisoner!"

She flung her dagger at him, her aim true. It struck Rarick in the chest, causing a grotesque contortion on his face as he tumbled backward.

The iron door slammed open, smashing into Rarick's body and crushing him against the stone wall of the corridor. His lantern shattered, spilling oil, which caught fire in an instant. In the sudden glare, Ankarette saw the hulking shadow of Bidigen Grimmer as he emerged from the cistern. Her plan had been to lock him in there, not face him in the corridor alone.

"Don't kill me!" Krupp wailed, dropping to his knees.

Ankarette saw the silver glow in Grimmer's eyes and felt the sudden churn of magic sucking hers away. She turned and bolted back up the stairs. If she was going to fight him, she'd choose the time and place. Not give *him* all the advantage.

Grimmer gave chase and she heard a sickening crunch as he passed where Krupp knelt. Of course the young Espion had been killed. Ankarette's heart thumped wildly in her chest as she raced down the corridor. She heard the man behind her, his grunts and hisses of breath. He wanted to catch her, to strangle her, to bash in her skull.

Ducking down a side corridor, she ran at full speed, hoping she'd lose him in the dark. But no, she heard him race after her. It was dangerous running headlong into the dark like this. She could slam into a stone wall and stun herself.

She felt a warning from her failing magic and flung herself toward the wall of the passageway as Grimmer's weapon sailed by her. It clattered against the stone. His steps thumped closer. Gagging down her terror, she continued her flight, reaching another set of stairs. As she clambered up them, one of her hands brushed against the fallen weapon. A war hammer. Seizing it, she hurried up the steps.

At the top of the steps was another Espion doorway, one she could lock. Her mind was still shocked with panic, but she remembered where the trip latch was to open it. As soon as her feet had finished the last step, she reached for it in the dark. Where was it? Her fingertips scraped over stone. Grimmer was pounding up the steps behind her, jets of magic sucking away her power.

She wanted to weep from fear, but she kept searching and found it. After activating the lock, she shoved open the door and then slammed it shut behind her.

A roar of fury sounded through the thick oak planks. With his hammer clenched in her hands, she smashed the trip-latch mechanism, breaking it off. Gulping air, trying to quell the wild beating of her heart, she turned and ran down the corridor, carrying the hammer. Once she was far enough away, she felt the draining of her magic recede. She'd not been sucked dry, but already her stores of magic were nearly nonexistent.

Loud thumps sounded against the door as Bidigen Grimmer threw himself against it, trying to break it down with his body.

She hoped it would hold.

When Ankarette reached the Star Chamber, she was dripping with sweat and trembling from the surge of fear and energy. Master Nichols was seated at his desk with neat stacks of correspondence across its surface. He blinked in surprise at her harried arrival.

"Are you all right, Ankarette?" he asked in growing alarm, seeing the war hammer in her hand.

"Bidigen Grimmer. . . is in the castle," she panted.

He flew from his chair instantly. "Where?"

She swallowed, her throat thick with thirst. She tasted bile. "He was waiting at the cistern. But he's loose in the tunnels. Have. . . have the king's guard summon crossbowmen and get them in position at the docks. There's a ramp for boats down there. He may try to escape."

"I know it," he said, nodding.

"He's here for Morvared. I'm going up to the tower and making sure she stays there. One of Lewis's spies is also in the castle, impersonating me. We need a password. It will be *Victoria*. If someone who looks like me doesn't know that word, you'll know it's the imposter."

He nodded in understanding. "Where did you get that hammer?" he asked. "It's a soldier's weapon, is it not?"

"He tried to kill me with it," Ankarette said. "He killed Krupp with it first." She'd seen the bloodstain on it after coming into the light. Still fresh. "He was in league with them."

"By the Veil," Bensen gasped with resentment. "I sent him to get you! Because of the cipher."

"I know. It's all a diversion. Have the Espion flood the tunnels. He has some uncanny magic, but he knows he's in a precarious situation. I think he'll try to flee back to his master. We have to stop him else he takes Nanette with him."

"Indeed," Bensen said. "Go to the tower. I'll have the Espion search the tunnels. Barbed crossbows, I think, will be the most useful."

"And polearms," she said. "In close quarters, he's too deadly. At least I have his weapon," she said, brandishing the hammer.

"He's dangerous enough without it," Bensen answered. "I'll raise the alarm. We must act quickly."

He was right.

Yet she still feared they were too late.

It was time to face the mad king's wife once more. Her heart quailed from the task. Ankarette had poisoned her husband, and there was little doubt the older queen knew it.

CHAPTER

TWENTY

INTO THE TOWER

The last time Ankarette had climbed the stairs to Holistern Tower, she had come to poison the mad king. The last time she had met Queen Morvared, the woman had just learned she'd lost her only son and heir. It was a reunion that neither would care for.

Reaching the top, she found it guarded by ten soldiers—the king's guard. They were armed with weapons and wore hauberks beneath the tunic bearing the Sun and Rose.

"Greetings," the captain said in salutation. She recognized him. Barrent was his name.

"Has anyone tried to see the queen?" Ankarette asked.

"Nary a soul," Barrent replied.

"Have *I* come to see her?"

Barrent's face wrinkled in confusion. "Pardon?"

"Someone who looks like me may try to rescue her."

"No, my lady. You're the first to come."

Ankarette felt a prickle of relief, but she didn't want to trust it. "Unlock the cell for me. If anyone comes without the password after, you are to assume they are here to break her out. Be vigilant."

"If she's this much trouble, why not end the suspense and put her over the falls?" the captain demanded.

Ankarette knew the answer.

"It is the king's decision to let her live," Ankarette said.

"And the password?"

She stepped close to him and whispered it in his ear. *"Victoria."*

He pursed his lips and nodded. "Very well. Unbolt the door."

One of the soldiers produced a ring of keys and went to unlock it. Ankarette reached out with tendrils of dwindling magic. To a man, the guards were true. And she sensed the queen's presence in the cell beyond. Holistern Tower had long been reserved for noble prisoners. Ankarette recalled that the first Argentine queen's husband had imprisoned his wife for years in one of the towers. That was centuries ago, but the palace walls had seen and endured much.

The locking mechanism released, and the guard opened the door. Ankarette raised her cowl and walked into the room. It was finely furnished, containing a single bed with lace curtains. A small writing table by the window. A garderobe.

She spotted Morvared pacing by the south window. A diminutive woman, she had a singsong voice that belied her utter ruthlessness and implacable nature. Occitanian by birth, she had married the mad king when his malady was just manifesting itself. She'd come to Kingfountain as a young woman and had managed to clench the reins of power with admirable, if brutal, efficiency. She'd won lords to her side, men like Devereaux. And she'd alienated others, like Eredur's father.

The curtains were closed, drawing that portion of the room in shadow. Ankarette turned away, looking at the door and nodding to the soldier to shut it. As soon as the door shut, Ankarette addressed the queen in Occitanian, using the accent of Pree.

"The time has come, Your Majesty. The wait is over."

How much did Morvared know about the escape plan? Had messages been smuggled into Holistern Tower? Or was she ignorant of the machinations happening on her behalf?

"You think I don't know it's you, *Poisoner*? You think I would forget?"

"But you were expecting someone else, surely," Ankarette answered, turning her profile to the queen amidst the shadows, resuming her normal speech.

"Indeed. You've done well, girl of Yuork. Your master should be so proud." She said it with contempt dripping from her voice.

Ankarette turned and faced her enemy. "No one is coming for you today. You are our prisoner still."

"I know. I am patient. But I will have my revenge."

"On Warrewik's daughters?"

"A life for a life," Morvared said sweetly. "Nanette for my dead son. Murdered by that wretched duke of Glosstyr. And my life for sweet, darling Isybelle. She is with child, Poisoner. A son, I hope. Will you kneel to serve him, I wonder? Or will you come to Lord Hux as he says? Hmmm?"

Ankarette's throat tightened with worry. "So Nanette is already dead?"

"Is she? Don't you know? I'm disappointed."

"Where is she?" Ankarette asked with an edge to her voice.

"My kishion does not tell me such things, demoiselle. You cannot force a secret I do not know with nightshade. Nor would you risk it on me anyway, lest I perish. . . and you die." She stepped from the shadows, a beautiful and cunning smile on her mouth.

"Your kishion?" Ankarette asked. "Bidigen Grimmer?"

"You are so naive, pretty thing. Yes, I have a kishion still. They are more dangerous than even you. I'm surprised you're still alive."

"Maybe they are not as formidable as you think."

"You are Fountain-blessed. That helps you, I think. But not against a kystrel. Do you know what that is, girl? Have you worn one?"

"You speak of the medallion around his neck."

"Do you know what it is? Or where they come from?"

Ankarette knew the queen would only reveal what she wanted to. She was trying to dominate the conversation. To negotiate for her freedom by hinting at information that Ankarette wanted. Eredur had no intention of letting Morvared go. That's why the Wizr pieces had been arranged so. They wanted to *force* Ceredigion to relinquish their prisoner.

"I know that he's powerless without it," Ankarette said.

"Oh, you would be surprised," Morvared chuckled with a feathery laugh. "There are magics from the Deep Fathoms you know nothing of. I want my freedom. You want your friend to live. Let me go, and I will grant that wish. A life for a life."

"I don't think so," Ankarette said. "We've uncovered the plot. Every Espion in Kingfountain is hunting your kishion and the spy. If Nanette is dead, there will be war with Occitania."

"You think Lewis does not know this? Your king is weak. Your enemies multiply. It is not too late to save Isybelle and her child. Unlike the last time. The babe you could not save."

Ankarette hated this woman. She'd landed a blow that was still painful. Isybelle had gone into labor after fleeing with Dunsdworth and her father for Callait. The miscreant Vauclair, who was bought and paid for by Lewis, had refused them refuge at the harbor, but he'd offered a bottle of wine to ease Isybelle's discomfort. It had been poisoned. The babe had died.

Ankarette, whom Warrewik had originally hired to be a companion and midwife for his daughter, had not been there and had been unable to prevent it from happening. It still hurt. Which is exactly why Morvared had pressed her there.

Ankarette walked toward Morvared purposefully and caught her by the wrist, pressing her thumb into the spot where she'd once thrown a dagger at the other woman. A dagger that had stopped Morvared from murdering Isybelle after the Battle of Hawk Moor. She squeezed deliberately, invoking a gasp of pain from the other woman. Morvared's lips twitched, but she controlled her features.

"Where is Nanette?" Ankarette demanded.

"I do not know the widow's fate. I told you this."

"How was she taken from the Arbon? Who kidnapped her?"

"I do not know. I've been here at the tower all along. If I could fly away, would I not have escaped already?"

"How did Lord Hux escape the palace? There's a magic you spoke of. Is that how he got away?"

"You are Fountain-blessed and know nothing of the ley lines? He can come and go as he pleases. But he cannot come up here to the tower. Let me go, and you can save your friend. When Dunsdworth rules, you will be taught secrets you cannot yet imagine. This is your last chance, girl."

Ankarette heard the door thump open, and Captain Barrent emerged. "Come quickly," he ordered.

Ankarette released her grip and watched as Morvared's eyes flashed with hatred while she massaged her wrist. Ankarette knew the dagger wound had never healed properly, making it so that Morvared could not fully use that hand anymore.

"What is it?" Ankarette said, turning to the captain worriedly.

"They went into the river."

That made no sense to her. "What? What of the crossbowmen?"

"They shot the two of them in the boat as they tried to escape. The big man fell into the river. The girl slumped over in the boat, and the guards watched the river carry it away. It was careening toward the falls. The king wants you to come. Now. The Espion have been dispatched to the bottom of the falls to recover their bodies."

Ankarette's chest seized with pain. If she was right, then the Espion dressed to look like Ankarette had been shot with Grimmer, but what if she was wrong?

What if that girl in the boat had been Nanette? Had

the king's men just killed Severn's beloved? On *her* orders?

Morvared laughed, that feathery, annoying laugh. "Oh, the sweetness," she crooned.

Ankarette wanted to smack her across the mouth to silence it. She fixed a finger at Captain Barrent. "Be on your guard."

"Aye, my lady. With vigor."

Ankarette looked at Morvared once more. She'd just learned that her escape had been thwarted, that her kishion had fallen into the river. No one could swim against the power of that river, especially no one who'd been wounded. Grimmer would surely go over the falls, and they'd find his drowned corpse in the harbor below. It was still daylight, so there would be plenty of eyes watching for it.

But why did Morvared seem gleeful?

Ankarette would not believe Grimmer was dead until she stared down at his body with her own eyes. But could a man truly survive a waterfall?

There was one thing Ankarette did know. Judging by the haughty look in Morvared's eyes, the Occitanian didn't believe for a moment that her kishion was dead.

The two were connected somehow, through the medallion or some other means.

It was a connection Ankarette intended to sever.

CHAPTER
TWENTY-ONE
PRISONER

Grimmer's hammer was heavy in Ankarette's hand as she descended into the dungeon area of the palace of Kingfountain. She'd left the weapon in the Star Chamber before seeing Morvared and then returned to fetch it before going down to get John Thursby released. War hammers were becoming a preferred weapon for many knights and soldiers. They could do more damage in one blow than a sword could, especially against a helmet. It was three weapons in one really—a square blunt end for a direct hit, a spear tip at the top for thrusting, and a hooked blade for ripping into armor or pulling a knight from a destrier. There were two metal plates along the length of the wooden haft fixed with rivets and a knobbed end that could also be used as a blunt weapon.

This particular weapon was well used and tarnished, each nick a testament to a battle that Grimmer had survived.

She opened the door to the dungeon, smelling the musty odor of stone and privy waste. The guard stationed there had been lounging on a stool, but he hastened to his feet.

171

"Are you the only guard?" she asked, her eyes flashing in annoyance.

"The others went to the river," he stammered. "They left me in charge."

"Do your duty, sentry," she admonished. "Show me the cell with John Thursby."

"Yes, my lady," he said. He glanced at the war hammer in her hand and swallowed. "Got the warrant of his release. The king's pardon if you will."

Ankarette nodded and followed him down the center aisle. The cells contained prisoners, mostly those who'd broken the king's peace. Some were awaiting trial for crimes, anxious about the consequences to follow. Near the end of the row, they reached the right cell, and the guard unlocked it.

From the torchlight, she saw John Thursby standing against the far wall. He'd turned to face them, his eyes wide with surprise.

"Ankarette!" he gasped. "Are you hale?" Then he noticed the war hammer in her hand and gawked. "Is he dead?"

"We don't know," she answered. "Come, I'll tell you about it on the way."

He didn't need to be told twice and left the dank cell with a scowl at the guard. "I want my weapons back. And my armor if you please."

The guard grunted in acquiescence and returned to the main room, where the items were retrieved from the top of a very large chest. She noticed knives, pouches, even an extra pair of boots. John Thursby grabbed his armor—the pauldrons to protect his neck and shoulders. Ankarette watched him put it on quickly and deftly, securing it with leather straps and rings. He tilted his head back and forth to adjust the fit and then strapped on his sword belt, which also contained the dagger sheath.

"That's his hammer," John Thursby said to her pointedly. "I recognize it."

"He threw it at me," she answered. The sentry gaped at her. It would have been a fatal blow if it had struck.

The night watchman's mouth drooped into an angry frown. "You went after him without me? He could have *killed* you!"

She handed the hammer to him. "He was in the Espion tunnels here at the palace. I didn't seek him out deliberately."

"I'll knock his head off," he whispered grimly. His hand clenched around the haft.

"Come on," Ankarette said, no longer wanting the guard to eavesdrop. They went to the stairs and started up.

Partway there, he caught her arm, stopping her. "Wait," he said. "Before we go any further."

She paused, turning around in the narrow area. There was a torch just up ahead, splashing light down at them, but the stairwell was dank and confined. She was taller than him, being a few steps higher. She tilted her head inquisitively.

He didn't release her arm. "I've been worried about you," he confessed. "Worried to the point I nearly broke that lone guard's neck and escaped. When you didn't come for me right away. . . I wondered, and I feared you might not come back at all."

"I sought the king's pardon for you first thing on reaching the castle. I wasn't going to let you languish there."

A thankful smile brightened his face. "I see that

now. But I was fearful. I don't want anything. . . well, I don't want any ill to befall you. It would grieve me."

"I trained at the poisoner school in Pisan, John Thursby. I'm not easy to kill."

He climbed one step higher. He reached out hesitantly, fear dancing in his eyes. She wondered what he was about to do. Was he going to kiss her? In a dungeon stairwell? Instead, he stroked her hair. Just a single swipe. A look of tenderness overcame the fear on his face.

"I know who you are, can imagine what you've done. I care about you, lass. I can't. . . help. . . it. I'm not used to giving pretty speeches. Most of my words are stolen from the books I've read. My feelings are real. They are deep. If that blackguard hurt you. . ." His eyes flamed as he said it. "I'd do my worst. I'm a soldier. I know I don't deserve someone like you. But every day is a gift. None of us know which hour will be our last. So I'm bold. Maybe reckless. I care. I've said it. Now we can go."

If it had been any other man than John Thursby, she would have suspected ulterior motives beneath such a confession. It was too soon for such declarations. But through her Fountain magic, she already knew his heart. It matched what she was seeing in his eyes. She was flattered, yes. Grateful even. His words awoke feelings inside her heart that had been dormant for years. She'd loved Thomas Mortimer fiercely and loyally, holding nothing back. Yet he'd chosen, in the end, someone else. John Thursby was choosing *her*. And wasting no time about it.

Still, she could not forget the poison coursing through her, even now, killing her slowly.

"Let's depart," he said, motioning for her to precede

him. He was blushing like a lovestruck fool. Her silence deepened his embarrassment.

"I see you, John Thursby," she said to him, meeting his eyes. Her heart was swimming with feelings she couldn't untangle and wasn't certain she wanted to. "I don't want any ill to happen to you either. Let's do our duty first. Then we can talk of such important things?"

Amidst the blush, he gave her a relieved little grin. "Aye. It was going to continue torturing me if I didn't blurt it out. I don't mean to presume."

"You didn't," she answered. "You've done nothing wrong."

"Except getting arrested," he corrected, chuckling.

"That was entirely not your fault," she said. "And I've asked the king to reprimand Lord Axelrod."

"You can *do* that?" He sounded impressed.

"If he does something like that again, I'm going to remind him of my profession. Not fatally. But enough to make him remember."

"Remind me to stay on your good side." He chuffed.

She smiled at him, then turned and started back up the steps. She didn't have leave to take him through the Espion tunnels, so when they emerged from the dungeon corridor, they walked the palace halls. Servants were bustling about, agitated, gossiping. John Thursby gazed at the murals and decorations adorning the walls with an appreciative eye. The palace of Kingfountain was centuries old, built before the Argentine dynasty. Back in the dawning of another age.

"Have you been here before?" she asked him.

"With Lord Devereaux," he answered with a curt nod. "I was never invited to participate in any council meetings, of course. Not like *you*. So what else have you learned while we were apart?"

"Bidigen Grimmer was intent on freeing Morvared. An Espion was bribed to switch sides and guided them into the tunnels. He tried to lure me away as well so that an Occitanian spy could dissemble as me. I interrupted the plan and was about to alert the guards when Grimmer chased me through the tunnels in the dark. He threw the hammer at me and missed, so I thought I might as well keep it out of his hands."

"Wise of you," he praised, hefting the hammer. "It's a brute. I've seen what these can do to a mounted knight. I prefer blades myself, but I know how to use one."

"What is the metal part with the rivets doing on the haft? Wouldn't wood be easier to grip?"

"Aye, but then the handle can be cut or broken, and that's not good in a fight. It takes two hands to get a good grip on it anyway, and you can use the haft to deflect a sword." He demonstrated for her. "How did Grimmer escape?"

"There's a cistern under the palace. There's also a ramp leading to the river and a boat lashed to a mooring. He and the spy went that way. I asked the king's guard to watch for them with crossbows when they hit the river. I've been told both were shot. Grimmer fell into the river, but the girl slumped down after being struck. We think they went over the falls."

"Ugh," John Thursby said, shaking his head. "Will they find the bodies, do you think?"

"We're going down there to find out. I'm concerned the girl might have been our quarry, Lady Nanette. If it's my fault she died . . ."

"You didn't have much time to react, Ankarette. Don't be hard on yourself."

"The Espion are searching the base of the falls for the bodies... or any survivors."

"No one can survive the waterfall," he said doubtfully. "I've never heard of anyone doing it all these years."

"Or does that mean everyone who is thrown over the falls is guilty?"

He grunted. "I doubt *that*, lass."

"Well, I was just with Morvared, and she didn't seem at all troubled by the news that they went into the river. She and Grimmer have some uncanny connection. I don't trust it."

They left through the front gates of the palace and came down the main road through the wall gates. None of the guards accosted them, for she was recognized on sight, and there was usually more of a suspicion of people coming up the hill instead of down.

After leaving the main gate, they started down the ramparts leading to the king's docks. The trade from that side of the river was still operating, with supplies for the castle and those dwelling inside, along with the king's fleet of warships. As she was coming down, she noticed Master Nichols coming up. He'd gone down himself to lead the search for the bodies. The look on his face implied the news wasn't good.

They met at a landing halfway down.

"We found the cistern boat," he said. "Wrecked. And a woman."

"Who was it?"

"No one recognized her, but she had some resemblance to yourself. She was dead before she went over the falls. Two of the bolts struck her, one in the heart. She was wearing a gown that I swore I've seen you wear, and her cloak also was remarkably similar."

"You're saying she was beautiful, then?" John Thursby asked.

Ankarette felt her cheeks heat.

"Yes. And Occitanian. She had a coin purse as well as a badge from the Duke of Garrone. Nothing tying her directly to Lewis, though."

"Naturally," Ankarette said. "But the look on your face says you didn't find Grimmer."

"He may be on the bottom of the bay. But there's no sign of his body. Not a trace."

"So he lived," John Thursby said in wonder.

"But how?" Master Nichols asked, perplexed. "The current of the river is too strong. No one can swim it. And he was wounded. One of the guards swears he saw him take a bolt in the shoulder. He couldn't have swum with such an injury."

Ankarette remembered how he'd still been quite hale even after a dagger stabbed him. Maybe the necklace he wore granted him special healing powers in addition to magic. She didn't know. But she agreed with John Thursby.

They had to assume he was still alive.

And still trying to accomplish his mission.

All warfare is based on deception. This is the first adage learned in the poisoner school when advising kings. When a force is ready and able to attack, they would do best to appear weak. The appearance of inactivity in a camp could be a calculated ruse to belie the true state of readiness. When a force is near, it must be assembled so as to appear far away. Or the opposite. The outcome of every battle, every stratagem, hangs on perception.

— ANKARETTE TRYNEOWY

CHAPTER

TWENTY-TWO

THE DEAD CAN SPEAK

The remains of the smashed boat had been dragged to the rocky shore. It had clearly struck a rock, or else the mighty power of the waterfall had pulverized the wood. She swallowed, feeling a sense of dread.

"There's not much left of it, is there?" John Thursby said, arms folded.

Ankarette crouched, examining the splintered wood. Grimmer's plan didn't make sense to her. If his goal was to get Morvared out of the castle, did he intend to bring her to the sanctuary of Our Lady? Would Tunmore even allow her sanctuary? Or was that where Lord Hux would be waiting to whisk her away?

Or could this be misdirection?

It was part of the poisoner's strategy to never reveal their full intentions. All warfare was based on deception. And who was better at that than Lord Hux?

Ankarette straightened and walked over to Master Nichols. John Thursby followed her.

"Where is the message from Lord Hux?" she asked.

He reached into his doublet and produced a note, the seal broken. She recognized Hux's penmanship. And yes, it was in a cipher that the Espion didn't know. The message was intended for *her*. There was no date on it, so she had no idea when it had been sent. But as she scanned it, her mind quickly replaced the garbled text with the real message. She could almost hear the playful sound of his voice as she read his words.

CHER ANKARETTE,

I propose an exchange of hostages. Two daughters for one queen. Even in the game of Wizr, no piece of true value is surrendered freely. Go to the Genevese docks. Seek Captain Anselm of the ship Baracruese. *He will negotiate the terms and provide the exchange. Decide swiftly, demoiselle. This offer will not be available for long. Remember the terms of our agreement. If the queen dies, so do you.*

Until we meet again,
With utmost affection,
SHX

SHE LOWERED THE LETTER, gazing at the deep river leaving the city of Kingfountain for the sea. The shoals were rocky and filled with sand and debris—trinkets and waste cast into the river from above. It was wide and deep enough for ships from all kingdoms to maneuver upstream to Kingfountain.

"What did he say?" asked the master of the Espion.

"He offered to exchange hostages," Ankarette said.

"Lady Nanette for Morvared?"

Ankarette pursed her lips, her insides clenching with dread. "He mentioned *both* sisters. Two for one."

"The Duchess of Clare is still at the Arbon," Nichols said.

Ankarette believed the letter was a ruse. A deception. "He's trying to trick us. To turn our gaze away from the objective. He mentioned a Genevese ship, the *Baracruese*. It's a decoy. He sent the letter to trigger a reaction while Grimmer was going to rescue the queen. Only. . . the timing is wrong."

"I'll have the Espion look for that Genevese ship," Nichols said, "but no ship on that side can leave, per the king's mandate. They're not going anywhere."

"Agreed. The captain's name is Anselm. Bring him to the palace for questioning."

"Of course," Nichols said. "I'll also send word to the Arbon in case Grimmer tries to abduct the duchess. Do you wish to see the body we recovered?"

"I do. She's over there?" Ankarette had noticed the bundled corpse when they'd arrived.

"She is. I'll have it taken to the coroner afterward. But there's little good it can do for us. The dead can't speak." The master of the Espion walked away.

Ankarette sighed. Together with John Thursby they walked up to the body covered by a dampened blanket. Ankarette crouched again and pulled the blanket away, revealing the dead woman's pale face. She'd seen enough death and corpses not to be disturbed by this one, but the woman *did* bear an uncanny resemblance to Ankarette.

She heard John Thursby suck in his breath and glanced up at him.

He was frowning, one hand clenched into a fist. The quarrel barbs still protruded from the body. The gown and cloak were similar to ones in Ankarette's possession. She examined the stitching and material and thought they were brilliantly done. It wasn't an Occitanian fabrication. The clothes were from Ceredigion. How long had the woman been in the city? She hadn't come expecting to die. Yet here she lay—pallid, her life snuffed out because of Ankarette's warning.

"It doesn't make sense," Ankarette murmured to herself.

John Thursby squatted next to her. "Not much in life does. Each of us is always hoping for clues or meaning. We grope for sense where there is none. I gave up on that search long ago."

Ankarette covered the body again with the blanket. "People do things for a reason. If you can discern the strategy, you can—"

He shook his head, cutting her off. "Life is like war, Ankarette. We're seeing this through slits in a visor, ears ringing from the noise."

She saw the haunted look in his eyes. He was talking about the warfare he'd endured. Being so close, she could smell the iron of his armor. She could almost hear the clash of arms ringing through his memory.

"You're remembering Borehamwood," she said with sympathy.

"Aye," he answered, not meeting her gaze. She saw his cheek muscle twitch. "We had the larger force. And two cunning battle commanders—Warrewik and Devereaux. A common enemy. Eredur." He said the name as if tasting something awful. "I'll never forget that day. Not just because of my wounds. But how it felt to lose *everything*." He sat down on the riverbank, looking forlorn and devastated.

She reached out and touched his arm. She'd come after the battle, fearing the worst. For her, it had been bittersweet. Warrewik had perished at the battle, so her loyalties were no longer conflicted. The man who'd made her the poisoner of Kingfountain had ultimately fallen victim to his pride. Still, the victory had been glorious. Borehamwood hadn't ended the war, but it had altered its trajectory.

"Such memories are painful," she said sympathetically. "I didn't see that battle firsthand. I did see Hawk Moor play out, though."

"We weren't ever going to win after Borehamwood," he said sullenly. "I was too injured to fight, but I've spoken to soldiers who were there. It was a last gamble. A final toss of the dice. But Borehamwood was an odd one." He looked at her. "A great mist welled up that morning. So thick. Like Old Rose's porridge. We'd shot arrows all night at Eredur's lines, but they'd crept closer to escape the volleys, and we didn't know it. They never shot back, so we had no notion of how close they were."

She knew this part of the battle. The king himself had told her that they hadn't returned fire because they hadn't wanted to reveal their presence to Warrewik. Their silence had aided in the deception.

"In the fog, we couldn't see each other very well. Because our armies weren't lined up well, we overtook Hasting's flank. We routed them, destroying that part and thinking we'd won. I know some of Devereaux's men chased Hastings all the way back to Kingfountain. The others started looting, believing the battle was over even when it was still raging in the mist. Devereaux sent me and my men to bolster our left flank, which was hit hard by Glosstyr's folk. But when we arrived, we mistook our men for Eredur's in the fog and attacked our own allies. In that fog, all was seen wrong. We fought our own kinsmen that day. They cried treason and attacked us back in fury, all while Glosstyr pressed from behind." He shook his head in misery. "It was that accursed fog. If we'd combined against Glosstyr, we would have ruined him, and the battle would have gone the other way." He sighed and shook his head. "So it wasn't just Eredur's brilliance that won the day. It was our own folly."

Her heart hurt for him. There was no contest so grievous and final as war. Most kings preferred to avoid it at all costs, because the winner was not always the most numerous, well positioned, or even bravest. Eredur had exploited his enemy's error in Borehamwood. And he'd won the day.

"So you were wounded by your own friends," Ankarette said with compassion.

"Aye. I'm not the only one who fell that day. But the shame of it still stings."

"You had to fight hard just to stay alive," she said.

"And kill many a man whom I'd drunk with days before. Who believed, as I skewered them with my sword, that I was a traitor to them. Some wounds heal faster than others. Part of me died at Borehamwood. It's why I can't sleep at night. Too many regrets."

"But you know what really happened. It wasn't your fault."

He pursed his lips and shrugged noncommittally. "Anyone with gumption and a sharp mind will take the measure of two things, Ankarette. What's said and what's done. And what's done is done. That's why men like the constable can never fully trust me."

"I trust you, John Thursby. Because of what you've said and done."

A little smile quirked on his lips. "Thank you, lass.

Sorry for being morose. The past can drown the pleasures of today. Let's be going."

She wrinkled her brow. "Going? Where?"

He rose to his feet and cracked his neck and back. "Your Espion friend was wrong. The dead *can* speak. I meant to tell you so sooner, but the whirlwind distracted me."

"Tell me what?"

"When we went to the warehouse, with all the dead hanging and killed. I knelt and examined one of the bodies. The man wore a guild ring on his little finger."

"A guild ring?"

"Aye. And I recognized it, for one of my brother soldiers used to be part of that guild before the war, and he showed his ring to me. If Grimmer hired that guild to help him smuggle away the duke's daughter, then he wouldn't want to leave evidence of that treachery. I say we call on the guild master and see what he knows. It's not much, but it's something. And I'll tell you true, he won't be on Grimmer's side anymore, not after the way he slaughtered the dockmen."

Ankarette felt the smile brightening her face as he spoke. It was a small detail he'd noticed. One that had slipped past all the high constable's men.

"Well done," she said and watched as he blushed.

TWENTY-THREE
THRUSHING MEEKS

The daylight was beginning to wane. If night fell again without finding Nanette, Ankarette feared that they wouldn't find her alive. The head of the Espion had sent men to interrogate the captain of the *Baracruese*. If he proved reluctant to leave his ship, it would require some strength from the king's guard to persuade him. Nichols said the captain would be brought to the Espion inn on Bridge Street.

She and John Thursby walked back to the South-wark wharf where they'd been earlier. The tension in the air was palpable as cargo lay spoiling in ship holds, threatening to ruin many a merchant depending on the trade. Sailors were carousing the streets in varying stages of intoxication. Ankarette kept her cowl up as she walked among them, feeling the anger and desperation in the air. John Thursby scowled, leading the way. He'd mentioned that the members of the guild they were looking for wore rings on their littlest fingers. Her eyes darted from person to person and then found a small group of men, about six, standing together in a crowd, with surly faces. Some were vocally complaining about the lack of good ale. They were all wearing rings, so she tapped John Thursby's arm and pointed surreptitiously to them.

"Good eyes, lass," he said. "Let me do the talking if you don't mind. They might get too friendly to such a pretty face."

"I've handled their type before," she said.

"I've no doubt of your abilities, Ankarette. I'm just offering."

She didn't want to let her pride get in the way, so she nodded to him and then blended in with the crowd as he approached them. A whiff of spoiled meat soured her hungry stomach. How long had it been since she'd stopped to eat? She maneuvered through the crowd until she was close enough to overhear the conversation.

"Can you tell me where I can find your guild master?" John Thursby asked.

"You one of the king's men?" asked a dockman challengingly. "Why should I tell you?"

"Nay, I'm a member of the night watch."

"It ain't night yet," said another man.

"With all the trouble in Kingfountain, you think daylight matters anymore? I need to speak with him. Where does he dwell?"

"Not 'ere," snarled the first man. "Thrushing's in Queenshithe."

"Is that his name?"

The other added, "It's what we call 'im. He's got this rash, you see. Blotches on his face and arms. He's been done an ill turn."

"You gents talking about the warehouse?" John Thursby pressed.

"Aye," said the first. "Strung from ropes like poppet dolls. Nasty business that."

"What was the job?"

"Don't know nuffin' about it. But old Thrushing does. Won't say a word 'bout it now. Say, do you know when the king will let the ships go? Southwark is full, and new ships are rotting off the waters. Won't let them in. How long is this gonna last?"

"I don't know," John Thursby said with a toss of his head. "It could be a while."

"Lady's legs," cursed another dockman. "Thought the king was a truer man than that. It's all squabbles from the nobility, and we suffer for it."

"Aye, we do," agreed another man.

"If Thrushing's his nickname, what else is he called?" John Thursby pressed. "How can I find him?"

"His name is Meeks. Don't know where he lives," replied the man. "Just know he's somewhere in Queenshithe."

John Thursby reached into his purse and handed out some coins. "Thanks for your help." He left the crowd and started walking down the pier. Ankarette followed and then joined him. He glanced back at her.

"Did you hear any of that?" he asked. "I saw you behind them."

"Thrushing Meeks. An interesting name."

"And Queenshithe isn't small. Let's grab some dinner. I can ask some of the night watchmen from that ward. They'll know of him, I hope."

"If he has a skin condition, then an apothecary might be able to help us. I know one in Queenshithe. Danner Tye. Let's see him first."

He gave her an approving nod, and when they reached the end of the docks, they began climbing up the wooden ramparts to the higher portion of the city. She knew her way easily to Queenshithe. By the time they reached the apothecary's shop, the sun had fallen and most of the businesses were closed. Including the apothecary.

She knocked on the door, waited a few moments, then knocked again more firmly. With daylight fading, people were retreating inside. Those who could afford the luxury of candles had lit them already, but many of the shops were dark, including Danner Tye's.

"Should I break it open?" John Thursby suggested with a half-joking smile.

"What? And have someone call the night watch on us?" She smiled. "He might be gone for dinner himself." The streets of Queenshithe were well tended and so were most of the shops. She knocked once again, listening for sounds.

The noise of boots coming from the upper rooms could be heard in the quiet street. Moments later, she saw Danner's face peering through the curtain. He unbolted the door and cracked it open.

"Ankarette?"

"Had you gone to bed already?" she asked him.

"No. . . the. . . uh. . . garderobe actually." He glanced at John Thursby. "Who's this? Are you injured?"

"No, just need some information," she said. "We're looking for a guild master who lives in this ward. Meeks is his name. Has a skin condition. The dockmen call him—"

"Thrushing," Danner said, nodding in understanding. "He resents the nickname, you know. But yes, he's another patient of mine. He was here earlier today for a calming tonic."

"Do you know where we can find him?" Ankarette asked.

"He was afraid to go home," Danner said. "Some evil

befell his business today. With the city docks closed, there's been all sorts of trouble. I think he's lost a great deal of money."

Ankarette looked at John Thursby and back. "If he's not home, do you know where he is?"

"This is the king's business, then?" the apothecary asked warily.

"Yes. We have to find him at once."

Danner Tye nodded. "In that case, I'll tell you. He is staying at the inn on Saint Pancras street. It's not far from here."

"Time is of the essence. Can you bring us there?" Ankarette asked.

"Very well. Let me put on a cloak."

Soon the trio were walking the streets of the district, wandering past a few empty lots until they found the inn at another crossroads. It had four rooms, and there were candles burning in all but one.

"Likely that one," said the night watchman in an undertone. Ankarette agreed.

"Should I rouse the innkeeper?" Tanner asked.

"No. Let's not bother him yet," John Thursby said. He walked to the door and knocked firmly on it. He gripped his sword hilt.

"Who's there?" asked a nervous voice from the other side.

"That his voice?" John Thursby asked the apothecary softly. A curt nod confirmed it, and the night watchman stepped back, then kicked the door open and entered.

"Don't hurt me! Don't hurt me!" wailed the man inside. Ankarette noticed a candle and taper on the windowsill.

"Would you light a candle, please?" she asked the apothecary.

He struck a spark, lit the taper, then the candle. The soft glow illuminated the room. In the far corner was a heavyset man with splotches on his cheeks. He had white hair and very pale skin. He stood, trembling, gripping a walking cane with both hands as a weapon. Ankarette reached out with her Fountain magic, trying to determine what threat they faced. The man cowered in fear, his eyes going from face to face worriedly. He was terrified and expecting to die. She knew that even without the magic. But the level of his fear suggested he knew too much. He was implicated in this nefarious business and didn't know where to turn now that Bidigen Grimmer had killed so many of his men. That made him desperate.

"Wh-who are you?" he whispered, the cane trembling in his hands.

"Are you Master Meeks?" Ankarette asked him.

"Who *are* you?" he shouted.

Ankarette closed the door behind her, watching him.

"You're hiding from Bidigen Grimmer," she said, watching for a reaction.

He started involuntarily at the name. "Did you come to kill me?"

She shook her head. "I can help protect you. But you have to tell me what you know. This deal didn't end up as you intended, did it?"

He lowered the cane and shook his head. "Please. I don't want to die. Not like the others."

"I want to help you. I serve King Eredur. He sent me to find Lady Nanette. Do you know where she is?"

He trembled with agitation from head to foot. "No. She's. . . she's still alive?"

"We're hoping you can help us find her. Tell me what you know, and I'll ask the king to have mercy on you."

"I c-can't!"

"You must. Bidigen Grimmer wants to kill you because you know too much. Share that knowledge, and your value diminishes to him."

"Should I be hearing this?" Danner Tye asked worriedly. "I know nothing of this affair."

"The damage is already done," Ankarette said. "We're trying to catch a killer. The man who killed your guild members. Do you want him to go unpunished?"

"But if I talk, *I* could be guilty too! I could go over the falls."

Ankarette wondered if she should use nightshade on him. But she felt she was close to getting him to divulge everything.

"You're worried about going over the falls?" she pressed. "The only crimes worthy of that are unhallowed acts and. . . treason."

The guild master nodded vigorously and began weeping. He believed he was guilty of treason and would suffer a traitor's fate.

"Were you trying to help Morvared escape?" Ankarette asked.

Through snuffles and sobs, the guild master nodded. "She's our true queen."

"You knew about Lady Nanette's abduction?" Ankarette pressed.

"Not at the time, no! Since she disappeared, everyone's been looking for her. But she was never abducted by Grimmer. When they went to snatch her away, she was already gone!"

Ankarette turned to look at John Thursby and saw the same surprise she felt, evident in his eyes.

"She was?" the night watchman asked incredulously.

"Aye! The man at the porter door smuggled her away. He wouldn't go along with our plan. He was more loyal to Warrewik than his master!"

"You mean the Duke of Clare knew of this?" Ankarette demanded.

"Only part of it! He wanted her kidnapped. Taken away so he couldn't reveal where she was. And that's why I'm a dead man! I know it, and he *knows* I know it! If Grimmer doesn't kill me, Dunsdworth will! But Nanette is gone. No one knows where she is except the porter, and his skull was crushed in!"

Ankarette was so dismayed, she couldn't hide her feelings. She thought again of Lord Hux's note to her, his offer to exchange hostages. He was bargaining with collateral he didn't even have. It was a classic poisoner trick—make your enemy believe you are close when you are far away. Make them believe you have something you do not. His plot had *failed* because of the integrity of a lower servant. Hux knew he could dupe Dunsdworth into thinking hiding Nanette away was his idea. He knew he could suborn guards, sentries, and even Espion. But this plan had hinged on getting Nanette out through the porter door. And he hadn't counted on a native of Yuork, a man named Moser, being loyal to the young widow. The heiress.

If only she had listened to her gut....

She turned to Danner Tye. "Do you know the apothecary on Wrexham? By the Arbon?"

THE WIDOW'S FATE

"Aye, I do," he answered.

"Come with us. We need to try and revive someone with a head."

"But what about *me*?" Master Meeks begged. "I've done wrong, but I can help! I'd rather be alive in the king's dungeon than dead on a rope. Please, I beg it of you!"

"That, I believe, can be arranged," John Thursby said with aplomb. "I happen to know there is a spare room in the dungeon at this moment." He stepped forward. "I arrest you, Master Meeks, on a charge of high treason."

Ankarette saw the darkness outside the window. It was nighttime, the first hour of the night watch.

195

CHAPTER
TWENTY-FOUR
THE APOTHECARY OF WREXHAM

With so much intrigue afoot, Ankarette's circle of trust was diminishing rapidly. She trusted John Thursby to do what he said he'd do. She trusted the head of the Espion, for the most part, and some of the members she'd known for years. She trusted the king and queen. No one else, truly. That limited her options, and she knew it.

"Take Master Meeks to the Espion inn on Bridge Street," she said to John Thursby. "Inform them of what we've learned. I trust Hugh Bardulf's judgment about whether to keep him under guard or send him to the palace. I'll go with Danner to Wrexham. It's near the Arbon. Meet us there."

"I will," he answered with a stern nod. "I'm wary to leave you, though."

Touched by his concern, she put a hand on his arm. "Why?"

"Grimmer is a formidable chap. I'd like to be there when we meet him next. Don't go off chasing after him without me."

She smiled. "I'm not planning to. There've been no sightings of him since the river. He may have drowned."

He offered a weak shrug. "He's used the river before. The little sewer tunnel. The wharves. The cistern. He *likes* the water. I don't think we've seen the last of him."

"For the same reasons, neither do I. I'll be careful."

"You do that, lass. For my heart's sake," he added in an undertone. Then he turned and gripped Master Meeks by the arm and escorted him from the inn.

Ankarette shifted and faced Danner Tye. "We'll go back to your shop so you can gather your things. It may take more than medicine to heal this man. Your skill in battlefield injuries is highly desirable at the moment."

"Head injuries are awful things," replied Danner with a sigh. "I'll assume he's been given a sleeping draft. For an injury as grievous as this, trepanning is a common remedy."

She'd heard of the technique in poisoner school but had never seen it done. "That's relieving pressure to the skull by cutting a hole in it?"

"Aye. Not cutting exactly, it uses a special kind of auger."

"Have you done it before?"

"Yes, several times actually. During the Kingmaker Wars, especially following battles, it was unfortunately a common treatment. I did one several months ago for a child who fell from an upper window and landed on the street."

"Sometimes I forget the depth and breadth of what you're called on to do, Master Dye. I appreciate your expertise in this matter. The king will also."

"Assuredly, Ankarette. I had no notion that the guild master was involved in this affair. It's quite disturbing how many in this ward still nurture old allegiances. The folk in Queenshithe were rather partisan to the mad king."

"And what about your loyalties?" she asked pointedly. She didn't distrust him, but she realized that the shift of power from one king to another, and the instability it caused, had far-reaching consequences.

"I'm in the business of healing maladies, Ankarette. Not fostering them. King Eredur has been just and fairminded. But there are some who will not bury old resentments, no matter how long ago they were suffered. It is part of our nature, I think."

He was right, of course. She nodded for him to go ahead of her out the door and closed it behind herself. They traveled quickly back to the apothecary shop the way they had come, and while he was gathering his things, she paced around his front room until he was finished. He extinguished the lamps, locked the door behind them, and walked with her through the darkened streets of Queenshithe.

They encountered, coincidentally, a member of the night watch on patrol and were hailed for being out of doors at so late an hour. The guard was at least seventy years old, had a decisive limp, and was wheezing when he caught up with them.

"What's this?" he said with a phlegmatic voice. "Don't ye know it's dangerous being on the streets at night? What's the bother?"

"I'm Danner Tye, the apothecary. We're going to see a patient."

"I've not heard of ye. Where do you hail from?"

"Queenshithe. I'm going to assist a fellow on Wrexham."

"Old Moser? He's a fair gent."

"The very one. We're in a bit of a hurry if you don't mind."

"By all means but be careful. There's a killer loose

they say. I brought me little flute tonight, in case I need to call for help. Go on your way." He gave Ankarette a probing look and then backed away and started to limp off again.

"Poor fellow has the gout," Danner said. "He shouldn't be walking the streets at night, but what other business can a man his age do this late in years?"

The contrast between him and John Thursby had been notable, but she agreed with the apothecary's assessment. So many of the aged were forgotten and abandoned by the world, some so immobile they could only beg by the streetside.

After an interminable walk, they reached the apothecary at Wrexham. They did so without encountering any of Dunsdworth's men, which was no small relief to her. The shop was closed up, and it took some pounding on the door to rouse the apothecary.

"Y-yes?" he asked after unbolting the door. He held a candlestick, and the light illuminated the full face of a middle-aged man with pepper-colored whiskers and shorn hair. He looked from Danner to Ankarette without recognition.

"Who is it, Papa?" asked a child's voice from inside.

"I don't know yet, lad. I don't know. Is there trouble? What's wrong?"

Ankarette thought it best to establish her authority quickly. "My name is Ankarette, and I'm here on orders from the king. Can we come inside?"

"The king?" His eyes flashed with worry.

"It's about the duke's servant, the man Moser. I was told he was here." Ankarette watched him for a reaction.

"Oh, he's here. But he hasn't spoken since his injury.

He slips in and out. Awful business. Sanctuary men knocked him on the head."

"We'd like to see him anyway," Ankarette said. Her suspicions and alarm were growing.

"I don't know what good it will do. He can't speak. Been having fits and seizures."

Ankarette pushed on the door, felt the apothecary resist slightly, but then he backed away and gestured for them to enter. He snuck a furtive look behind them to see if anyone else had come. That was suspicious.

There was a little lad, about eight, wearing a nightshirt.

"I'm Danner Tye, an apothecary from Queenshithe," Danner said, extending his hand in greeting. It was an unusual handshake, a locking of wrists and a tapping of fingers, a code of sorts from one guild member to another. Ankarette knew most of the guilds had such secret ways of distinguishing each other, though it wasn't knowledge shared outside the initiated.

"I'm Chastain Bell. Apothecary. You. . . you want to see him?"

"Yes, that's why we came," Ankarette said. She was suspicious enough of him to want to use her power but had already drained so much of it.

Like many of the small houses in Kingfountain, all cramped together, the living quarters were upstairs and the shopfront below. The smell of herbs and remedies was layered with the scent of bile and sickness. Ankarette had visited enough sick chambers to be familiar with its different odors. Chastain led them with his candle to a room with a couch and hearth, which held sizzling coals and exuded warmth. Moser lay on the couch, a blanket tugged half off. Ankarette recognized his face, although it was covered in bandages and flecked with crimson from the bleeding. He was breathing raggedly, but his body was very still, in a stupor.

Danner Tye asked for the candle and then knelt by the couch. "What have you tried so far?"

"Milkwort for the swelling. Some tincture of gib weed to suppress the tremors."

"What about the injury itself? There are a lot of bandages here. Did you try trepanning?"

"No, sir. That doesn't work in these cases."

Danner touched Moser's neck, then began examining his chest. He leaned close to listen to his breathing.

"For a fractured skull? His brain has been swelling. The smell of vomit is stifling. He looks to be in great distress."

"I'm not the Lady of the Fountain," said Chastain defensively. "His life is in *her* hands. I told the duke's wife to drop coins in the well for him. If he revives, it's the Lady's will."

Danner shot him a disgusted look. "You haven't even tried *all* the remedies yet." He gave Ankarette a decisive nod. "I need to do a trepanning."

"I'm saying it won't help," Chastain blustered. "This case is beyond the aid of man."

"What can I do?" Ankarette asked, coming up next to him.

"It's too warm in here," Danner said. "That's only making it worse. Let's carry him to the table in the main room. I'll grab him by the arms. You take his legs."

Together, the two of them hefted Moser and carried him into the other room, being careful to support his head and neck. Chastain followed them and started talking in a low voice to the boy, who was staring at the intruders with fright. He knelt by the lad, gripping him by the neck and offered some soothing words.

"It'll be all right. Go on, now."

The boy nodded and then went down the corridor. She heard the stairs creak as he climbed them.

"I need more light," Danner said.

"Why not wait until morning?" Chastain suggested. "It's too dark to try it now."

Ankarette felt the deliberateness of the obstruction. "Bring us six candles," she ordered.

He gave her a resentful look and then went and gathered more, though he took his time doing so. She snatched them and then used the first to light the rest.

"It seems he's done the very least to help this man," Ankarette whispered to Danner, trying to keep her voice low enough that the other couldn't overhear them.

"Indeed. He's probably uncomfortable with the procedure. It's not for the faint of heart."

"Or he's been told not to," Ankarette suggested.

Danner sighed and began unwinding the bandages. She followed his instructions, fetching water, rags, and preparing some shaving lather to clear the spot on his head. Moser groaned and twitched but was otherwise unresponsive.

A short while later, the sound of horses came down the street. Ankarette imagined John Thursby would come on a single horse, not many. She left Danner Tye and hurried to the window, parting the curtain to gaze outside.

Knights were riding up to the apothecary's house. Knights wearing the badge of the Duke of Clare. Then she recognized Dunsdworth himself leading them. The Arbon was close by.

How had they known Ankarette was there?

She looked at Chastain and saw a relieved cast to his countenance. He'd been expecting them.

"You sent the boy?" she asked him, her suspicion spiking. The lad must have climbed out the upper window and down the wall. She hadn't heard a sound.

His resentful smile was his only answer.

In the profession of a poisoner, there is always the risk of capture. Being captured by an enemy ruler can put at risk the monarch's secrets, which various devices of torture have been invented to extract. The rack, for example, can pull someone's limbs out of socket and is excruciatingly painful and risks permanent disfigurement. Manacles, another technique, dangle one from iron cuffs at a height. There is a torture device in Occitania, I'm told, called the scavenger's daughter, which compresses the body in a tight band until breathing is nearly impossible.

Poisoners always keep a suicide ring at the ready. Cherry laurel extract is the preferred toxin as it tastes pleasant. Its cyanide content is very high. If capture is inevitable, it is usually the wisest course to ensure that the cost of capture far exceeds its benefit.

— ANKARETTE TRYNEOWY

TWENTY-FIVE

DEATH OR REASON

"**A**re we in danger?" Danner Tye asked, his eyes widening with the possibility.

Chastain ran to the door. Ankarette caught him before he could turn the handle. She torqued his arm violently behind his back and then shoved the crossbar into place to secure it.

The knights were dismounting rapidly. She only had a few seconds to decide what to do. When she'd last met Dunsdworth, he'd been in an intoxicated stupor, and she'd used force on him to achieve compliance.

Was this his attempt to return the favor? Was he coming to stop her from trying to help his servant? Or was something else afoot? As she gripped the moaning apothecary and held him against the door, her mind went through her options. She could try reasoning with the duke, but if he'd sent his knights to take her, it would be a one-sided fight unless Ankarette used her deadliest poisons. Still, they were in cramped quarters and would likely overpower her.

She could kill Dunsdworth. That would throw off his men and also eliminate a threat to Eredur. They'd probably run her through with their swords afterward, but at least she'd remove the king's brother as a contender for the throne. She had the king's permission to use her judgment.

The handle rattled and then a fist pounded on the wood. She heard Dunsdworth's muffled voice on the other side. "Open at once!"

"It's my master, the Duke of Clare!" Chastain snarled. "Release me!"

"Ankarette, I don't understand what you're doing," Danner Tye said, watching her grapple with the other man. "If it's the king's brother—"

"Then we're in more danger than you know. Go help Moser. Let me deal with this. Go!"

The weight of a body slammed into the door. She heard Dunsdworth order his men to break it open. Danner retreated to the other room, looking fearful at what he'd gotten himself into.

She shoved Chastain aside and then positioned herself on the side of the door opposite the hinges. She undid the bolt quietly and twisted the knob to release it so it would fly open on the next charge. It did, and a large knight stumbled onto the floor.

She backed away and exposed her needle ring. Then she drew her dagger, retreating to the corner. The stairs leading to the bedchambers above were on her right, giving her a way of escape.

"Ankarette!" Dunsdworth barked from outside. "Show yourself!"

"I'd rather we speak in here, my lord."

The knight who'd tumbled onto the floor was rousing himself. A kick to the head would knock him out, but she didn't want to be the one to instigate the brawl. She'd use reason first.

"Go in there and drag her out!"

"I would advise against that, Dunne. I'll kill any knight who crosses this threshold, beginning with this one."

"I've brought enough men to subdue you, Ankarette."

"You don't know me as well as you think. This is what will happen next if you all want to live."

"If we all want to live?" Dunsdworth snarled incredulously.

"I'm glad you heard me, my lord. This is an apothecary. There are powders here that can choke your breath. Poisons that can clot your blood. Ones that can make you blind—permanently. Believe me, my lord duke, if you send any men in here against my will, you'll be sending them to their deaths."

She was using fear of the unknown to rattle Dunsdworth's men. He might be the world's greatest fool. But they'd all heard rumors about her. She'd play on that.

"I just want to talk, Ankarette. That is all." His voice sounded nervous. She heard murmurs of worry from the knights. A few of their boots scraped in retreat.

The knight sprawled on the floor came slowly to his knees, his hands held up passively.

"Don't. . . move," she said to him in a low voice, giving him a menacing waggle of her dagger. He swallowed and closed his eyes and began whispering a prayer to the Lady of the Fountain.

She walked up to him and exposed herself in the doorway. She gripped his hair and held her dagger to his throat, but her eyes sought out the duke's.

He stared at her. There were eight knights total, including the one sniveling at her feet. They had the advantage in numbers and strength. But right now, she was the master of the situation. They didn't know what she could do to them. There is no fear so great as that of suspense.

"I'll release my hostage if you come in, Lord Dunsdworth," she said. "His life for yours. If I'd wanted to kill you, I'd have done it at the Arbon. Your men stay outside. You, I will allow to come in unharmed."

"Captain Rufus," Dunsdworth said, his cheek twitching with anger. His eyes were bloodshot.

"A-aye, my lord?" The captain stood next to him, sword drawn.

"Think very carefully before you utter your order," Ankarette said. "I will offer no quarter. I'll kill you all."

She wasn't bluffing. That was something you did playing games of chance. If she was going to die, she would take as many of them with her as possible.

Captain Rufus backed away a step. Dunsdworth shot him a blistering glare, but then turned back to face Ankarette. She could see his mind working. Eight against one. He'd been sure that he could best her. But seeing his knights hesitate, seeing them slowly inch away from the door, he was realizing that none of them wanted this fight. None of them wanted to die that night.

"Order them to drop their weapons," Ankarette said.

Resentment flashed in his gaze.

"P-please, my lord," groaned the man at Ankarette's feet. He was weeping. "Don't let her. . . kill me."

A reputation was a powerful thing. She saw that on clear display. She'd bested some of Dunsdworth's and Severn's knights, and they'd talked.

He was still hesitating.

"My lord," Rufus whispered. "She's *Fountain-blessed.* We don't stand a chance!"

"Come inside," she said to Dunsdworth. "Let your man free. Your duty as a lord is to defend your men."

"Their duty is to obey me," the duke growled in return.

"Please, m-my lord," Rufus begged. "Don't do this."

Dunsdworth realized his men wouldn't obey him. And he couldn't bear to give an order that he knew they'd shun. His honor was compromised. So was his dignity.

"We are not enemies," Ankarette said to him. "I know why you're here. I know more than you do right now. Come inside, and we'll discuss your fate. Let this innocent knight go free. *You* are the guilty one."

A mottled look came to the duke's cheeks. He gazed down and then met her eyes. "Let him go."

He'd surrendered. She could see it in his eyes.

She lowered the knife and released the man's hair. He dropped his face to her feet and continued sobbing. Every person reacted to the threat of imminent death in a different way.

"Come inside, my lord. You wouldn't want your men to hear what I have to say."

"I will, Ankarette. Now, let him go."

He was telling the truth. Trying to salvage some shred of lost dignity.

"Off with you," she said to the knight and tapped him with her boot. He hurriedly rose and backed out of the apothecary shop. She lowered the dagger and used her other hand to gesture for the duke to enter. He did, without hesitation.

"Captain Rufus, if you'll stand guard outside?" she suggested. Then she gave Chastain, who was staring at her in wide-eyed terror, a commanding look. "Go help

Master Dye with the procedure. Give him your best work."

Chastain looked submissively at the duke and then walked to the room where Danner was working on the trepanation.

"Were you really going to kill me, Ankarette?" he asked softly.

"If you left me no other choice," she answered. "I'm tired, Dunne. Let's cut the gibberish. Nanette is alive. She's not a hostage. Only Moser knows where she is. Which is why you were willing to let him die."

He flashed his teeth at her. But he wouldn't deny it.

"You believed the secret of your treachery would be safeguarded by his death. Alas, that is not so. What you don't understand is that you've been duped. Bidigen Grimmer is a kishion, a killer, hired by the court of Occitania to secure the release of Queen Morvared."

His eyes narrowed in confusion. "I have nothing to do with that!"

"I know that as well," Ankarette said. "You're guilty of being a selfish and self-interested noble of Ceredigion. It made you a willing, but ignorant, accomplice in this plot. Your refusal to let Nanette marry Severn provided the oil to start this fire."

"He should marry someone else!" Dunsdworth complained. "Anyone else!"

"I remember vividly your own chafing when Eredur refused to let *you* marry Isybelle to prevent giving Warrewik any more power. And you married her anyway, despite his prohibition. Nanette and Severn care for each other. Their love doesn't rob you of a farthing!"

"How can you say that? Of course it does!"

"You were never going to keep the entire inheritance for yourself," she reminded him. "It was always to be divided. *Always*. Warrewik had *two* daughters. Is that not so?"

"Obviously!"

"Then they would each get a portion. You convinced yourself that you could control Nanette's destiny. That you'd keep the majority of her fortune by choosing for her a man loyal to you. But she refused to comply. She argued with you, and you couldn't abide it."

His mouth twisted with guilt and anger.

"She had a champion. An advocate if you will. One even more powerful than yourself. Your younger brother. And he fought for her, and that only made you more angry and desperate. Resentment festers and grows. You were willing to do anything to secure what wasn't truly yours. Even work out a deal to allow someone to kidnap your sister-in-law. What did you think they were going to do with her?"

"I was drunk," he spat. "I barely remember the conversation. At the time, I didn't care so long as they took her far away."

It was an admission of guilt. And she could see that he was tortured by it. He'd agreed to something he'd later regretted but could not undo.

"I know. And so did they. The plot was to kidnap your *wife* as well."

"No!" he shouted. "That was never part of the deal!"

"And who approached you about the deal? Who was the go-between?"

"A guild master. In. . . from. . . Queenshithe. Meeks."

"Where did you meet him to discuss it?"

His jaw trembled. "The Flyte Tavern. It was all arranged just days ago. A solution to my problem. I left orders with Moser at the porter door to let them take her away. And to lie about it. I didn't know they were going to hurt him."

Ankarette nodded. "But he was more faithful than that, wasn't he? He snuck her out. That's why I'm here, Dunne. You've done very little to help him recover. So I brought an apothecary to help revive him. We can still find her."

The noise of hooves came from the street outside. It was probably John Thursby, for it sounded like a solitary steed.

"Now that I know the truth," Ankarette said, "let me try, once again, to reconcile you with your brothers. There is no reason why an elder sister cannot have a larger portion of her father's inheritance. But she cannot have all of it. You must relent on this count. The king demands it."

"I will accept that," Dunsdworth said. "Although it chafes me."

The rider approached. "Where's Lord Clare?" he demanded breathlessly.

She didn't recognize the voice.

Captain Rufus spoke up. "What's the matter? Why aren't you at the Arbon?"

"I just came from there! Lady Isybelle has been abducted! A brute of a man came for her. He slaughtered six knights. I barely escaped with my life! Where's the duke?"

Ankarette looked at Dunsdworth and saw the growing look of horror spread on his mouth.

"Help me!" he begged her. "Help me save her!"

Now, at last, he understood how his brother Severn felt.

CHAPTER

TWENTY-SIX

THE POISONER'S GAMBIT

There was no doubt in Ankarette's mind that it was Bidigen Grimmer who'd abducted Isybelle. He'd survived the falls and was making one final gamble. He'd been unable to get Nanette. His initial attempt to rescue Morvared had also failed. But rather than skulk back to Occitania in shame, he'd seized Dunsdworth's wife. He would use her to win Morvared's freedom. Or kill the duchess if they refused. He'd proven his willingness to commit violence time and again.

"I cannot lose her," the duke said, his voice throbbing with worry. "She's with child. My heir!"

She gripped his shoulders in her hands. "Will you heed me? Do as I say?"

"What choice do I have? I can't bear to lose her. To lose the babe. Not again. I beg you, Ankarette Tryneowy, do not let that happen!"

"She's my friend. I don't want anything to happen to her either. But this man is desperate. I think he was hiding nearby. Watching the Arbon. When you left with your men to come here, he saw an opportunity and took it."

"Where would he take her?"

"Like before, he'll go to the river. He's still in the area. We have to act fast. It's time to raise the hue and cry. We need every able-bodied man and woman on the street looking for them. Give them no place to hide. Have Captain Rufus spread word, then call in the night watch. From every ward. They know the streets of King-fountain better than anyone. Let them lead the search."

"But what about you? What will you do?" he demanded.

"When the horn is blown and the hounds are loosed, what does the beast do?"

"It flees."

"Where?"

"To safety. Its lair or some place to hide."

"And that's where I'm going. I'm going to the river. Because that's where you'll drive him."

"What if we find him in the streets?" Dunsdworth asked.

"Don't go near. Call for help. Block the street on both ends. Sound a horn three times. Then again. I'll come to you. But he has a head start. I think he's going to the river."

"Very well. I'll do as you say. We must act quickly, and I'm too distraught to argue."

She patted his arm and then went to the room where Danner Tye and Chastain were working on poor Moser.

"Master Chastain," she said. "I need a lock and key. Do you have them to guard your stores?"

"Aye. What do you need it—"

"Just fetch it for me."

Dunsdworth had returned to the door and was giving orders crisply. "Sound the hue and cry. Rouse the city. We have to find him before he escapes. The duchess's life is at stake! Go now!"

Chastain hurried to a chest beneath the main counter and unlocked it. He handed the heavy lock to Ankarette and gave her the key.

She took both, and as she went outside, she said, "Keep working on Moser. If my man is hindered in any way, you'll regret it. Also, I need a horse."

The rider who had come from the Arbon gave her his. She mounted it, kicked its flanks, and sped down the road. People were coming out of their homes, some carrying lanterns, some candles. The glow began to spread as the cry was shouted from street to street. It was the law of the realm that when the authorities or citizens called for the hue and cry, the people were to respond immediately. A false alarm was a grievous crime, and the punishment was severe—two days in the public stocks, with passersby pelting them with rubbish.

Ankarette believed she knew where Bidigen Grimmer was headed. His influence lay in the Queen-shithe ward. When he'd taken that girl, he'd retreated into the sewers that led to the river. Vintrey didn't have sewers. The muck was held in cesspits and then carted out of the city. But Queenshithe lay along the river. He'd go to that place where he'd escaped before—where he'd escaped into the river.

And she was going to use the lock to prevent him from fleeing.

AFTER SPENDING SO many days in the city with John Thursby, she'd come to learn its byways, its shortcuts. She knew he'd respond to the hue and cry. But there was no time to intercept him, to get him a message of where to meet her. What she'd told Dunsdworth and Captain Rufus—she was going to the river—was the clue he'd need to find her.

Her cloak billowed out behind her as she raced down the streets of Queenshithe. There were lit windows now, people in the streets asking what was going on. The echoes of the hue and cry came over rooftops, spread from family to family. But no horn blasts rent the air. They hadn't found Grimmer yet. Ankarette rushed past these people, the horse's hooves thundering on the cobblestones.

She reached the alley she'd gone to before. On horseback, she believed she must have overtaken Grimmer's escape. He'd fled on foot, carrying a body. While he could have stolen a horse after leaving, only a very large animal could accommodate his weight and that of another person. No matter how strong he was, carrying Isybelle would tire him. Ankarette's horse was fresh. As she breached the mouth of the alley, she reached out with her Fountain magic, sensing for danger. There was no indication of any. No sensation of worry.

She rode to the sewer covering and leaped from the horse. She squatted down, heaved up the heavy metal grate, and dragged it aside, grimacing with the effort. Then she jumped down into the shaft, landing with a sludgy splash in the muck. The awful smell surrounded her, soaked into her. She carefully retraced her path to the gate that blocked the way to the river. The previous time they'd come, she'd heard Grimmer hammering away at the lock and chain that had closed the gate. She wasn't sure if another had been put in its place. But she knew he didn't have his hammer this time.

In the darkness of the tunnel, she groped her way forward, hearing the noise of the rushing river grow louder. When she reached it, she saw the gate was still open. Had he already come that way? She began to doubt herself but still swung the gate closed—it swiveled with a rusty groan—and used the lock to secure it.

Now it was time to execute the rescue part of her plan. She had to catch Grimmer unawares, to kill him with a single stroke before he could summon his magic against her. Her poisons had been powerless against him.

She heard the noise of another horse coming down the alley above. If Grimmer had stolen one, he would see hers waiting at the grate. She rushed back to the opening.

"Ankarette!"

It was John Thursby. She exhaled in relief and gazed up through the sewer hole. He approached the edge and looked down.

"I'm here," she said. He knelt by the edge and reached for her. She grabbed his wrist, he grabbed hers, and then he pulled her up.

He was out of breath, his eyes blinking with relief. "You. . . you scared me, lass. I thought you were going to face him alone."

"That was my plan actually," she said. "Come, we need to stow the horses. I'll explain on the way."

"I figured he'd come here too," John Thursby said, grinning. "He's no time to think up another way."

"And he's hoping we don't remember it," she said.

They took the reins of their mounts and led them back up the alley.

"When I came up the street, I passed a place where I smelled manure. I think the owner has a cart horse."

"Then he should have a stall," Ankarette said, admiring his acumen.

He led her a short distance toward a gathering of townsfolk.

"You're with the night watch," one of them said. "What's the hue and cry for?"

"Some matter in Vintrey," John Thursby said. "Have you seen anyone skulking about with a body?"

"No," the man said with a chuckle. "Is it Glosstyr and Clare fighting again?"

"Could be," said John Thursby. "Be a friend and watch our horses a moment? Do you have a stable?"

"I do. A crown will do if you want me to feed them too."

"That would be grand." He offered the man a coin and then went back to the alley with Ankarette. "I thought the less they know, the better. Now, what's your plan?"

"It's dark in the sewer," she said.

"Aye, and it smells foul."

"Decidedly so. He abducted Isybelle, Duchess of Clare. He'll lower her down first before coming himself."

"Remember what he did to the last girl he brought down there?"

"I do. We were chasing him. This time, I'm going to be waiting for him. I want you to put the lid back in place. When he lowers her down, I'm going to drag her the other way and free her if I can. She may be unconscious. Then I'll take her cloak and lie in the muck.

When he comes down, he'll think I'm her and drag me to the gate. The darkness will conceal all."

His eyes widened with worry. "I don't want you anywhere near the river. He broke the lock last time. I doubt they've replaced it."

"I've locked the gate afresh. You have his hammer. When he realizes it, that's when I'll strike. I'll rip that medallion off his neck and plunge a dagger into his heart."

"What if he has a lantern? He won't be so easily deceived."

"He'll still need to lower her body down first. If he's a fool and goes down first himself, then you take her and flee back to the street and raise the cry. But he's no fool."

"What if we attack him before he jumps down? Two against one? I like those odds better, lass."

"If he hears us, he'll use his magic again. And then her life will be forfeit. I can't risk that."

"I'm not keen on risking *you*."

She was about to touch his face but realized her hands were soiled. "And I you. But we do our duty."

He sighed. "He could come along any time. Or not at all."

"I told the duke to blow a horn in three bursts if they find him. We might both be wrong about where he'll take her. But this is where I believe he's going because he knows he can escape in the water somehow. This is where he'll come. I'm sure of it."

"Very well. Why don't you go back down there? I'll hide myself over there amidst the broken rubble. I'll just play a drunkard if he sees me. That happens often enough in the city at night."

She nodded and went to the lip of the entry. When

she was about to jump down, he took her hand, kissed her knuckles.

He sniffed. "Can't smell your perfume anymore. All that filth. But I'll have you any way I can."

She was touched but pulled her hand away. He then lowered her down as before. At the bottom, she gazed up at him and waited for him to put the grate back in place. The moon illuminated his face in a pleasing manner.

A prickle of warning came from her magic.

"He's coming," she whispered.

CHAPTER
TWENTY-SEVEN
THE QUEEN'S REVENGE

"**B**e careful. Be safe," Ankarette whispered to him through the bars of the grate.

"We take him down together," John Thursby said. "Once I hear you attack, I'm coming down."

"Hopefully, he'll be dead before you reach me."

"I won't object to that. Let me hide myself."

Ankarette watched him leave her sight and felt her stomach constrict with dread and the early pangs of the poison. She hastily pulled out the vial of remedy and took a quick sip, then twisted the cap on and put it back. She had her daggers, her needle rings, even some powders she could blow into Grimmer's face to blind him. In the confined shaft of the sewer drain, her smaller stature and speed would be an advantage. Her plan was a good one. If Grimmer dragged her to the locked gate, that's when he would be the most vulnerable. It would give her a chance to snatch the medallion while stabbing him in a vulnerable spot. The rush of the river beyond the gate made it difficult to hear anything aboveground.

She wanted to pace out her nervous energy, but the

splashing noise it would make would alert Bidigen Grimmer to her presence. She heard John Thursby settling in the alley and then fall quiet. The noise of the river added to her concealment. She waited, straining to hear a sound. She felt the malevolent throb of warning again. Then the scrape of boots and the huff of breathing.

Ankarette swallowed. She'd positioned herself so that if a body was lowered down, she could quickly drag it away from the gate. A dirk was at the ready to slice through any bonds used to confine Isybelle.

The noise of labored breathing could be heard approaching the dead end above. Ankarette's nerves were as taut as bowstrings. It was her friend, her childhood companion, who was at risk. A friend who was pregnant. Failure would bring unspeakable suffering.

The wearied exhales approached the grate. Ankarette kept perfectly still. Then a shadow fell over the grate.

A body.

Ankarette heard the rustle of fabric, a muffled moan, then Grimmer's voice.

"We're going down," he muttered in a low growl. "Into the sewers. Don't make a sound, wench. Nod if you understand me."

Ankarette heard a frightened murmur and imagined Isybelle complying.

"We're going into the river." Ankarette discerned Isybelle trying to wriggle above. "Don't thrash about, or I'll box you! We'll be safe enough. I can cross the river unharmed. You'll see."

There was a skittering noise, the squeak of rats. "What's this?" Grimmer whispered. Ankarette felt a throb of magic chilling the air, drawing darkness. She recognized it.

"Who's there?" Bidigen Grimmer said gruffly. Isybelle's body was still blocking the grate.

Ankarette's throat tightened. In her mind, she heard whispers, more like the mewling of cats. Fear tugged at her chest, but she quelled it.

More squeaks. Bidigen Grimmer's footfalls echoed below in the sewer.

"I see you," he said with a snarl.

Ankarette's mind whirled. She was trapped down in the sewer. Did Grimmer know of her? Or had his magic helped him sense the threat of John Thursby?

Then she heard the sound of a sword being drawn from a scabbard, followed by another blade. "Thought you might come back this way," John Thursby said, his voice edged with hostility.

"I've seen your face before. From the war."

"Aye. You look familiar too."

Grimmer grunted. "You were one of Devereaux's men."

"I was. Not anymore."

The two combatants were sizing each other up. Ankarette gazed down the dark shaft. If she went upstream, there would be another sewer grate. She could try to wrestle it open from below and get up there, but she'd risk revealing herself to the kishion. The thought of John Thursby facing him alone terrified her.

"So you're on Eredur's side now? Working for his poisoner?"

"I'm a night watchman of Kingfountain, and you're under arrest."

"I can take you to Devereaux," Grimmer said. "Help me on my mission, and you'll be greatly rewarded." As he said the words, Ankarette felt a sudden rush of magic, a feeling of desire and greed following it.

"Do you pay in fractured skulls, perchance? I've thought you might have taken a fancy to mine."

"You have my hammer."

"I do. Now you've got naught but a dagger. I've always preferred blades. Very efficient. Shall we get this over with?"

"You'd throw away a fortune?" Grimmer sounded amused. "You think you'll win?"

"Never start a fight believing you'll lose it."

Don't fight him! Ankarette pleaded in her mind. *Call for help! Raise the hue and cry!*

But he didn't. Maybe he didn't want the bystanders in the nearby street to be killed, or perhaps he thought he could succeed. Either way, he'd made up his mind to fight. A soldier to the last. Ankarette clenched her fists, consumed by worry.

Isybelle began trying to yell, but a gag muffled her words. There was no question she was terrified, though.

Then Ankarette heard the confrontation begin. Not being able to see it, to assist, was its own acute torture. If she tried to get up there, she'd lose the element of surprise. How much time would it take to trudge through the muck and get back? How long would the fight last?

If she left, Isybelle might die.

Grunts and curses sounded from above. John Thursby was fighting for his life. She could sense his determination to prevail. To win the day so that Ankarette wouldn't have to face Grimmer alone.

Her mind worked quickly, going over the situation again and again. Somehow, Grimmer had been alerted to the night watchman's presence. It was his magic assisting him no doubt, just as she could often sense danger through hers. Had the rats warned him? The skittering noises had happened first.

"You're controlling your fear," Grimmer said, impressed.

"Only way to survive a battle," John Thursby grunted.

"We could use a man like you on our side."

"I'd sooner sleep in the Deep Fathoms!"

"There is no afterlife. Only darkness and sleep."

"Doesn't sound so bad." John Thursby chuffed.

There was the sound of a blade clattering on the paving stones. A boot kicked it away. John Thursby let out a curse, and they were fighting again. Blow after blow, grunt after grunt. It was a battlefield of just two. In her mind, she pictured John Thursby at Borehamwood, fighting against his own side because of the fog of war. Killing men he'd supped with the night before. Confusion, chaos, blood—those were the trinity of conflict.

If she were up there, she could stop it.

She heard the sound of a breath sucked in, the sound a man makes involuntarily when a blade ruptures him.

John Thursby groaned, then gasped. Ankarette heard the slump of a body falling.

"Bravely fought, for what it's worth," the kishion said with no emotion. He must have pressed the blade deeper because a choking noise came from John Thursby next.

Hot tears squeezed past Ankarette's lashes. Pain lanced inside her heart. He'd lost the fight. She heard him panting, then muttering something about a soldier's death. Maybe it was the fragment of a poem.

Tears trickled down her cheeks. Her heart seared with anguish and hate. She was going to kill Bidigen Grimmer. She was going to slay him for this!

"I'll have my hammer back now," Grimmer said. She heard the sound of a weapon clearing leather. He adjusted his grip on it with a gloved hand. Even that made a distinctive sound. Grimmer was going to crush John Thursby's skull. She waited for the blow, silently weeping, hand pressed over her mouth.

The fight had ended so quickly. Then again, most battlefield confrontations lasted only a few seconds. She'd heard that from some of the survivors. It rarely took long to find an opening. Even a hauberk could be pierced by a blade if the thrust was hard enough.

Why hadn't he just run away and called for help? That would have made Grimmer even more urgent to leave, which would have brought him within reach of Ankarette's dagger that much sooner.

But no. Not John Thursby. He wouldn't run from a confrontation. He'd fight, soldier to soldier.

And he'd died for it.

There was no crushing blow. It was an unexpected mercy. The kishion obviously knew Lord Devereaux. Whatever the connection, he'd chosen to spare John Thursby an ignoble last moment, a blow struck when one was already helpless. He'd bleed to death quickly enough.

She heard the heavy sound of boots coming to the grate. Isybelle was weeping, sitting up atop the grate.

"You're never going to be a mother," Grimmer said menacingly. "My queen wished you to feel the pain of loss. This is her revenge. For the prince's death that she suffered so greatly because of *you*."

Grimmer lifted Isybelle to one side, and then she saw his fingers grip the grate.

His words thrummed in Ankarette's mind. She realized, belatedly, he'd spoken them not to Isybelle but to *her*.

The grate hissed against the stone as it lifted up.

"I'm coming for you, Poisoner," Grimmer said down the shaft. "Just as I promised."

Water doesn't complain. When a boulder falls in a river, the water finds a way around it. What stands in the way becomes the way. Just as nature takes every obstacle, every impediment, and works around it—turns it to its purpose, incorporates it into itself—so, too, a canny poisoner can turn each setback into the raw means to achieve her goal.

— ANKARETTE TRYNEOWY

TWENTY-EIGHT

THE WISDOM OF WATER

Ankarette had learned to fight men larger than her in the poisoner school in Pisan. Size could be overcome with the right strategy, so long as she could avoid being struck. One blow from Bidigen Grimmer's war hammer, and she would be broken, but the cramped sewer drain would ensure he didn't have enough room to fully swing it. The darkness would also be her ally unless he could see in the dark with his glowing eyes.

While every primal instinct screamed at her to run down the shaft and escape, reason prevailed. This man, this kishion, was the most dangerous enemy she'd faced. Not as cunning as Lord Hux, but more physically powerful and dangerous.

Ankarette retreated down the shaft, moving away from the gate she'd locked and the river. She unhasped her wet cloak. It would only be an obstacle if she wore it now, another thing for him to grab and yank. She dunked it into the putrid waters, soaking it full. Even a cloak could be a weapon.

The scrape of metal on stone sounded above as

Grimmer lifted the grate. Had Hux ordered the kishion to kill her if she stood in the way? Probably so. She had every intention of killing him.

She felt the whoosh of air, and then he landed with a noisy splash in the middle trench of the sewer. Immediately, she felt the sucking sensation of his magic draining hers. She had to get that amulet off him quickly.

Ankarette flung her wet garment at him like a net. It was her intention to make him react to her every move. Just like in a game of Wizr, she would keep pressing her advantages, forcing him to respond. The wet cloak slapped against him, and he grunted with surprise, finding himself tangled in it. She drew her pouch of hogweed. The pollen of that plant caused temporary blindness and irritation in the eyes. He'd not been affected by her other poisons so far, but she wanted to try a new one. Many of the paralytics had antidotes, which Lord Hux had probably provided.

Grimmer thrashed for a moment, and she used the noise to approach from the side. When he flung away the wet cloak and turned, she saw his eyes glowing silver in the dark. She'd been expecting that. When they'd first met in the cellar beneath the Flyte, it was one of the first things she'd noticed about his magic.

And it showed her exactly where his eyes were.

She flung the hogweed pollen right at his face as she charged him, drawing a dirk with her left hand. She lunged low and stabbed it into his leg, aiming for where she thought his knee was.

He roared with pain and rage and swung at her with the hammer. It crashed into the wall right above her head, causing sparks and a bone-rattling impact up his arms. Ankarette didn't wait. She wrenched the dirk out and swept around behind him. Another wild swing nearly caught her as he tried to reclaim the offensive. She felt it swipe just in front of her face. He also knew that one blow was all he needed.

"I'll kill you, wench!" he roared at her in frustration. She couldn't see his eyes. He was closing them because of the pain. He stumbled forward, driving her back toward the gate. She dodged another wild swing, having listened for the grunt of breath that preceded it.

Ankarette dropped low again and then uppercut with the dirk, aiming for his groin. In the dark, she couldn't tell what she'd hit, but the sudden gasp of agony revealed she'd connected again. He landed backward with a noisy splash.

The poisoner leaped on him, plunging the dirk into his body. With frantic hands, she reached for his neck and sought the chain of the medallion. She was panting already with the effort. Where was it? She clawed through his shirt, feeling the metal bite against her fingernails. He had a fruity smell to his breath. He was chewing something. Her Fountain magic sensed the medallion but also another magic at work. His injuries were healing rapidly. She'd hurt him, but he was recovering swiftly.

She grabbed the medallion and yanked it off his neck, snapping the chain. Then she hurled it toward the gate, hoping it would go through the bars and land on the other side. But the metal pinged against the bars and plopped into the sludgy water. As soon as it was gone, she felt the draining power wink out.

Grimmer's hand seized her throat and squeezed.

With the heel of her palm, she smashed him in the

nose. It should have broken it, but it didn't. He grunted, rising from the ground with power and determination.

"Give... it... back," he growled at her.

Spots were beginning to dance in her eyes. She grabbed his little finger and tried to torque it, but his grip was incredibly strong. Another kind of magic was thrumming through him. He slammed her hard against the wall, stunning her. He was going to use the hammer on her. She knew it instinctively.

Unable to break his grip on her throat, she held her forearm in front of her at a slightly bent angle. In the poisoner school, she'd learned a technique called "the unbendable arm." She caught the hammer blow on her forearm, blunting the full force of the swing. A shard of pain went down her arm, but she held it at bay, her whole body taut with pressure. The pressure against her throat would make her black out in seconds.

"Ankarette! I've freed her! Get out of there!"

It was John Thursby, shouting down the shaft. He was alive? Hope lit brightly in her heart. Still, although she'd restrained the kishion from making the killing blow, she couldn't wrench his hand free. She kicked at his chest.

Water flows around obstacles.

Ankarette stopped trying to pry his hand lose and used her legs. Since he was supporting her weight already by her throat, she snaked one of her legs around his neck, using her other hand to lock her ankle behind her other knee. That allowed her to use her stronger leg muscles to choke him. It also locked his arm in place, the one with the hammer. At the poisoner school, it was called a triangle choke, pitting her legs against his arms. It was incredibly effective against larger opponents.

And it was working.

She felt his rise of panic as he collided into the sewer wall. Spots danced in her eyes. He dropped the hammer and wrenched her legs apart with sheer physical strength. She groaned as she tried to prevent it, but he overpowered her.

Ankarette tried to wriggle free to go at him again, but he took her by the back of the neck and forced her head under the sickening water. She heard John Thursby call for her again to run. Her lungs burned for air. She hadn't been able to take a breath before he'd pinned her underwater.

The more she struggled, the more quickly her air would deplete. She slumped as if she'd passed out.

Grimmer pulled her body from the sludge, and she heard him exploring the water until he had his hammer. Then he dragged her to the gate while she pretended to be unconscious.

"Ankarette!" John Thursby roared.

Grimmer deposited her at the edge of the gate. "Where is it?" he grunted and began searching the water.

She felt the metal edge of the medallion bite against her side. She deftly snatched it and then threw it past the bars.

"No!" he roared in anger. He shoved at the bars, which refused to budge. Then he whipped the hammer down and smashed the lock in a single blow. He was desperate not to lose that medallion, which was being swept away by the flow of the water toward the river.

Ankarette's strength was nearly spent, but she summoned her Fountain magic, trying to find a weakness in him.

The dregs of her magic revealed that he was spent

as well. The magic he'd used to heal himself was fading.
He had none left to replenish it. He would soon be vulnerable to her poison. He was fatigued by the ex-
hausting ordeal he'd gone through, including carrying
Isybelle to the sewer. Their fight had taken a lot out of
him too. But he was determined, as was she, to escape
with his life. He didn't want to die. And he'd never been
so close. In moments, he'd be vulnerable.

Ankarette drew her hairpin and jammed it into
his arm.

He hissed in pain and swiped at her with the hammer, but she rolled away, and it struck the bars. The
gate creaked open.

"Die. . . curse you!" he snarled, shoving her back
with his hand. He tried to land another blow, but she
rolled away again, and it splashed ineffectively into the
water. He began to rise and flee.

She wrapped her legs around his, trying to hold
him back. He kicked her in the ribs with his other boot
but lost his balance and went down. She grabbed his
belt and then pulled a dagger from her boot. The
magic was dwindling. She was ready to land the killing
blow.

His boot struck her head in his frenzy to escape.
Ankarette reeled from it but managed to stay conscious.
Her grip eased, and he slipped away from her, scurrying
toward the river.

Ankarette hoisted herself up, stabilizing herself on
her arm, and watched his silhouette against the sewer
opening. He was going to jump into the river. She saw
his body framed by the moonlight in the dark shaft.

She felt his magic extinguish.

Raising her arm, Ankarette threw the dagger at his
back. She was aiming for his spine, to sever the nerves

that would make his legs work. It wasn't a killing blow, but it would keep him immobile the rest of his life.

Bidigen Grimmer's back arched in pain as the dagger struck true. She'd always been a good thrower.

His legs crumpled, and he sagged against the side of the opening, the clean water of the river just ahead. He reached behind his back and plucked the dagger from his spine, groaning in pain as he did so. He started to arm crawl forward, hammer in one fist, her dagger in the other.

Ankarette rose to her feet, gasping for breath, and stalked him.

"Ankarette," John Thursby moaned, his voice thick with despair.

"I'm all right," she called, panting. "Give me. . . a moment. I need him alive for a minute longer."

He couldn't escape. He certainly couldn't swim.

He was still grunting, pulling himself in agony toward the lip of the sewer. She was filthy from head to foot, but she'd won. She'd fought a kishion and won. A little throb of pride beat in her chest. Reaching into her bodice, she removed a pouch of nightshade.

Bidigen Grimmer twisted his neck and looked back at her, seeing her approach.

"You don't have a suicide ring, do you?" she said mockingly.

He would have used it by now if he had.

"No," he panted. He'd twisted onto his side. "Mine. . . is. . . much more. . . powerful."

What did that mean?

He looked at her and raised his hand. She felt the sizzle of a new magic. There was a ring on his hand that suddenly vibrated with unseen power. She hadn't sensed it at all before.

THE WIDOW'S FATE

Suddenly the river was rushing into the sewers, slamming Ankarette back into the iron bars of the gate leading back to the street, which kept her from sweeping with the waters back into the sewer. The rush blinded her, choked her.

She started to drown.

CHAPTER
TWENTY-NINE
WHISPERS FROM THE DEEP FATHOMS

Ankarette clenched the bars of the sewer gate, eyes tightly shut against the flood rushing past her. She was pinned against the bars, her lungs screaming for air. She sensed the magic radiating from Bidigen Grimmer, but she was powerless to stop it. She couldn't even take a breath. With the magic of his ring, he had turned part of the river and sent it into the sewers.

She tried to wrestle against the gate, to pull it open. If she did, she could let the current take her through the shafts. Hopefully it would lose power with distance, and she could try to get out through one of the grate openings. But she was no match for the power of the river. Weariness began to sap her strength, the waters whispering for her to succumb to death.

Involuntarily, she hiccuped and began to choke on the water. The burning pain in her chest eased. Soon she'd black out. They'd find her body wedged against the gate. It was not how she wanted to die.

A little Fountain magic still remained with her. With it, she sensed Grimmer's strength failing. He was trying to maintain the magic long enough to kill her, but he was in excruciating agony. He couldn't hold it forever. The river's flood wasn't affecting him—she didn't know why, but she sensed him just at the edge of the chute, at the river's edge.

Once more she tugged at the gate, but it was unyielding. If she didn't get air soon, she was going to die. But how could she breathe when the entire shaft was filled with river water? Was there a gap higher up?

She tried to pull herself up the bars, but the pressure against her back was too intense. Her arms and legs weren't strong enough.

Help me, she thought frantically, feeling her lungs quiver with need. She'd trusted her magic in the past. She'd invested in it, building her power with it by embroidery. In her mind, she imagined doing the stitches, the poke of the needle through the fabric, the tug and pull on the thread, the little knots to tie them off. She believed in the Lady of the Fountain.

Please help me, she thought again, surrendering herself to the magic. If there was a way to escape, she didn't know it.

Nesh-ama.

The whisper came to her thoughts as she was about to black out. It was a word she'd never heard before. She hadn't spoken it, but *someone* had. She felt something brush against her lips. It felt tender, like a kiss.

And then her chest filled with air. Even with the waters swirling around her, she could breathe. Even having gulped down some of it, she could *still* breathe.

Relief surged in Ankarette's breast. She clung to the bars, each breath coming steady and strong despite the ravaging current. She gripped it tightly, enduring the pressure. Finally, after an interminable time, Grimmer's strength of will failed, and the magic stopped coercing the river. The tide fell, and she found herself free of its grasp.

Her hair hung in clumps across her face, and she wiped the wet strands away. Turning, she saw Bidigen Grimmer lying on his back, arm outstretched. She sensed the fading power of the ring on his hand—a ring that was now invisible.

She started toward him, her legs weak but determined.

When he realized she wasn't dead, he grunted and huffed, twisting around, and began crawling into the river. Was he going to drown himself instead of facing defeat? She watched him drag himself over the edge, watched as the river began to tug him away.

Ankarette leaped forward and caught the edge of his boot cuff. The river yanked them both, but she reached with her other hand and grabbed his belt. She pulled with all her might to haul him back into the sewer tunnel, but the river had caught him, and its pull was powerful.

He was heavier than her, more determined. She wouldn't let go, though, even as he started to fall into the river. She remembered the word that allowed her to breathe underwater and uttered it.

Still, breathing underwater wouldn't save her from the crushing force of the falls. If they went over together, they'd both die.

Or would they? That ring he wore was his secret. It was the thing that gave him power to defy the river. She knew such powerful magic was precious, worth a king's ransom.

They both tumbled straight down. The current parted around them, and they went sprawling into the boulders and stones at the edge of the river. The stones were too heavy to be pulled by the relentless pressure. She saw masonry parts that had fallen into the river. Rusted chunks of iron. She was sprawled atop Bidigen Grimmer, and he groaned in agony from his injuries but also from the magic invoked by his ring. She saw it once again, its white gold blasting the waters away from them, opening a pocket in the river. The turbulent waters rushed all around them, but they were safe.

The ring was *hurting* him.

This was how he'd escaped before. It gave him power over the water but at a terrible cost. She saw his finger already was blackened from using it to summon the water into the sewer.

She pulled herself higher up his body until their faces were level.

"Where did you get that ring? Whose is it?" she demanded.

He was suffering. He knew he was going to die. And he didn't care. Death was preferable to the agony he was suffering.

"It's King Lewis's," Grimmer said with a snarl. "I lose my life if I don't bring it back. I'm dead. . . either way. H-he warned me. About you."

"Who? Lord Hux?"

He groaned and nodded. "Said you were Fountain-blessed. To be wary."

The roar of the waters pounded against her ears. She didn't know how long the ring would work. Would that magic fail if he died?

It would, her magic whispered to her. He was using

241

the last of his strength to stay alive, but only because he wanted her to die too. The magic would snuff out, and they'd both be dragged with the current to the waterfall. She felt his hand squeeze into her dress, gripping tight.

She was shocked to discern that her clothes were totally dry. So were his. Looking at the hair draped over her bosom, she saw it too was dry. The magic was incredibly powerful. And it was about to fail.

Cut off his hand.

The thought came to her mind as a realization. The ring would protect her as long as Grimmer lived. There was some magic binding him to it. A magic that ended with his life. If she was going to claim the ring to protect herself, she needed him alive for a few seconds longer.

Ankarette whipped out her last dagger and sawed through his wrist. He bellowed in anguish, his eyes wild with panic. He tried to grab her with his other hand to stop her, but she clubbed his temple with the hilt of the dagger and went back to work. She knew where the ligaments and bones were located. The hand separated quickly. She saw the glowing gold band of the ring. There were two colors of gold—white and yellow—overlapping in concentric circles.

She scrabbled up the boulders toward the edge of the sewer entrance. She needed a better grip, so she ditched her dagger and clambered up the rocks, pressing the hand with the ring against her chest.

The magic failed just as she reached the edge. The glow winked out, and the river came rushing at her. She was doused but managed to pull herself into the opening before collapsing against the wall of the tunnel, breathing hard.

In the moonlight, at the edge, she stared at the withered hand. The ring finger was totally blackened, the fingernail gray. It was grotesque. Ankarette pried the ring from the finger and then gazed at it in her hand.

She heard a low moan coming from the sewer shaft and remembered John Thursby. She stuffed the ring into her pocket and went to the gate. It opened freely now, creaking noisily.

"A-Ankarette?" he begged. "Please let it be you."

"I'm alive," she said reassuringly. She went to the grate opening and saw his arm hanging through it. He was lying down on the street, weak as a cub.

She pulled herself out, and he tried to sit up. One hand pressed some fabric against his belly. His face was pale with pain. Blood stained his fingers and the rag.

"I thought... I thought he had killed you." He closed his eyes, rolling onto his back.

"I told you I'm not that easy to kill," she said wryly. "Let me see the wound."

"I've... had worse," he grunted.

A voice shouted from the alleyway. "This way! Bring the torches quickly!"

Ankarette lifted her head, having recognized Isybelle's voice. She heard the sound of the horn being repeated all over the city of Kingfountain. The Duchess of Clare arrived with some of her men-at-arms, soldiers wearing her husband's badge.

Ankarette's dress was sopping wet, but she ignored it and bent close to examine the wound. Putting pressure on it was the right thing to do. He'd stanched the bleeding. But there would be internal damage, wounded organs.

Isybelle arrived with the men and gasped when she recognized Ankarette kneeling there.

"Ankarette? Where's the man who abducted me?"

"Dead," Ankarette said. "He's in the river now."

She saw the looks of surprise from the soldiers who'd accompanied her. Looks of respect quickly followed.

"Who is this? He saved me," Isybelle asked. She was wearing a robe over her nightdress. Someone had provided it. Bystanders were gathering in the alley. The soldiers kept them back.

"I'm with the night watch, my lady," John Thursby greeted.

"I need to bring him to an apothecary," Ankarette said. "He's wounded. Our horses are tethered nearby."

Another sound came, then a barked a command to clear the way. Lord Dunsdworth arrived with some of his knights and disbanded the crowd. He came off his horse, and Isybelle fell into his arms. He looked so relieved to see his wife whole, healthy.

"Are you okay, Belle?" he asked tenderly, touching her face, exploring her for signs of injury.

"I am hale," she said. "Thanks to Ankarette." She nodded to where Ankarette was kneeling in the street.

The Duke of Clare looked at her with gratitude. Then he hugged Isybelle tightly, kissing her hair, and began to shed tears.

"Is she truly well?" he asked Ankarette, his voice choking.

"I'll examine her. But I need to help this man first. We need our horses."

John Thursby tried to rise, but the shock of pain made him go down again.

"You can have mine," Dunsdworth said. "Captain

Rufus, help him! Help them both. Shall we take him to the apothecaries working on Moser?"

Ankarette shook her head. "We're going to the Hermitage. To Old Rose."

She put her hand on John Thursby's and squeezed gently. He smiled in relief and then put his other hand on top of hers.

One of the healers at the poisoner school liked to say this: Fire is the test of gold. Adversity is the test of strong wills. The fear of pain does more harm than pain itself.

— ANKARETTE TRYNEOWY

CHAPTER

THIRTY

MORTAL WOUNDS

The birds were singing. Carts rattled down the street, preceded by the snorts of horses and the murmur of voices. The midmorning sun came through the threadbare curtain. Ankarette was reading one of John Thursby's books at the table by the window when he finally roused from his deep slumber. She heard him shifting on his pallet and set down the book.

"You're still here?" he asked, rubbing his eyes. He tried to sit up and winced, the blanket falling down his bare torso.

Ankarette rose from her seat and went to his bedside. There were battle scars across his body. He'd been a soldier since his youth. She brushed her hand across his forehead, and he closed his eyes at her touch and shuddered.

"No fever yet, that's a good sign," she said.

He tried to sit up again, his face twisting with the pain, and she helped him. The wound in his side was stitched and bandaged. She'd done her best to try to repair his inner injuries too. He looked down at it, then at her.

"You have a delicate touch," he complimented. "I'm

used to more rough handling by my doctors. You've been here while I slept? Why?"

She reached down, gripped his hand, and squeezed it. "After all you did, I wasn't going to abandon you, John Thursby."

"What of old Moser? Shouldn't you check on him?"

"I will. Danner Tye is a skilled apothecary. After a trepanation, it'll take some time for Moser to recover, if he does at all. I wanted to be sure you didn't get the blood sickness. A wound like that can be mortal."

She lifted her hand from his and gazed into his eyes.

"I like your hair like that," he said, reaching tentatively, brushing a few locks from her shoulder. "You normally keep it coiled in braids. I prefer it loose."

The admiration she saw in his eyes made her heart beat faster. "That's good to know." Then she leaned forward until their foreheads touched. "I feared I lost you last night. I thought Grimmer had killed you."

He snorted and stifled a chuckle. "I tried my best to slay him. But he was better than I, and I knew it. When he wounded me, I feigned more hurt than I felt. Because of our shared history with Lord Devereaux, I thought he just might let me bleed to death instead of smashing my skull with his hammer."

She shuddered at that thought and ran her fingers through his cropped hair.

"When he went after you, I crawled over to Lady Isybelle, cut her loose, and told her to flee for help. But I was worried sick that he'd kill you. I prayed. . . to the Fountain. . . that you'd be spared his wrath. And then. . . then I saw a miracle."

He pulled back from her, his fingers sliding into her hair at the nape of her neck. "Water from the river gushed through the sewers, spewing like a fountain. I took a blast in the face and was shocked, confused. There was all the ruckus down the street, the cries for help. I couldn't hear what was going on down there. Then it all went quiet. What happened to you?"

Ankarette liked the feel of his hand touching her. She wanted him to continue stroking her hair. To kiss her neck.

She and Old Rose had bathed him after removing his hauberk and tunic. It was important to defend him against the blood sickness, especially for such a deep wound that had cut into his organs. She'd tended victims of war before, had attended mothers in the most intimate parts of their bodies during pregnancy and childbirth. So she was accustomed to seeing bodies unclothed. But helping scrub dirt and blood from John Thursby had evoked some interesting feelings inside of her. The smell of the lavender from the apothecary shop added to the moment.

"I broke the medallion from him, but he had another magic too. One that I hadn't sensed before."

The medallion was lost to the river. It might have been carried downstream and gone over the falls, but it was likely heavy enough to become lodged in the river boulders at the base. It would be impossible to find.

"What kind of magic?"

"He wore a ring. One that was invisible until he invoked its power. I've never seen such magic before. It is clearly from the Deep Fathoms. It gave him power over water. He sent the river up the tunnel and tried to drown me." She showed him her dress sleeve. "I was filthy with the sewer sludge, but you can see how clean I am now. Maybe your prayer was answered—I don't know—but I survived the flood. I had thrown a knife into his back, which paralyzed him, so all he could do was crawl away from me. We went into the river together."

John Thursby's eyes bulged. "Nay!"

"The ring he wore created a shell of sorts around us. The waters couldn't touch us. In fact, it dried my dress and his clothes. It even dried my hair. It... repelled water. But it came at a cost. I could sense the magic would fail as soon as he died. The river would have swept me away." She tilted her head slightly. "So I cut off his hand. I made it back to the sewer as he perished."

He stared at her, dumbfounded. "That was very clever of you, Ankarette of Yuork."

"I must give proper credit. The Fountain guided me. Just because the sextons rake the coins out of the Fountains doesn't mean its power isn't real. Now you know the rest of the story."

"What did you do with the hand?" he asked, arching his brow.

"I took the ring, of course. The hand is in the rubbish bin. I don't know how Grimmer endured such wounds. He had some sort of healing magic as well, but it ran out, and I was finally able to injure him."

"Would I had been there. I would have landed some smart blows."

"Indeed you would have. My brave soldier."

Their noses gently touched. And then she kissed him on the mouth. The prickle of his beard was pleasant. The warmth of his breath soothed her aching heart. His fingers entwined with her hair, and he kissed her back with passion and fervor that pleased and surprised her. He pulled her even closer, pressing her near, and suddenly hissed in pain. His hand shot down to his side.

"Gently, John Thursby," she teased. "Don't exert yourself too much."

She saw the coy smile on his mouth. He took her hand and kissed her knuckles. "I fear this is only a dream. That I'll awaken and you'll be gone. I care for you, Ankarette. Even if I'm dreaming, my words are true."

"You are awake, sir," she said, squeezing his chin. "I don't know when the last time you slept so long was, but it seemed needful."

"Aye. After your *ministrations*, I fell into a slumber and didn't dream of the battlefield, or death, or murderers with hammers. I dreamed of Yuork. Is that strange?"

She put her hand on his chest. "That sounds pleasant. I haven't dreamt of it in years."

"It *was* pleasant. It brought back the days of my youth when I'd wander the gorse after sunset. There was a family of badgers near my father's cottage. The smell of the sea in the air. Fresh sprigs of wild thyme." She saw his face brighten with the memories of smells, but then, like a cloud dimming the sun, the expression faded. "And then there was war. Nothing but war." He gazed at her, the pain still there in his eyes. "I'm not that young man anymore. He died long ago."

She listened to him, nodding gently, and then kissed him again tenderly. A thought came to her mind. A quote she'd heard once. She didn't remember where she'd heard it, but it came from the heart. *"Misfortune brings a blessing. Whom it assails, it eventually fortifies."* She slid her hand down his bare arm. "You are stronger because of what you've suffered, John Thursby. None of us were meant to stay in innocence forever."

He pursed his lips and thought on her words. "Well said."

She felt a little tug of pain in her heart. "I must go. But I shall return."

"You'll seek Moser?"

"Yes. And I must report back to the king. But I'll come back and see you."

He took her hand and squeezed it. "Don't say it and not mean it, Ankarette. I couldn't bear it."

"I only speak when I'm certain what I'll say isn't better left unsaid. I *will* come back. The blood sickness is dangerous. Old Rose will tend to you. If a fever comes, there are remedies. But don't lie abed all day. After such an injury, it's best if you walk around a while. Don't test your strength yet. Don't raise a sword. That would be too much. But your body will heal itself. It was made to."

"And what of my heart? Will it heal as well?" he asked, a sad smile revealing itself.

She knew what he meant. He was afraid they wouldn't see each other anymore now that her mission was coming to an end. Losing her to death would have been a torture. But losing her to her indifference would be a mortal wound.

She took his hand and fondled his fingers. "I care for you as well, John Thursby. But my duty binds me."

"I would never ask you to forsake your duty," he said firmly. "Not for me."

"It's not only that. I'm dying. I was poisoned before the Battle of Hawk Moor. The vial you stole from Dragan prolongs my life, but it can't heal me. The Fountain hasn't fated me with a long life. Nor can I have children." She looked down, feeling twinges of guilt for sharing her burdens with him. "It's the Fountain's will that I won't die of old age."

He touched her hair again, and she peered into his

253

sympathetic eyes. Nothing she'd said had shocked him, but her words obviously grieved him.

"Each day I've had with you has been a gift, Ankarette. One day more is all I ask for. I don't pretend to be as wise as you. I certainly don't deserve you. You fill something inside me I never knew was empty. I take my solace in books, as you know. When I was bedridden after Borehamwood, there was a line that helped me endure the pain, the struggle, the halting strides. These aren't my words, but I've made them mine day by day. *It's fortunate that this has happened and I've remained unharmed by it—not shattered by the present or frightened of the future. It could have happened to anyone. But not everyone could have remained unharmed by it.*"

He stroked his thumb across her cheek. "You remind me of that poem, Ankarette. What you've done. What you've endured. It made you who you are."

She felt a tear trickle down her face.

"Be safe, John Thursby," she whispered, brushing her lips against his cheek.

THIRTY-ONE

A WIDOW'S FATE

When Ankarette returned to the apothecary, she found several knights with Dunsdworth's badge, guarding the door. She was weary and sore from the conflict, but her concerns subsided when the knights looked at her with fear and respect in their eyes and promptly stepped aside.

"How is your lady?" she asked them after dismounting. She handed the reins to the knight she spoke to.

"Safe and sound," he replied. "Resting back at the Arbon."

Passersby came up and down the street, casting curious looks their way. Ankarette nodded to the knights, and one of them opened the door and held it for her.

Inside, she smelled a cleaning agent and found Chastain Bell minding the shop. One look at her, and he flinched and drew back.

"It's all over," he said. "He lived."

Ankarette breathed in relief. "Is he resting?"

"Aye, and Captain Rufus is in there as well. You can go in. I. . . I was following orders, my lady. I meant no disrespect."

She gave him a cool gaze, said nothing, and went to

255

the room where Moser lay. Danner Tye was sleeping in a chair, looking exhausted from the long labors of the night. Captain Rufus sat in another chair but came to his feet when she entered.

"She's back," he said gruffly, rousing the apothecary from his slumber.

"Isybelle is well?" Ankarette asked the surly captain.

"Aye. A midwife was sent for. She and the babe are healthy. No harm was done."

"I'm glad for it," Ankarette said.

"I heard about last night," Rufus said. "That you killed Grimmer all by yourself."

"And that surprises you, Captain?"

He did give her a surprised look. "Blessed be the Lady," he said. "I'm grateful the duchess is in good spirits. And so is the duke."

"The trepanation went well," Danner Tye told her, rubbing his eyes. "There was swelling and bleeding of the brain. But I think it's been relieved. His pulse is steady and getting stronger. His breathing less ragged."

"Has he regained consciousness at all?"

"No. It could take hours still. Maybe days. The paralytic I gave him should have worn off by now. It'll be a long recovery."

"Why are you still here, Captain?" she asked, turning to the knight.

"Lord Dunsdworth is just as anxious to recover his sister-in-law as you. This man holds the secret to resolving his conflict with Severn and the king."

"So you're saying it's in his best interest to bring her back alive?" She arched her eyebrows. She wasn't entirely convinced of the duke's sincerity. After his involvement with the conspiracy, he probably wanted to know in advance if Nanette bore him ill will.

"That is his intent, yes," said the captain with a diplomatic nod.

"And you have no other leads as to where Nanette might have gone?"

Rufus shook his head. "All have been explored. The trail goes cold after Moser."

"Why don't you return to the Arbon? You need not remain here."

He fidgeted uncomfortably. "It is my duke's will—"

She gave him a stern look, and he stopped speaking. He gave her a small bow and promptly departed.

After he was gone, Danner Tye chuckled. "Thank you for sending him away."

"I thought it odd that you didn't try spirit of hartshorn to revive him."

Danner Tye grinned. "I thought you might prefer to be present when he was roused."

That's why he'd claimed, in Rufus's presence, that it could be hours or days before the man awakened. His allegiance to her was comforting.

"I've no doubt that Lord Dunsdworth is expecting to turn this to his favor," she said. "He wants to get credit for finding her and restoring her to the crown. He'll likely demand a *reward*. Shall we ask Master Bell for the hartshorn?"

"I always carry a supply with me to use after a procedure like this," the apothecary replied. He returned to his bag and produced a vial with a marbled texture on it. "I prefer hartshorn to sal ammoniac. I mix mine with a little eucalyptus oil and apply a touch just below the nostrils." He unstoppered the cap, producing an immediate and powerful smell. He dabbed a bit on a cloth and then hovered it in front of Moser's nose.

The man's eyelids fluttered, and he reflexively turned his head away.

Looking pleased with himself, Danner Tye corked the vial and put it away. Moser winced and then opened his bleary eyes. Ankarette felt a throb of relief. The older man looked from apothecary to poisoner and back again.

"You had a serious injury to your head," Danner Tye explained, slipping his calloused hand into Moser's. "I'm an apothecary. You've been unconscious for several days. Do you understand me? Squeeze my hand if you do."

Ankarette saw the muscle flex with the faint squeeze.

"Your name is Moser? You serve the Duke of Clare?" Ankarette asked.

Another squeeze.

Ankarette's heart began to beat faster with anticipation. She leaned closer so she could speak very softly.

"I serve King Eredur. He is concerned about Lady Nanette, the duke's sister-in-law. The king wants to protect her rights of inheritance. Do you know where she is?"

He blinked rapidly. His eyes darted from Danner's to hers. He didn't do anything. Didn't squeeze the hand.

She spoke calmingly. Coaxingly. "I was going to take her to the sanctuary of Our Lady," Ankarette said. "She'll be safe there. No one can make her leave. I know about the man sent to abduct her. He's dead. The duke is back at the Arbon with Lady Isybelle, who was also abducted. It's not your fault, Moser. Do you know where Lady Nanette is?"

"He squeezed my hand," Danner said softly. "Very faintly."

"Where is she?" Ankarette whispered. "Where did you hide her? You will not be punished for telling me."

Moser licked his lips and swallowed.

"He's thirsty," Ankarette said, looking for a pitcher of water. Danner, still gripping the man's hand, pointed to a nearby table with a pitcher and cups. She filled one partway and then returned. With Danner helping Moser sit up, they held the cup to his mouth so he could drink. He drained it.

"Tell us," Ankarette said smoothly.

Moser looked worried and a little fearful. But he nodded and then winced at the motion of his head. "Agnuhz," he rasped.

Ankarette looked at Danner Tye in confusion.

"Say it again?" the apothecary coaxed.

"Uh. . . uh. . . gnuhz." Moser looked disoriented. He tried speaking again, but only gibberish came out.

"It's the trauma to his skull," Danner said. "It could take a while for his normal speech to return."

That was time they could ill afford. The docks were still closed, the merchandise spoiling at the wharf. The two brothers were still at odds.

"What is your name?" Ankarette asked.

"Moh. . . zur," he said, his voice thick. He tapped his throat worriedly.

"He's slurring his words," Danner said. "This is common. At least he knows his name."

"And he knows where she is," Ankarette added. She knelt by the table, took his hand, and squeezed it. "Can you write, Moser?"

He shook his head no. Very few of the lower-class servants could.

"Are you telling us the name of a person?" she asked, urging him to respond.

He squeezed her hand and offered a gentle nod, which made him wince again.

"It's a person, then," Danner said. "Someone's name. Agnuh?"

Moser looked frustrated. "Ag-nuhz." He made a frown, his lips contorting.

"He's getting upset. That won't help."

"It's a name. Probably a common name," Ankarette said. "Anne? Amanda?"

Moser squinted and frowned. "Ag-nuhz," he groaned. "Muh... seester."

"His sister," Danner said excitedly.

A memory dashed through Ankarette's mind. "Agnes?" she asked.

Moser squeezed her hand emphatically. His eyes brightened, and he began to nod until the pain was too strong.

"Agnes," Danner said. "There could be a thousand women in this city with that name. But it's a start."

"Is she in this ward?" she asked Moser, her excitement growing. She'd heard that name recently. At Old Rose's.

He shook his head slowly. He tried to speak. "Urm... grage."

"Do you understand him?" Danner asked.

"I think so. Is she in the Hermitage?" Ankarette whispered.

He squeezed her hand again, even harder. Another flash in her mind. Another memory.

"Did her husband die? Were you helping to take care of her?"

He squeezed hard again, his eyes worried. It had to be the same person. The mother who'd come to Old Rose after she'd cut her hand. Ankarette had helped suture the wound since the barber nearby hadn't answered his door. Memories of the conversation flitted through her mind. She'd recently hired a new scullion who didn't. . .

Who didn't know how to cut vegetables. A new scullion. Sent to another ward in disguise, to hide her from the duke and his wine-besotted greed.

Moser had hidden Nanette in a humble place, in another ward, where the duke wouldn't be able to find her. He would trust his sister to protect her. But his livelihood was at risk if the duke found out.

Moser knew how fickle Dunsdworth could be. How greedy. But the man was loyal to Isybelle and Nanette. It was very common for families to care for their own when disaster struck. A widow without resources, without friends or family, could suffer a fate worse than death.

While hardly without resources, Lady Nanette was a widow, and her future had been tossed to the wind when her father died and could no longer protect her. Morvared was a widow too, her days spent in Holistern Tower, relying on her brother to try to win her release. He'd even sent a magic ring, likely a family heirloom of tremendous value, to try to win her freedom.

Agnes was the key to finding Nanette. Old Rose knew her. And so did John Thursby. She'd been within reach the whole time.

"I will guard your secret," Ankarette promised. "I won't tell the duke where I found her, but the king will reward you both for helping me."

"You know where she is?" Danner Tye asked with incredulity. "How?"

"I believe so. Or at least, I know how to find her."

To avoid being followed, Ankarette returned to the Hermitage using a circuitous path. She sensed she was being shadowed by one of Dunsdworth's men in the beginning, but that feeling began to abate once she was out of Vintrey, so she changed direction and headed back toward the Hermitage.

She reached Old Rose's apothecary shop in the late afternoon and found, not to any significant surprise, John Thursby up and about, pacing with a limp.

"I thought I told you to rest," she said, arching her eyebrows when he opened the door.

"I thought I'd not see you again," he answered, his features softening as he added, "so soon." A slight flush came to his cheeks. He was wearing his hauberk again, a fresh tunic without bloodstains, and even had his dagger in his belt.

"Were you going to walk your ward tonight?" she asked, seeing his state of preparedness. "That will not do."

"I'm more hale now than half the night watch on an ordinary night. And I've neglected my duties for too long. But all for a better purpose. The least I owe these people is the comfort of knowing I haven't forgotten them."

Old Rose opened the main door, catching Ankarette on the porch. "I was just about to bring him some soup. Would you care for some as well?"

"She spoils me," John Thursby said with an indulgent smile.

"I would enjoy some, yes, but not if it takes away from your own supper," Ankarette said to the apothecary.

"I have plenty, to be sure. Let me get another bowl."

"Would you like to come in?" he invited.

Ankarette agreed, and soon the two of them were sitting at his humble desk by the window with two potters bowls filled with steaming soup fragrant with bay leaves, rosemary, leeks, and some strips of meat. She noticed John Thursby holding his face above the bowl and inhaling the smell of it before he started eating. His love of smells was an endearing quality.

"How fares old Moser?" he asked after wiping his mouth.

"He survived and is conscious. His speech is altered. It's difficult to understand him. And may be for some days."

He looked crestfallen at the news and took another mouthful of soup. "I'm sorry. Can he spell it out?"

"He can't write." She ate more, enjoying the warmth of the broth. "But I think he's told me enough to find her."

He nearly dropped the spoon. "Truly?"

She lowered hers and reached across the table, tracing her fingertips along his hand. "I need your help again, John Thursby."

He looked down at her hand touching his, and his flush came back. "What can I do?"

"If I'm right, Nanette is here in the Hermitage, right now."

His eyes widened with surprise.

"I need *you* to take her to the sanctuary of Our Lady. Once she is inside the sanctuary grounds, she cannot be expelled by force. Then I can notify the king and Duke Severn and arrange for her release if *she* so chooses. For too long, her life has not been her own. I want her inheritance situation resolved so that she controls her own wealth and can decide her own future."

John Thursby nodded emphatically. "I cannot agree more. I'm happy to escort her to the sanctuary, but what if I'm accosted by Axelrod's or Clare's buffoons? I'm in no condition to put up a fight."

"I don't intend for you to do any fighting. In fact, the idea came to me as I walked here. I'd like to borrow *your* ruse, the one you used at the sanctuary gate to trick Dragan. I'll let her wear my dress and cloak. I even picked up a wig to conceal her hair. You and I have been seen on Bridge Street multiple times in recent days. Act as if you're traveling to the Espion safe house and then cross to the gate instead. I'll follow in her attire at a discreet distance, to make sure no one interferes. Once she's inside the sanctuary, I'll rejoin you and get permission from Deconeus Tunmore for her to stay."

He looked thoughtful for a moment and nodded. "It's sound. Then you can tell the king you've found her, and this trouble will be over."

"Actually, I need to protect my source. I'm going to tell the king that *you* found her."

His brow furrowed. "But I—"

She patted his hand. "You did, indirectly. I'd like you

to get the credit *and* the reward for finding her. This is how you can help me. I need you to be the hero."

His look darkened a little, his lips pursing. She could see he liked the idea not at all.

"I'm not the stuff of heroes, Ankarette."

"Let our opinions differ on that score. You are loyal, faithful, and true. You deserve more than scorn and derision for those traits. It would please me to see you honored in this. And it would help fulfill my mission for the king."

He sighed and pushed his bowl away. He folded his arms with a surly look. "You didn't tell me where she is."

"Moser spoke in gibberish, but he kept saying a name over and over. Agnes. Do you remember the woman—"

"With the cut hand, yes. I asked Old Rose about her earlier today, wondering how the wound was healing."

"She said she's brought on a new scullion," she said meaningfully. "One who wasn't skilled."

His eyes bulged with realization. "Lady Nanette? The duke's daughter?"

"Agnes is Moser's widowed sister. I'm afraid our missing heir might be nervous about losing her freedom. She could flee like a bird. I'd like you to check in on Agnes. Ask to see the scullion and see if she responds to her true name. I'll circle around the back in case she tries to escape. She knows me. I think I can get her to trust me, so she'll go with you willingly."

"She'll trust you," John Thursby said with certainty. "As do I. If we want to get to the sanctuary before the bells toll and the gates are locked, we'd best get going."

"Thank you."

"You thank me? This is all your doing. Your cleverness. If you hadn't had the compassion to help that woman to begin with, we'd not have learned any of this."

"I always prefer using my talents to heal rather than to harm."

AGNES LIVED in a tiny dwelling on a cramped street only a few blocks away. John Thursby brought Ankarette to the alley behind the houses, which had strings of laundry drying from many of the homes. A rat slunk away.

"I'll go around to the front," he said in a whisper, grazing the hair by her ear with his fingers in a playful manner. She leaned into the caress and then watched him go.

Waiting in the shadowed alley, Ankarette was hidden by the drapes of clothing but close enough that she heard the knock on the front door. The sound of voices came as children excitedly went to answer it. From the muffled noises, she could discern John Thursby's deep voice speaking to a woman. Ankarette felt tingles of excitement go through her, but she tried to quell them. She didn't sense any danger.

Then she heard the back door gently creak open and the brief scuff of footfalls. Ankarette waited patiently, listening keenly. A young woman dressed in sooty scullion garb emerged from behind the wall of clothing, looking back toward the house. There were smudges on her cheeks and chin, but Ankarette recognized her instantly as Warrewik's lost daughter.

Nanette was startled by Ankarette's cloaked presence, gasped in shock, and bolted. The poisoner caught her arm and restrained her.

"It's Ankarette," she whispered in Nanette's ear. "I'm here to help you."

Nanette tried to wrestle free of her grip, but Ankarette had positioned herself with her back to the alley so Nanette couldn't get past her.

Then the struggle slowed, and a look of recognition came to the other woman's eyes.

"Ankarette? Is it really you?"

The poisoner kept one hand fixed to Nanette's wrist and lowered her cowl with the other.

Then Nanette's face crumpled with tears, and she hugged Ankarette fiercely and began to cry.

"We're going to the sanctuary of Our Lady," Ankarette soothed. "You will be under the deconeus's protection. The king sent me to save you. He's on your side."

Nanette pulled back, her look of anguish beginning to lift. She covered her mouth with a hand. "I thought I was in disfavor."

"Not at all," Ankarette said. "You are a royal ward now, under his protection. But you have a say in your future. I'll see to that. No one will force you to marry. It will be your choice."

"Dunne said Severn doesn't really w-want me," Nanette said thickly through her tears. "That he only wants my wealth."

Ankarette's heart ached for Warrewik's daughter. For the widow whose life had been bent and twisted but not broken. "That's not true. He's been scouring the city for you. Moser was injured. He's been unconscious for days. We only learned you were here today."

"Bless the Lady," Nanette cried, hugging Ankarette again. "Every day, I was getting more and more frantic. I feared Dunne would search house to house. I despise him. He's done nothing but try to keep us apart! Greedy, selfish man!"

"You can add dishonesty to his list of flaws," Ankarette said.

The back door opened, and a woman—Agnes—called out. "It's all right! You're safe!"

"We're here," Ankarette said in reply. Still holding Nanette like a lost sister who'd finally been found, she parted the curtain of laundry, and they saw Agnes and John Thursby standing in the doorway, with her brood of children peering out from behind their legs. The night watchman gave Ankarette a congratulatory smile.

"Now, let me tell you how we're going to get you to the sanctuary without being discovered," Ankarette said coaxingly. "It involves a little trick about you pretending to be me and me pretending to be you. This is John Thursby, the night watchman of this ward."

"I've heard of him," Nanette said, gazing at the soldier with a look of respect. "Agnes speaks highly of you. I'm sorry I ran. I was so afraid you would bring me back to the Arbon."

"I've no such intention, my lady," he said. "But I can see why you feared it. I'm loyal to the crown."

"You knew my father, didn't you?"

He smiled sadly. "For a brief time, my lady. I served Lord Devereaux."

"I remember him at Shynom. He was at. . . my. . . wedding." Her throat caught again, and she looked so devastated and mournful that Ankarette hugged her again, kissing her head. She was barely eighteen, but she'd been through so much. The past would torment her.

But her future, as one of the wealthiest heiresses in Ceredigion, would be very different. Ankarette was sure of it.

She will be queen.

The whisper from the Fountain was so subtle and piercing that Ankarette nearly gasped when she heard it. It took every measure of composure not to react visibly to it. This glimpse of the future. . . it had shaken her to the core.

The thought flitted by, and then it was gone.

THIRTY-THREE

RINGING OF THE BELLS

It was a vastly strange experience for Ankarette to watch John Thursby walking alongside a woman who looked like her. It triggered a memory of seeing another woman who had looked like her just the previous day. She followed the two to Bridge Street without trouble. Ankarette had disguised herself with smudges on her face and wore the smock and kirtle of a scullion while toting a small crate of carrots, onions, and squash. The roar of the falls was an omnipresent sound as they approached the sanctuary of Our Lady, with the spire rising in the background.

They reached the gates before the bells tolled, and she watched as the two figures slipped inside without notice or fanfare. She noticed the night watchman's limp had increased during the walk and could tell he was stifling feelings of pain. She'd get him a remedy for it when it was all over. He needed rest most of all.

Ankarette entered behind them. She'd told John Thursby to seek out the deconeus immediately, and there was no deviation from his path as he escorted Nanette up the wide steps toward the massive sanctuary, a complex of brilliant windows, smooth stone walls, and arching buttresses.

As she watched them climb the steps, she felt the shudder of Fountain magic from an invisible source, which immediately began to follow the two. It was Dragan, up to no good.

Ankarette's stores of magic were very low and needed to be replenished, but she had enough left to send a prod of warning to halt the thief. She sensed his pause, and he turned.

She strode toward the steps in his general direction. "You'd best steer clear of them both," she said under her breath in passing. "It doesn't concern you."

He'd been caught off guard, and she could feel his fretting and fear of her.

"My mistake, lass," he offered gruffly. She felt his magic graze her. Was he prodding her for weakness as well? Or something worth stealing? She had the ring still. That would be a tempting prize. She couldn't stay in the sanctuary. In her wearied state, it wasn't prudent. Dragan and his sanctuary men would rob her if she did.

"If you come near me again, I'll put a knife in your back," she said confidently.

"Glad we understand each other. That's a nice. . . trinket. Grimmer had it, didn't he?"

She said nothing, but she didn't need to in order to communicate with him. He chuffed. "You killed the sodding bloke. I'm impressed."

"You thought he'd kill me, which is why you had courage enough to steal from me. That was not very wise, Dragan."

"Ah, but what's life without a little risk, eh? I'll stay out of your way from now on. But that trinket, that *ring*, if you ever want to—"

"No," she said firmly.

"Ah. Well, I don't blame you. They're about to ring the bells and shut the gates."

"I'm on my way. And I delivered my warning. I only warn once."

"Very generous of you, lass."

Ankarette turned and walked to the gates. She turned back once before leaving, finding Dragan had lowered his magical invisibility. They nodded to each other, one Fountain-blessed to another. She couldn't understand why the Fountain had granted gifts to such an unworthy and unsavory man, and yet it had. Somehow, he'd learned how to tap into the magic and replenish it.

She left the grounds and walked to the Espion tavern nearby. When she entered, she saw Hugh Bardulf, who took one look at her and dismissed her as a waste of time until she approached him.

"I need a room. . . and some of my clothes," she said, startling him with a recognizable voice.

"By the Lady, Ankarette! Where have you been?"

"Here and there, Hugh. Lady Nanette has been found. She's at the sanctuary of Our Lady. Can you send word to Master Nichols? It's best he learn of it before the king finds out."

"Why aren't you with her?" He gazed around for someone else and looked about to fall out of his chair. "How did she get to the sanctuary?"

"Just send the message. I imagine the king will want to open the wharves again and let trade commence. It'll be a busy night, and ships will leave with the tide."

"Indeed so. This is welcome news. Did you find her or someone else?"

"Does it matter?" she answered cryptically. "Send the message. Quickly."

He obeyed, and Ankarette was given her usual room. After shutting the door, she leaned back against it, feeling exhausted and relieved. She'd done it. But she wasn't sure she could have managed it without John Thursby. They'd agreed that he'd spend the night at the sanctuary, watching over the heiress.

A barmaid arrived with a tray of food for her, which she accepted gratefully before she wolfed it down. The last thing she'd eaten was Old Rose's fragrant soup.

She stripped down to her chemise and pulled out a gown from the chest beneath the bed. Then she replenished her stores of poison, tucking the ring into her pocket to safeguard it.

She had just started brushing out her hair when the bells of the city began to toll.

It was dusk. The night watch would commence. And John Thursby would get all the credit for finding the missing heiress. Ankarette smiled, pleased with herself.

EARLY THE FOLLOWING MORNING, Ankarette watched from the window of the inn's common room as a group of knights with the badge of Glosstyr—the White Boar—gathered outside the sanctuary gates. There was Severn himself, astride his saddle, fidgeting with a dagger in his belt. He loosed it from its scabbard, pulled it partway out, then slammed it back down. She enjoyed her breakfast—a meat pasty and fruit—all the while watching for the gates to open.

When they did, she pushed aside her plate and rose from the table.

"The king still wishes to see you," Hugh said. He'd wanted her to go to the palace after changing clothes, but she'd remained behind and slept at the Espion inn.

"I know. Tell him I'm coming. There's one more piece of information I need to gather for him first."

"Of course. We're still short on men down here. It'll take weeks to recruit new ones. What about that night watchman you worked with? Thursby? Think he'd be interested in joining us?"

Ankarette gave him a sidelong look. "No. I don't think he would be."

"Well, I heard the lord high constable pissed his milk when he found out Lady Nanette was safe and sound. He'd offered a reward of fifty crowns to whoever found her, and it galled him to have to hand it over to a lowly night watchman. Especially him." Hugh grinned.

"There will be a reward from the king as well," Ankarette said. "Mark my words."

"I don't doubt it! I'll send word you're coming in your own due time. I know *I* couldn't get away with such cheek."

Ankarette gave him a charming smile and then walked out onto the street. There were people already coming and going, especially those who'd spent the night at the sanctuary. She caught sight of John Thursby walking slowly down Bridge Street, heading back to the city proper, away from the palace. He had a satchel around his shoulder.

She caught up to him and walked alongside him.

"I smell your perfume," he said, looking ahead.

"That's why I wore it," she answered. "How did the deconeus react when you brought her in last night?"

"He was pleased as Old Rose's cat with a bowl of cream. Only too grateful to take custody of her. She slept in the deconeus's manor with all dignity and respect." He clapped his hand on the satchel. "I have your dress here. Wasn't sure when we'd see each other again."

He stopped, and for a moment they both stood in the street, the city dwellers flowing around them as the river had parted around Ankarette and Grimmer.

"Did you get any rest last night?" she asked him.

He smiled sadly. "No. I've had enough of that to last a while. We spoke late into the night. Shared memories of Yuork. Of her father. I pity the lass, truly. Forced to marry her enemy's son, then to live with a brother-in-law who hated her. Nearly kidnapped or murdered. She's a strong one, though. Determined not to lose her freedom again. I don't blame her."

"She'll need some time to recover. Time to feel safe."

"Aye." He looked at her, his expression changing. "When will I see you again, Ankarette? I know I have no business asking, but. . . I must ask anyway."

"I need to speak with the king. I'm sure he'll wish to reward you. It may take a few days."

"I didn't do this for the glory or the reward. I did it for *you*."

"If you don't want Lord Axelrod's money. . ."

"Oh, I'll keep it. Just because it pains him to give it to me. What I need, money cannot purchase." He stepped closer to her, brushing her loose hair over her ear. She smiled at him.

"What I give, I give freely," she said. "We'll see each

other again. Soon, I think. The king asked to see me, but I wished to see you first."

"Might he not throw you in the river for such impertinence?"

"I'm worth more to him alive than dead. Take care, John Thursby. Until we meet again."

"It cannot be too soon," he answered.

She left him and walked the short distance to the gates of the sanctuary. She wanted to ask the deconeus about the ring from the Occitanian king. She knew he had a strong mastery of history, the Deep Fathoms, and artifacts related to the Fountain. That information would be helpful to Eredur. Yes, she'd accomplished the mission he'd given her. But the relic she'd secured would be quite valuable to him. A ring with wondrous power.

The sexton informed her that the deconeus was in the gardens behind his manor, which were adjacent to the sanctuary and off limits to visitors, but he recognized her and used his ring of keys to unlock one of the garden gates so she could enter. The smell of the flowers was intoxicating, and a cool breeze blew through the grass and hedges. She found the deconeus standing at the end of a footpath, eyes fixed on a scene. He looked troubled. Brooding, even.

"Pardon the intrusion, Deconeus," Ankarette said, approaching him from behind.

He turned, but his gaze returned to their former focus—Severn and Nanette, walking hand in hand down another garden path, heads bowed in deep conversation.

"I was surprised a night watchman in the city found her. And you didn't." He gave her an incredulous look.

Ankarette said nothing for a moment. "What matters most is she's safe now."

"Oh? You think so?"

"Why wouldn't she be?"

He rubbed his chin, a faraway look in his eyes. "I'd rather not say."

"Did the Fountain. . . speak to you?" she pressed.

"Indeed."

"What did it tell you?"

"I cannot speak it. Especially not to you."

She had a suspicion the Fountain had told them both the same thing. She'd wrestled within herself all night whether to reveal her impression to the king. If Nanette would become the queen, that meant, in all likelihood, that *Severn* would be Eredur's heir. But such news would only haunt Eredur, not help him.

Some secrets were not meant to be shared.

Every decision you make narrows the future. It alters future choices, reduces options. One must be very wise and consider the long-term consequences. But you can also commit injustice by doing nothing.

— ANKARETTE TRYNEOWY

279

THIRTY-FOUR

THE RING AND THE MAID

Ankarette blew out the candle and watched as the wisp of smoke curled about the wick. The little ember at the end sizzled and then winked out, plunging her room into total darkness. She was in her private chamber in the palace of Kingfountain. No windows led to it, and the door was barred and locked with a key that only the master of the Espion had a copy of. After days of searching the city, the room seemed. . . small. Confining. That night, the stone walls of the castle felt like a glamorous prison.

She longed to see John Thursby again. That she was missing him already made her wonder at herself.

She set the candle holder on the table, then walked to the secret door and triggered the latch. Even in the total darkness, she knew the way to go and followed the corridor with a precision and expertise born of years of experience. Sir Thomas had educated her in the ways of the Espion. Should she confide in him the whisper from the Fountain?

She felt a throb of warning in her heart not to tell anyone. She and the deconeus were the only two who knew, the only two whom the Fountain had trusted with the revelation. Some secrets weighed on the heart and the soul. Like this one. No, it would be best if she never met Thomas again. Even the ashes of memories could be dangerous if rekindled.

After navigating through the tunnels, she reached the private quarters of Eredur and Elyse. She peeked through the spy hole to be sure she wasn't intruding on anything intimate, but she found the couple talking by the fireplace, each holding an ornate goblet.

She triggered the latch and swung the door open.

Eredur turned his neck and spied her emerging from the opening. "Ankarette! I've been expecting word from you all day! Where have you been?"

"You sound almost accusing, dearest," said the queen. She stroked Eredur's arm. "I'm sure she had good reason for the delay."

The king set his goblet down and rose from the couch, looking at Ankarette expectantly. "Don't tell me the night watchman discovered Nanette on his own. I'm happy to pay the man a reward, but I know it was you. It had to be."

Ankarette stared at them, sensing the curiosity raging in both. The queen was more patient than her husband.

"I wouldn't have found her without his help," Ankarette said. "He deserved the recognition."

"You're driving me mad with suspense!" Eredur chuckled. "Out with it!"

Ankarette walked over to rest her hand on the mantel above the fireplace, gazing down at the flames. "It was your brother's fault," she said carefully. "But not in the way you might think. Dunne was duped by a dock merchant in Queenshithe into permitting Nanette to be smuggled away. It turns out the merchant had loyalties to Morvared. Many in that ward still harbor prejudice against you." She turned and looked at Eredur. "Dunne was drunk at the time. Wasn't thinking clearly. Lord Hux manipulated him into cooperating with a kidnapping scheme, and his wife nearly paid for it with her life."

"By the Fountain," Elyse whispered in shock.

Ankarette felt the warmth of the flames seep through her gown. "This is what I've discovered. The Occitanians used the friction between Severn and Dunsdworth over the inheritance to try and liberate Morvared. And Morvared also wanted revenge against Warrewik's daughters. Hux's plan should have worked. Only they underestimated someone."

Eredur grinned. "You."

Ankarette shook her head. "I'm not prone to false modesty. They underestimated Nanette herself. She convinced the guard assigned to watch the porter door —a man named Moser, as you know—to smuggle her away before the kidnapping happened. He sent her to his widowed sister in another ward, one far enough from Vintrey and Dunsdworth's influence and loyalty. She bided her time, watching the windows for signs of Severn's men. She hid herself as a scullion. And her disguise fooled everyone."

Elyse beamed and took a sip of her wine. "I've always admired her. Even after being forced to marry the prince, she was determined not to play the victim."

"She's weary of her fate being manipulated by others. Which is why she agreed to go with John Thursby to the sanctuary of Our Lady and seek the deconeus's protection. Even now, as a ward of the crown, she fears *you* will try and force her to do something against her will."

"Me?" Eredur exclaimed. "I was doing this for Severn's sake! He dotes on the girl, surely."

"I saw them together at the sanctuary this morning," Ankarette said. "But I've counseled her not to rush her decision. Let her make up her own mind. They'll both be happier if a little time passes before she leaves sanctuary. Let the duke woo her. It'll do them both some good."

"Severn? Woo? Do you know my brother at all?"

"I've taken his measure," Ankarette replied with a disarming smile. "I heard from Master Nichols that trade has been reopened?"

"Yes, thank the Lady," the king said with a sigh of relief. "Petitions for relief have been flooding the castle all day. Every merchant wants to be made whole for the inconveniences. What a bother."

Ankarette looked at him pointedly. "You should relieve the suffering."

"It will cost a fortune!"

"I've counseled him to do the same," Elyse said. "Help me convince him, Ankarette."

The king held up his hands. "This is unfair! I don't need another set of spurs at my withers."

"Now you're being dramatic," the queen said, shaking her head.

Ankarette knew Eredur could be stubborn. It reminded her of the adage *He that complies against his will is of his own opinion still.* Telling Eredur he was wrong wasn't going to alter his thinking quickly. If at all.

"Your husband is quite right; it will cost a sizable sum. I imagine the Genevese will be pressing the hardest for recompense."

"They are indeed," Eredur said with defensiveness.

"Their ambassador is expecting an audience tomorrow, though I'm of a mind to delay him a fortnight."

"And delaying the encounter will allow time to cool tempers," Ankarette said. "Surely their requests will be more reasonable if tempered."

"Exactly so," the king said, feeling now that Ankarette was on his side. "'Tis precisely what Hastings advised me to do. 'Stall them all.' They'll be grateful to get *any* relief, instead of demanding to be made whole. I'm glad you see it my way."

Elyse's doubtful look suggested she wasn't convinced.

"It would safeguard your interests," Ankarette said. "Preserve your royal treasury. It might even check Genevar's ambitions."

Eredur hooked his thumbs in his belt and rocked on his heels, giving her a nod to go on as if he believed Ankarette were trying to persuade the queen instead of him. He was enjoying the help.

"Every merchant takes a risk when he ships goods to another realm," Ankarette continued. "There is always the risk of shipwreck. Or pirates. Or a winter storm come early. These are facts to be mitigated. Should the king bear the risks of such events?"

"Indeed not!"

A smile quirked on the queen's mouth.

"And a man maimed at the Battle of Boreham-wood, one who can no longer work because he's missing a leg or his arm, should not require a pension or subsistence. He took the risk to fight for the king, come what may."

Eredur's expression altered, and he looked at her in confusion.

"And when he dies, nor should his widow have

284

claim on the crown. Let her beg in the streets for marrying a soldier."

"Nay," Eredur said, shaking his head. "Soldiers will not fight if there is no promise of a pension, one that would benefit their widows."

"But what of a merchant who buys herbs from Ceredigion to sell in Brugia? Wool may not spoil quickly, but cabbages will. Because a king ordered the ports closed for no reason they can account for. Will not these merchants also feel entitled to compensation for acts beyond their control? Will they not, perhaps, increase their prices to compensate for the injustices done to them? Will not that spoiled cabbage end up in someone's soup? And whose? The merchant's? Or a lowly widow who has no remedy, no recourse?"

He stared at her, his mouth tightening as he realized her logic had spun him completely around. He was not an unjust king. They both knew that. And to deny the impact of his decision on the people, especially the most vulnerable, scorched his conscience.

"If there's one thing I've learned during my days in the city, it's how precarious life is down there. We're shielded from suffering in this castle on a hill. And your lord high constable, Lord Axelrod, cares more about crime than the causes of it. Now is the time to be generous. Your people will love you because you helped them in their hour of need, not because you defeated an enemy in the past. Waste no time arguing about what a good king *should* be. Be one."

He looked chagrined. He looked humbled by her words. Elyse beamed at Ankarette and gave her an approving nod. And wisely, said nothing. The scales were tipping.

"I will address my privy council in the morning,"

Eredur said. "You give wise counsel, Ankarette Tryne-owy. Even if it stings."

She smiled and bowed to him. Then she reached into her pocket and produced the ring. The firelight glinted off the circular grooves entwining the band. Elyse rose from the couch, and both of them approached her to look at it.

"What is that thing?" Eredur asked.

"My gift to you, my liege. And the reason I'm so late seeing you. A ring."

His brow wrinkled in confusion.

"The killer Bidigen Grimmer was wearing it. I cut off his hand to claim it. I witnessed its power firsthand. It stayed the river's flow. It is powerful Fountain magic. And it belonged to your enemy, King Lewis of Occitania."

Eredur's eyes widened with surprise.

"I asked Deconeus Tunmore about it. He referred me to the archives in the sanctuary, the records kept by his predecessors. There's a story about the first Argentine king who faced an Occitanian invasion. He had a knight who was Fountain-blessed. Lord Barton."

"Was he the one who'd been a hostage to King Gervase?" Eredur asked.

"The very one. King Estian crossed the river with his army and the waters parted for him, allowing them to cross and attack the city. King Devon was nearly captured, they had to flee, and he died shortly after. Poisoned, I believe. This ring has been a secret for centuries. That's how Grimmer survived going into the river. He had another magic that healed his wounds, but he'd used it all up by the time I killed him. He tried to drown me with this ring. And without the Fountain's insight, I would have perished in the river."

Elyse reached out and squeezed Ankarette's arm with a worried look.

"This is one of Lewis's most prized treasures. I believe the ring dates back to the time of King Andrew. As I researched the archives, I came across another such relic the Occitanians treasure. One that has been missing for decades. Do you remember the story of the Maid? The peasant girl from Occitania who led an army against us years ago?"

"Who hasn't heard of her?" Eredur chuffed. "What about her story intrigues you? Aside from the fact that she was Fountain-blessed."

"The sword Firebos went missing around the time of her capture. As I read the account of her trial, I had an uncanny feeling about the sword. That it may yet be found. There is a power among the Fountain-blessed that allows us to reach into bodies of water and gain access to the Deep Fathoms. If I can learn where she hid the sword, I might be able to reclaim King Andrew's blade."

His eyes glinted with enthusiasm. "Might it still be retrieved?"

"I believe it is possible, yes. And Occitania would do everything in their power to stop us from finding it if they believed we were even looking for it. After their failed attempt to free Morvared, I think we should restart negotiations for her release. To draw their attention away from what we're actually doing, just as they tried to do with us. This is the first time Lord Hux has failed. Who knows what Lewis will do? I have no doubt Hux persuaded the king to loan him the ring to use on Grimmer's mission. His reputation will be damaged, especially if Lewis knows *we* have it."

"I like your thinking, Ankarette. It's time we turned the tables on that old fox."

"I agree. I propose sending a message to the king and Hux simultaneously. No doubt Hux will try to excuse himself."

"What about the tincture he gave you?" Elyse asked. "Might we not use our new leverage to demand a cure?"

"I'm not sure I dare hope there's a cure," Ankarette said. "But we will get more because we're in a better position now."

"Thanks to you," the king said. He took up his goblet again and saluted her with it. "What you've done will benefit Ceredigion for years to come. You found Nanette. You stole one of Lewis's greatest treasures. And you might be able to help us regain the sword of legends. What do you want, Ankarette? What reward can I give *you* for such loyalty? I know Lewis gave Hux a castle and its income. Is that what you want? How can I reward you?"

"There is something I would appreciate," Ankarette said. "And it's not a castle. I like staying here, but I would prefer to have a place of my own. In the city. A place I can keep a little window garden. Where I can hear what's happening in the city and not through the Espion informants. A little place all my own where I can rest."

"I'll boot Dunsdworth out of the Arbon. You can have his house." He laughed, but he was only half joking.

"I don't need something with servants and responsibilities. I'm busy enough. Just a little house on a quiet street and some. . . some books."

"Done," Eredur said, snapping his fingers. "You find the property you like, and I'll have my steward make the arrangements to secure it. Is there a ward you've become fond of? I don't know them very well myself."

"There is one," Ankarette said with a wry smile.

Elyse gave her a knowing look and arched her eyebrows.

THIRTY-FIVE

FREEDOM'S KISS

The morning bells tolled at the sanctuary of Our Lady of Kingfountain. Ankarette watched from the window of the Espion inn as the sexton unlocked the gates. She lingered at the curtain, observing the initial rush of people going in to petition the Fountain for a blessing. And she watched as, invariably, some sanctuary men slipped out to begin their daily pillaging.

Hugh Bardulf approached her at the window, his silver hair shining in the sunlight. "I thought you'd want to know we caught an Occitanian spy down at the Corfe last night asking after Grimmer. I had him sent to Master Nichols for questioning."

Ankarette let the curtain fall back into place. "It's not often we catch one of their spies. Well done."

He shrugged but gave her a gratified smile. "We try. I'm sure Lord Hux isn't used to losing a round. He'll be angry."

"It's my hope he'll be disgraced," Ankarette said offhandedly. "The king is sending his herald to Pree with a message and a threat. Additional soldiers will be sent to Castle Beestone to increase her war footing. I'm sure it hasn't escaped King Lewis's memory that our king has never lost a battle."

"Nor will he yet if it please the Fountain. Now, you're off to the sanctuary again. Three days in a row. Visiting Lady Nanette, I take it?"

"I don't discuss my assignments from the king unless I must," she answered cryptically. Hugh Bardulf's easy manner made him seem trustworthy, but men like him traded in secrets. Ankarette wasn't only visiting Nanette. She was spending time with the deconeus, learning all she could about the Maid of Donremy and where her sword might be. The herald sent to deliver the threat to Lewis had another mission to fulfill. To see if he could learn the whereabouts of any survivors of the Maid's battles. Someone who may have known her firsthand. They would be older, of course, since the Maid was put to death nearly thirty years ago. But there was much to be learned from a firsthand witness of past events.

She was heading toward the door when Bardulf halted her once more. "Another thing, Ankarette. The night watchman. Thursby. He came by yesterday looking for you."

Her reaction was very important. Or, more precisely, her lack of one. She turned her head, giving Hugh an indifferent look. "Oh?"

"I didn't know where you were and said so. Should I . . . deal with him?" It was an offer to warn off the soldier. A request to do her a favor.

The last thing she wanted was for anyone in the Espion to believe she cared for someone. That information could easily be turned against her. Poisoners were not supposed to fall in love.

"He served his purpose," Ankarette said casually.

"But don't warn him off. I may need to use him again in the future to find Lord Devereaux."

Hugh smiled like a wolf. "As always, you're a step or two ahead."

She took the compliment with a shrug and went into the street. She crossed to the gate of the sanctuary and then ventured into the deconeus's gardens. There was a little tamping down of her feelings after learning that John Thursby had sought her out—she admitted to herself she was touched, even though she'd told him that she would come to him. Another adage she'd heard flitted across her mind *Nothing important came into being overnight*. Even grapes and figs needed time to ripen. She'd wondered if the separation of a few days would cool her feelings for John Thursby. Pleasantly, it had not. She missed him.

She trod the yard and entered the gate, which the deconeus had kept unlocked for her. She found Nanette pacing, wearing a beautiful gown the color of jade, with silver armbands and pretty shoes. In her countenance, Ankarette could still recognize the young girl she'd first met years before. But she was a woman now, not just because of age but because of the hardships and suffering she'd endured.

Nanette turned when she heard Ankarette approach, her expression nervous and excited. And wary. She clutched her abdomen in a worrying gesture, then fidgeted with her hands.

"I feel like a hive of bees is inside me," Nanette said.

"Oh? Why is that? There is no rush to marry, as I counseled you yesterday. You can take as much time as you need."

"I know that. And I appreciate your counsel, truly I

do. You were always Isybelle's friend more than mine, but I feel you have my interests at heart."

Ankarette smiled. "Then why hurry your decision to marry again?"

Nanette fidgeted again. "Because I love him, Ankarette. I've always loved him. Even when I was a child and thought it was just a fancy. It broke my heart to marry that awful prince, but I wasn't given a choice. You know. . . how my father could be when he was determined to get his way."

Yes. She did. She gave Nanette a sympathetic nod.

Nanette turned away, bowing her head. "My father had intended Sev for me. From the beginning. It broke his heart too."

"Is he jealous?" Ankarette asked.

"No. Not really. Resentful, to be sure." She gazed up at one of the garden trees. "After Hawk Moor, he said we'd have to wait. To be sure I wasn't with child. But he said he'd want me regardless. And then his wretched brother kept us apart. That was unchivalrous of him." She turned and faced Ankarette. "I remember how besotted he was with marrying Isybelle. I don't know what he craved more, her affection or her dowry. Sev wants *me*. He's willing to accept a lower portion. He won't fight for more so long as we can marry soon."

"You love him that much?" Ankarette already knew the answer. She could see it in the rapturous look that came over Nanette's face when the question was posed.

"I do, Ankarette. I don't want to be parted from him anymore, not for a single day. It's been. . . torture being here." She gave Ankarette a sly look. "We kissed yesterday. For the first time in a *long* time. Here in this garden. None of us is guaranteed love or laughter or even being alive. Truly alive. That's how I feel when I'm with him.

He can make me laugh. Oh, his observations of people are so witty."

Biting, rather, Ankarette thought, but kept the observation locked away. This was more than a sign of infatuation. The two cousins had a deep bond. Their experiences together had drawn them close. Her previous marriage hadn't been an impediment to their love.

It struck her again, forcefully, that one day Nanette would wear the crown of Ceredigion.

The thought must have made her betray some mark of emotion, for Nanette noticed it and stepped closer. "You don't think I should marry him?"

"It's not that, Nanette. It's just that the future can be so. . . unpredictable. Dunne still wants to be king. His ambition sickens him day by day. If he ever became king, he could make your lives miserable. The ill blood between brothers needs to be healed."

"What you say is true," Nanette said. "I'm not blind to Dunne's ambition. And I've counseled Sev to try and get along. But he won't be trampled down. He's almost as powerful as my father was in his prime."

"Yes. That's a concern as well. Marriage to you makes him even more powerful."

"And there's nothing wrong with that," Nanette said firmly. "Loyalty should be rewarded."

There was no going back. Even though Ankarette could discern that the conflict between the three brothers wasn't over, that there were unknowable consequences lurking in the future.

Ankarette took Nanette's hand and squeezed it. "If you are determined to marry the Duke of Glosstyr, I bring you my first wedding gift. I was at the Arbon yesterday and helped temper Dunne's demands. I reminded him that the breach in your safety was his fault and that, had things turned out badly, he would have been found guilty of aiding in the conspiracy. The king will not reward him for his infidelity any longer."

Nanette smiled with the victory. Her animosity toward her brother-in-law was evident in the curl of her lip. "At last."

"He's agreed to split the inheritance in accordance with Severn's offer, and the king will reimburse the rest to you through additional grants of manors and castles. The portion you bring to the marriage is undiminished."

"I care not about it," Nanette said simply. "Can we marry today? Will the king object?"

"He will not. But he's offered you both a wedding befitting your rank and station."

"I don't want that. I want it to be private. Just a few in attendance. I wish to leave for Glosstyr tonight." As Nanette said these words, she was looking over Ankarette's shoulder.

The poisoner felt a gentle throb of Fountain magic. Not from herself. Not a warning. But a detection of another source.

She turned and found Severn Argentine standing in the shadows of the garden, looking at Nanette with adoring eyes. It surprised Ankarette. She'd never felt Fountain magic in his presence before, and the ability normally revealed itself in early youth. Something had awakened it.

Maybe his happiness with Nanette had allowed it to surge to life inside him.

Severn approached his cousin and bent down to one knee. He looked humbled and victorious. "I wish it as well," he said huskily. "Say you are mine."

"I am, my darling. I am yours."

Severn rose and kissed her. It was freedom's kiss.

AFTER A WHIRLWIND DAY and a hastily conducted marriage, Ankarette at last had time to depart for the Hermitage. When she arrived at Old Rose's, she found that her favorite night watchman had already started his rounds. The savvy apothecary gave Ankarette an understanding look but couldn't tell her where he'd gone because he varied his walks through the ward. He'd used some of his reward money to fix her shop and home. That was not a surprise to Ankarette, for she knew him to have a generous heart. The cat Ani purred against her legs, and she bent down to stroke its soft black fur.

"You could stay and wait for him?" Old Rose suggested warmly. "I know he'll be devastated that he missed you."

"How is his injury healing?"

"He still limps quite a bit, especially by morning, but he's getting stronger day by day." She looked at Ankarette pointedly. "He loves you. Surely you know that?"

Ankarette didn't need Old Rose's words. Fountain magic had revealed the depths of his feelings early on, and her own heart was twitching with anxiety and delight at the prospect of seeing him again.

"He's a good man," she responded simply, not wanting to reveal herself to the old woman. "Tell him I'll try again tomorrow night. Tell him to wait for me."

"I shall. Best get home before it's too dark out."

Ankarette had no intention of going back to the palace.

She left the old woman and her cat and walked the streets of the Hermitage, ears keenly listening for the sounds that might reveal him. But she had a destination in mind. A place she imagined he might show up sometime that night. When he'd first escorted her back to the Arbon, they'd taken a little street with houses clustered close together, each with a little window garden full of herbs and lovely smells. It was just at the edge of the Hermitage, near a major crossroads in the city of Kingfountain. It was in the shadow of Vintrey but outside of Dunsdworth's domain.

And there was a little house on that street that had been vacant and for sale. The key to it was in her pocket.

When she arrived at the alley, she found John Thursby already there. The moonlight glinted off his shoulder armor beneath his cloak. A swarm of stars flickered in the gap of sky high above.

She walked up to him and tilted her head inquisitively. "You seem to be waiting for someone?" she said in a low voice.

He tilted his head slightly, gazing at her with a look of unmitigated contentment and anticipation. He was pleased to see her. To be near her again.

"I heard a rumor that the empty house over yon was taken this week. I had a mind to rent it myself. They said the tenant was a woman of business. A lovely creature with eyes as light as moonbeams."

"Like moonbeams they say?" she asked. "How interesting."

"They said the woman's name was Krysia. That she was from Yuork."

"What a coincidence," she said, sidling closer to him. When she reached for his hand, his fingers brushed hers. That made them both hesitate for just an instant before she grazed her hand up his arm.

"That perfume you wear. I rather like it," he said huskily.

"Oh? It's my favorite too." She tilted her head, exposing her neck to him. She wanted him to kiss her there. She'd been daydreaming about it all day.

"I may be a thick-headed night watchman—a fool in love—but I'm not a lout. Tell me for certain, Ankarette. Did you get the house to be closer to me?"

She lowered her cowl, and her hair spilled out, unbraided. "I hear this is the safest ward in the city. That it's guarded by a brave night watchman from the North." She put her hand on his chest, felt the ridges of the hauberk beneath his tunic. She gripped it and pulled him closer. "I can't see the future, John Thursby. I don't know what lies beyond the next bend in the river. But I do know I'm sick and I'm dying."

"And I don't care," he whispered. "Be it one more sunrise or a thousand. I'll take whatever you give. It's more than a rascal like me deserves."

"Are you a rascal, then?" She liked the sound of that word. How he said it.

"I could be," he said with a grin. He lowered his head and brushed his lips against the slope of her neck, sending a quiver of delight down to her toes.

Then they were kissing in that dark alley between the buds and blooms of thyme and rosemary. She felt another part of her heart snick and unlock.

And found freedom inside.

EPILOGUE

A TWIST OF FATE

Ankarette arrived at the rear porter door of the Arbon in the middle of the night. Two sentries with torches were posted there, the flames chasing away the moonless dark. Moser no longer held his post anymore. Because of his head injury months earlier, he was still rehabilitating with his sister, Agnes, and her children in their ward. The king's treasury had generously provided a suitable reward for him.

"Thank the Lady you came," the sentry said. "My lord duke is raving. He's afraid Lady Isybelle is going to die. Hurry!"

Ankarette had been sharing a book and some tea with John Thursby when the Espion had arrived to alert her of the summons. The night watchman had offered to come along, but she was keeping their relationship hidden from others. Eredur and Elyse knew, but she valued her privacy and didn't want someone like Dunsdworth connecting the pieces.

"How long has she been in labor?" she asked.

"Started this afternoon. You can hear her keening from upstairs betimes."

Ankarette hastened through the inner gardens,

which were still run-down. The trees had lost their leaves with the onset of winter. There had been no snow as yet, but the air was chill enough that Ankarette could see her breath.

When she reached the inner doors, she was greeted by the butler, who had a frantic look on his face. "Come this way!"

She heard Dunsdworth's moans of despair, and when she entered the main hall with war instruments hanging from the walls, she saw him pacing, his shirt open, his chest bathed with sweat. The hearth was blazing, a raging fire that seemed to mirror the master of the Arbon's frenetic mood.

Then he saw her, hand still mid-swipe in his hair. He ran and dropped on his knees before her. "Thank the Lady! Blessed Lady! You came! Where have you been? I sent a rider to the castle hours ago."

"I wasn't there," Ankarette said. "But I've returned. I'll go to her room."

Dunsdworth gripped Ankarette's arms so fiercely it hurt. "You have to save my child! I beg of you! Do not let this one die. . . I couldn't. . . I couldn't bear it. . . not again!" He released her, biting the edge of his hand. He smelled of malmsey, and his eyes were delirious.

She still felt the imprint of his fingers on her arms.

Another wail came from upstairs.

"No, no, no!" Dunsdworth moaned, dropping to his knees. "Belle! I must see her! Belle!"

Ankarette blocked the way to the stairs. "Remain down here, Dunne. In your state, you'll only frighten her."

"Can you help her? Can you?" he begged.

"I'll do what I can. I will try."

"My lord, come sit down," the butler urged. "You're not yourself."

Ankarette turned and hurried up the steps. The last time she'd come to the Arbon had been in negotiation for Nanette's birthright, her dowry. Now, Nanette and Severn were happily ensconced at Glosstyr castle. With Atabyrion having withdrawn their troops from the North, the realm had enjoyed a relatively brief time of peace before winter hit, but there were rumors of Occitanian trouble brewing outside Westmarch. King Lewis was amping up tension with the negotiations for his sister.

Ankarette rushed down the corridor to the master suite, where she'd poisoned Dunne with a sleeping draft. The bedchamber smelled of blood and vomit. She found Isybelle on the bed, her chemise soaked with sweat. Another midwife was already there, trying to calm Isybelle and offer encouragement, but the woman looked desperate with worry.

"Ankarette, Ankarette, Ankarette," Isybelle gasped in relief when she saw her friend.

Gripping Isybelle's hand, Ankarette looking questioningly at the other midwife.

"The babe is breech," the older woman said. "I see the foot, that's all. She's hard pressed."

That was a difficult complication. It required a midwife with extensive experience. "Have you tried opening the womb with a blade?" Ankarette asked.

"I told the duke that option, but he said if I cut her open and killed the child, he would. . . he would kill *me*!"

"I'm so. . . so tired. . . Ankarette. . . so tired," Isybelle murmured. Then another pang struck her, and she let out another cry of pain, like the one Ankarette had heard from below.

"I've done this kind before," Ankarette said. "You can do this, Belle. It's not impossible. Courage. You need all your courage to help your babe."

"I wish I were dead instead," Isybelle said, sobbing. "Not. . . not again. Please, not again! Let me die instead!"

"Everything will be well," Ankarette said, gripping her friend's hand. "Trust me. I'm here. I'll help you."

"You. . . are. . . my friend," Isybelle gasped, squeezing Ankarette's hand as the pain became unbearable again. "My. . . sister!"

It was a hard delivery. . . and a painful one. But Isybelle refused to give in to despair, refused to quit trying. And with coaxing and help, Ankarette watched as the babe finally slipped out. Thankfully, the umbilical cord was not wrapped around the babe's chest or neck. The skin was gray with mucus, but after a quick handling and wiping, the pink skin shone through.

And he squealed.

"It's a son," Ankarette said, her voice thick with wonder. "A healthy son!"

Isybelle lay panting, completely exhausted. The midwife severed the umbilical cord and began to tidy the mess. Ankarette lay the newborn on Isybelle's heaving chest. It was always good for a newborn to begin suckling right away. He was a large lad, so it was no wonder the birthing had been so painful. Other than him being breech, all was normal.

Ankarette used a clean towel to wipe sweat away from her throat.

"L-look at him," Isybelle cooed through tears. "So. . . sweet. . . so precious."

"Did you and Dunne choose a name already?" Ankarette asked, using the towel to wipe Isybelle's brow next.

"Yes. We'll name him after. . . his father. Dunsdworth. The second. . . duke of Clare. He's so big! So sweet. Oh, he's suckling! Look, he's suckling!"

Ankarette grinned and offered a silent prayer of thanks to the Fountain. The bleeding had stopped. It had been a successful birth.

"Let me tell Dunne. He'll want to see him."

"Yes! Oh, yes, have him come! I want him to see his son."

Ankarette left the chamber and found the duke in the hall, being restrained by Captain Rufus and his butler.

"I heard a babe cry!" Dunsdworth said worriedly. Feverishly. "Then silence! Tell me!"

"You have a son, and he's nursing. All is well, my lord. All is well."

The two men released their hold, and Dunsdworth hurried to Ankarette, taking her hands. He was about to kiss them, but he saw the bloodstains there and grimaced. Then he shot into the room like an arrow and let out a cry of exultation that rang through the house.

Ankarette was weary. Sunlight shone through the upper windows of the manor. She stood on the balcony, gazing down at the room below. The child had been born into wealth and power. He would inherit lands, gold, fine horses. He'd be taught in war and diplomacy. If he served the king, he could become a great man in Ceredigion.

Or if ambition seized him like a fever, as it had his father, he might end up in a cell in Holistern Tower.

It all depended on how he was raised.

"I'll tell the other servants," the butler said eagerly. "This is cherished news indeed!"

"And I'll raise a cup with the men," Rufus declared. Both men hurried down the steps to spread the news.

Ankarette went back to the doorway, which was still open, and leaned against it, watching as Dunne knelt at the edge of the bed, peering in fascination as his son nursed. There was a look of pure transfixion in the father's eyes. His mind was whirling with thoughts.

Ankarette reached out with her Fountain magic. Just a little touch. She wanted to discern the duke's thoughts. To know his intentions. His desires.

This is my son. My heir. The future king of Ceredigion.

"Isn't he handsome?" Belle said huskily. "Like his father."

"He is," Dunsdworth said. The smile on his mouth was fearsome.

Ankarette's heart burned with dread, with disappointment. Dunsdworth had been twisted by Warrewik into believing that he was the true heir to the throne. He wouldn't let go of that ambition. Not even to spare his wife. And definitely not to spare his own child.

And the poisoner had another premonition, that one day, after all hope was lost, she would have to destroy this family.

She felt a tingle of pain in her abdomen. She needed the vial again.

AUTHOR'S NOTE

I wasn't planning on writing another Kingfountain novel. Nope. Wasn't on my radar or on my mind at all. In fact, you wouldn't be reading this if it weren't for Tanya Anne Crosby, who reached out around my birthday and asked if we could work together. She's the founder of Oliver Heber Books and a friend I've gotten to know through BingeBooks and Authors AI. She wanted more fantasy in her lineup and asked if she could acquire my Ankarette stand-alone novels. I was willing to, but then she popped the question. Would I be willing to write another one?

I usually plan out my novels for months or even years in advance. I need a little fire in the gut to persuade me to start. I spent the weekend thinking about it and then dug around in some of my old War of the Roses sources from my college days. I scoured them again looking for historical anecdotes I could weave into a story and came across a snippet I'd read about years ago: A nobleman's daughter who mysteriously disappeared. Two brothers at each other's throats. I'd first read about this instance in Sharon Kay Penman's novel *The Sunne in Splendour* back in college, but it was based on real history.

I dug deeper. Could Ankarette be part of this story? Would Eredur have asked her to find the missing heiress? Why not? I relistened to the audiobook of *The Poisoner's Enemy* to make sure I could get back to the world again. I'd just finished writing the final book in my new thriller series *The Dresden Codex*, so I'll admit a thrilling adventure sounded fun. And then in an obscure document, I found another clue about the real Ankarette that I've overlooked for thirty years. I found the name John Thursby. That's when I decided the story would be much more fun if Ankarette had a sidekick of sorts. I'd encourage you to listen to Richard Armitage reading Edward Shanks's poem *The Night Watch for England*, which also helped serve as inspiration for John Thursby's character. You can find it on YouTube.

I committed the book to Tanya, signed a deal with OHB, and started writing immediately. I wove in a bad guy from one of my unpublished novels (Bidigen Grimmer). And when I was nearly done writing the novel, my wife suggested I watch *Miss Scarlet and the Duke*. I love the chemistry between the characters, who very much had some Ankarette Tryneowy and John Thursby vibes. I finished this novel in record time, less than three months after starting it. I don't think I've ever written one so fast, and that includes spending spring break in England with my family, where I was actually able to visit Warwick Castle, Bosworth Field, and the Tower of London. So inspiring to say the least!

Now that you've read it, I hope you've enjoyed the little tale. While writing it, another story idea began to tickle my mind, related to the future events in the kingdom revolving around Lord Devereaux. We'll see how this book does first, though.

Thanks for reading!

ALSO BY JEFF WHEELER

ABOUT THE AUTHOR

Jeff Wheeler is the *Wall Street Journal* bestselling author of over thirty epic fantasy novels, including his bestselling and beloved Kingfountain novels. Jeff lives in the Rocky Mountains and is a husband, father of five, and devout member of his church. Learn about Jeff's publishing journey in *Your First Million Words*, and visit his many worlds at www.jeff-wheeler.com.